MW01688582

dedication

To my "Rockin' Readers" who asked for Brett & Julie's story to be told.

This one's for you.

Thank you for your support and for loving this couple! xoxo

table of contents

When one isn't looking, that's usually when another is found.
—Brett Chambers

~Part One~

chapter 1

Julie

I DID MY BEST to live a carefree life—it worked for me. My existence consisted of work, shoe shopping, and some play, but mostly work. I was employed at a prestigious marketing firm, and I loved it. Well, at least most of the time. However, last night, work had included ass-kissers and aloof people who were more concerned with what others had than bettering themselves. The thought of the business dinner I'd attended made me shiver. At times, the men at those functions acted like vultures on fresh meat. It hadn't been a "hook-up" function, but it sure felt that way. Okay, I'd confess that I may have gone home with someone a time or two in the past, but I hadn't done that to impress anyone—it was to scratch an itch, if you will. Boyfriends led to broken promises and heartbreak, so I was fine on my own.

Tonight was different. Our company was hosting a speed dating event at the White Orchid, a trendy nightclub. It was a different soiree, and as soon as it ended, I was going to plant myself at the bar and enjoy a drink . . . or five. Who knew, maybe I'd even dance a bit. But first things first, I needed to manage the event.

Aubrey, my closest friend, was in attendance to find a muse for her romance novel she aspired to write. When my eyes landed on her, I couldn't believe she was sitting with the club owner. Alex was a great guy, but he was a well-known player. I didn't want to see Aubrey's heart get broken. She was there to find a muse for her romance novel, not for a quick hook-up. That was Alex's M.O.

Once the event was over, I rushed to Aubrey and gently tugged at her arm. "What're you doing?"

Her gaze drifted from my eyes to my hand on her arm.

"Follow me," I said, ushering her to the ladies' room. As soon as I knew it was safe to talk, I spun around to face her. "Aubrey, you need to be careful with Alex. He has a bad reputation."

Her eyes had a faint glint of nervousness, and before I could continue, the bathroom door swung open, and the "mean girls" pranced in, giggling. Those women were known to go after men with money or clout. We ran in the same circles because of their fathers' businesses, so I'd had the misfortune of knowing one of them, Leah Pierce, for years. She was as bad as they came, and her friends' reputations were almost as horrible as hers.

Leah gave Aubrey the once-over with her big brown eyes and sneered. "So you're Alex's playmate of the night?" She leaned in and whispered something in Aubrey's ear, making Aubrey cringe and leaving her speechless. That apparently gave Leah the satisfaction she was looking for.

Aubrey may not have been able to say anything, but I could. “Why, Leah, is it the lighting in here, or are you turning green?”

“Go to hell, Julie. You know that I can have any man, anytime, anywhere.” She crossed her arms in front of her fake double D’s.

“Oh, I know all about your reputation.” I looked at Aubrey, who appeared extremely uncomfortable and in need of a cocktail, so we left the clique to their own devices—gossip and lip gloss.

The bass-heavy music boomed through the opulent club as we headed toward the bar. I couldn’t help but notice a tall blond bartender talking to Alex. He had the body of a runner: lean, toned, and tight. With each move he made, his muscles flexed and made every woman around him swoon. Then my eyes caught those of the other bartender. My breath hitched, and my heartbeat fluttered. He was one of the most attractive men I’d ever seen, and he had an indescribable aura. He was pouring shots for a couple of ladies sitting on the stools, vying for his attention. They all looked willing and eager to accept anything he’d give them, including himself. Not that I blamed them. I wasn’t sure I’d have turned him down, but I wasn’t about to flaunt myself to find out either.

His light brown wavy hair looked soft, and I pictured running my hand through it. How silky it would feel gliding through my fingers. Quick flashes of me doing that while his lips were on mine played in my head. Maybe I was dreaming, and he was something I’d conjured up as compensation for all of the trolls I’d dealt with lately.

Alex turned toward us. “Aubrey and Julie, I’d like you to meet my friend, Brett, and, Aubrey, you already met Tyler.”

Nope, not a dream. Brett shook my hand, and everything else around me faded away. Even Tyler's blond locks and model smile no longer fazed me. The bass of the music disappeared and was replaced by my pulse thundering in my ears. The warmth of his skin on mine made a chill run down my spine. All I could do was stare at him as I felt heat rise in my cheeks.

"Can I get you a drink?" Brett's voice was deep and sultry, which brought me out of my daze.

I glanced at Aubrey, who looked at me with wonder dancing in her eyes. I wasn't the shy quiet type, but around Brett, I was rendered speechless.

"Yes, I'd love a martini, please," I managed.

"Ahh, my specialty." He winked and made my drink. He placed the masterfully poured beverage on a burgundy cocktail napkin. "Here you are. A Chambers martini."

I raised my brow at the name of the drink he set in front of me.

"Chambers is my last name. And yours is?"

"Michaels." I cleared my throat.

"Well, it's a pleasure to meet you, Julie Michaels." His white-tooth smile beamed. "I hope you enjoy your martini."

Pride and confidence flashed in his eyes. Anyone could tell he loved his job and being a bartender meant more to him than slinging drinks.

I reached in my purse to pay for my cocktail.

"Your money isn't good here tonight." Brett's sexy voice stopped my movement. "Drinks are on me."

My lips curled into a smile. "Thank you."

"Believe me, it's my pleasure."

Pleasure. His voice was seductively deep and rang with promise. A promise that he could bring me more pleasure than the liquid in a triangular glass. When I looked at him, there was no doubt since my body tightened in anticipation.

Before I knew it, I was alone with him. Well, not alone since we were in a crowded club, but Tyler went back to making drinks. Alex and Aubrey must have slipped away at some point because when I spotted them, they were in an embrace and swaying to the music on the dance floor.

I turned to Brett, who was regarding me with delight in his eyes.

"So, you look familiar. Do you come here often?" he asked.

His voice did heady things to me. My brows rose, making him close his eyes as a chuckle vibrated from his lips, giving him the most adorable laugh lines.

"Okay, that wasn't a line." He wiped down the bar in front of me, although it looked spotless. Maybe that was a nervous habit. "I meant—"

I cut him off to help him out. "I was here last month to discuss tonight's event with Alex." Our eyes met, and a silent exchange passed between us. "But I don't remember seeing you."

Alex and Aubrey approached the bar. I glanced at them only to find her staring at Alex as if she'd met the man of her dreams. Maybe she had. Maybe I had too, and I'd never wanted to find anyone who made my heart flutter. But something about Brett was different from other men, and I needed to know what that was.

Brett's hazel eyes sparkled as Alex told him to take a break and join us upstairs in the VIP area. I prayed my feet would carry me up the steps gracefully, and thankfully they did. Alex had shown me the private area the last time I was there, and it was superb. The jewel-toned plush furniture transformed the club into something more luxurious than an ordinary nightclub—it was sexy.

Brett's presence changed the atmosphere. My stomach fluttered with his every glance. Some were teasing, and others lingered, and I couldn't tear my eyes away. Prickles flickered on my skin when he placed his warm palm on my thigh. He was subtle in his pursuit yet very present. I wasn't sure if it was the drinks I'd had or the gorgeous man next to me, but the temperature around me heated.

He leaned in and whispered, "You're captivating."

His fingers played with the ends of my hair as his knuckles grazed my shoulders, and an odd sense of . . . I don't know, excitement or nerves washed over me. His eyes expressed satisfaction and confidence. It was as if he knew his touch and words would make me his—that I would want him.

"You're pretty smooth, but you're a bartender, so . . ." I quirked my lips. "You must use that line a lot."

He shook his head. "Never." His breath caressed my neck. "No one has ever captivated me. Your lips, your eyes . . ."

I shifted in my seat while my hands began to sweat, and my thighs clenched.

"Everything," he said.

My breath faltered. I was completely taken aback by his comment, but when Brett threaded his fingers into my hair and crashed his lips onto mine, he knocked the wind right out of me. *Wow!* He moved fast, and I didn't resist. If he'd been like the guys from last night, I would have punched him in the balls by now, but he tasted too good. I'd never hurt someone I was sure could bring me carnal pleasure, so I went with it.

Our tongues tangled. He pulled me tighter, and I became lost in our own world. My hands were on his thighs, and I felt his muscles flex. His hands slid to my neck as mine moved to his defined arms. My body responded to him and the way he kissed me. To use his words, this man had captivated me—with one kiss.

Alex cleared his throat beside us and brought me back to the now. I flushed with embarrassment. I wasn't a shy woman, but playing tonsil hockey with a man I'd just met in front of a man I did business with was a different story. I slowly wiped my bottom lip with my thumb, gathering the moisture that had collected there. I was half tempted to suck it off of my thumb, but I refrained.

"Julie, I'm going to head home."

Aubrey's voice took me out of my dreamlike state. She stood at the end of the table with Alex, who was smiling, and he nodded. I wasn't sure if that nod was meant for me or was a congratulatory "way to go, bro" signal for Brett. Either way, I felt the blood drain from my head.

I wasn't ready to leave, but I also didn't want to assume Brett wanted me to hang around. Technically, he had to work. I started to rise out of my seat, but Aubrey stopped me and told me to stay. When I glanced at Brett, he looked relieved that she had. He stood and said good-bye to them then sat back down.

Brett grabbed my hand and laced my fingers with his. "I'm glad you didn't leave."

"Don't you need to work?"

He glanced over the railing toward the mahogany bar, which was crowded with thirsty customers. "I suppose I do. Care to keep me company?" His lips twisted into the sexiest grin as he brought our hands to his mouth and kissed my knuckles one at a time.

The back of my neck was sprinkled with goosebumps. What the hell was I doing? I'd let a man I'd just met devour me in a public place in front of our friends. I was all for having a good time, but even for me, that was quick. I remembered the way the ladies at the bar had ogled him. "Sure, if you don't think I'll be in the way. I don't want to cramp your style."

He stood and pulled me up with him until we were toe to toe and chest to chest. His index finger lifted my chin. "I don't have a style." He winked, and we walked downstairs to the bar.

As the night wore on, I couldn't help but notice all of the women flaunting themselves, primarily their breasts, at Brett and Tyler. All I thought about was how Brett's lips had felt pressed against mine. How his tongue had firmly stroked mine and twirled in my mouth as if it was on a mission to lick every facet. I swiveled my stool, so I faced the dance floor rather than the bottles lined up on the bar. I shot a text to Aubrey, telling her I was still at the club with Brett. I figured she was dying to talk to me about Alex, so I didn't want her to worry if she called and I didn't hear my phone.

I chanced a glance at Brett as he handed Leah, one of the skanks from the ladies' room, a shot of tequila. It wasn't my first time around women like her and her friend at the bar. I knew their moves and could tell that they were on the prowl—Brett and Tyler were their prey. I couldn't make out what Leah had said, but Brett's eyes flicked between her and me. He shook his head while Tyler held a wedge of lime between his teeth. The ladies poured their shots back, and Leah pushed herself up on the bar to take the fruit from Tyler with her teeth. The exchange ended in a heated kiss while the other woman's eyes shot daggers at Brett when he laid her wedge of lime on a cocktail napkin. On the inside, I laughed, but on the outside, I remained indifferent.

She slid off her stool and headed in my direction. I let out a breath, not wanting to deal with her. She stood next to me at the bar and tugged on her dark miniskirt and pushed out her chest, which was ready to spill out of her crop top. Her dark roots showed through her fake red hair. The smell of tequila on her breath made my nose crinkle.

"I wouldn't get my hopes up if I were you." She looked in Brett's direction.

When I did the same, I saw him staring at us. His brows lowered, and he began to walk toward us, but a thirsty patron stopped him.

"Leah's wants to be with Ty, and I've had my eye on Brett for a while now, so back off."

I smiled and in my sweetest voice said, "Does he know this? Because he didn't seem too eager to get close to you when his tongue was in my mouth a few minutes ago." I shrugged.

She straightened her spine. "You don't know me, but I'm Nikki Webster. When I want something, I don't stop until I get it." Her eyes devoured Brett's body as she gave him a once-over then brought her attention back to me. "I want more than a one-night stand with him. That's all you'll be, you know. I've known these guys a while, and all they care about is dipping themselves in something warm at night. Just ask Alex." She rotated, and her lips twisted before she peered at me from the corner of her eye. "Handsome, can I give you . . . I mean, can I please have a blow job?"

I glanced at Brett, who glared at her, and my guard went up. He grabbed a shot glass from the back of the bar, poured some Amaretto and Kahlua in it, topped it with a dollop of whipped cream, and placed it in front of her. She clasped her arms behind her back, wrapped her lips around the mouth of the small glass, and slowly tipped her head back while looking at Brett under hooded lids. When she came forward and set down the empty cup, she licked the excess cream off of her lips and moaned as if she'd just had an orgasm.

Brett wasn't fazed by her attempt at seduction. "That'll be fifteen dollars."

She dropped a twenty on the bar. "Worth every penny . . ." Her eyes caught mine as she ran her thumb along her lower lip before licking her fingertip. "And then some."

She twisted and walked away, making my stomach lurch. I didn't know why I'd let her comments and blatant come-ons toward Brett bother me. I wasn't the long-term type—at least, I hadn't been until he'd kissed me. Something inside me had changed. *Who am I kidding? It was one kiss.* I needed to get a grip.

I hadn't even noticed Brett standing in front of me. He must have come around from behind the bar.

"Are you okay? You look pale." The lines on his forehead deepened as he waited for my reply.

I forced a smile. "I'm fine. Maybe I should go."

Before I could get off the stool, Brett's hand went to my hip. "Please stay. Dance with me."

He cupped my cheek, and I leaned my head in his hand. Why did it feel so comfortable, so normal? I slid off the stool, and his hold on me tightened. Our fingers were interwoven as we strolled to the dance floor. The pace of the music was fast, but we kept rhythm to our own beat—a slow one.

"I saw your face when Nikki was talking to you. Do I want to know what she said?" His voice was steady, but his eyes were hooded and worried.

I shook my head. "She's not worth it. Sorry, but I've never been a fan of her *kind*. It isn't important what she said or how obvious she was when she ordered her shot. I'm in your arms right now, so let's enjoy this for what it is."

"Julie?"

His voice was like a warm blanket, and all I wanted to do was wrap myself in it like a cocoon. I met his beautiful hazel eyes, which had just the right number of golden flecks. They caught the lights above the dance floor perfectly. "Yes?"

His forehead was on mine. I closed my eyes and breathed in his masculine scent, which reminded me of amber—rich and earthy. "I'm going to kiss you again, okay?"

"I was hoping you would." I steadied myself and lifted my chin.

When our lips touched, something unspoken passed through me. It wasn't rushed or as demanding as the kiss we'd shared upstairs. This kiss was softer, deliberate. It claimed me in a way that I didn't expect. Brett changed me with that kiss.

He pulled back, excitement etched across his face as his eyes darkened. "Forget dancing. Let's get out of here."

His husky voice wasn't demanding, but I didn't hesitate to comply with his request.

Brett

THE LOOK IN her bright emerald eyes made me feel alive. I took her hand and hurried us off the dance floor. I wasn't scheduled to close tonight, but I made sure to give Ty a wave, so he knew I was leaving. Julie's slim fingers tightened around mine when we passed Nikki, who was giving Julie a death stare.

Once we were outside, the gentle breeze that cut through the humid air didn't do a thing to cool off what I felt for the woman beside me. I'd had my share of one-night stands, but judging by the way I'd felt when I kissed her, one night with Julie would never be sufficient.

"I don't want this night to end. Can I offer you a ride home?" I gazed at her in anticipation.

"I'd like that." Her voice was soft and soothing.

She was different from other women. Whenever I'd wanted to take women home, they were all over me, and when I thought about it, they sounded almost obnoxious, completely the opposite of Julie. It was then I realized I did have a style and a type—she was it.

We walked across the street to my SUV, and I turned her, so her back was up against the passenger door. Her hair blew in the gentle wind, and the scent of her shampoo infiltrated my nose. Her chest rose. I needed to touch her, to be closer to her. I took her hands and pulled them behind her back. My hips pressed against hers, and our mouths almost touched. After I absorbed her breath, her sweet scent of vanilla and looked at her beautiful eyes, I couldn't take much more.

"Let's go then." She swallowed hard, and I knew I'd gotten to her.

I released her hands and opened the door. She slid in. Once I was in the car, I didn't want to leave, but we couldn't stay parked. Julie gave me her address, and we drove to her place.

I thought about turning on some music, but I needed to hear her voice now. She had been with her friend tonight, so I thought of asking about her. That would be a safe bet to get her talking. "So Aubrey seems nice."

A genuine smile stretched across her face, which glowed. "She's the best. I hope Alex doesn't hurt her."

I glanced at her before looking back at the road. Her nose was crinkled, and small lines formed on her forehead.

"I'm sorry. I shouldn't have said that" she said. "I know about his reputation. Aubrey isn't as experienced as he is."

"Alex is one of the best guys I know. Yes, he's had his share of women, but he isn't a dick or anything." I shrugged and felt her stare on me.

"Well, he dated Leah. I remember seeing their picture in the society section. I have a feeling he had a go at it with your friend Nikki, so that doesn't say much about him. I can't help worrying about Aubrey." Julie let out a breath. "Here's my building."

"Nikki isn't my friend." I pulled up to the curb and turned off the engine. Julie placed her hand on the door. "Don't leave yet." My body turned toward hers, and she looked at me with expectant eyes. "I want to see you again. Can we get together tomorrow?"

"I'd like that a lot, but if you want to come up, that'd be okay too." Her lids slowly closed then opened to find me smiling.

I had opened my door before she changed her mind. I walked around the car. She was already getting out, so I took her hand and closed the door behind her.

Her place was nice, and I was enveloped by the scent that lingered in the air. Her perfume was intoxicating, and I was ready to get drunk.

She walked into the kitchen, and I couldn't stop looking at her tight ass as it swayed with each step. "Would you like something to drink?" Her purse landed on the table with a gentle clunk.

I declined, and she grabbed a bottle of water for herself before joining me in the living room.

"So speed dating . . ." I couldn't help but chuckle. "That really works?" I sat beside her on the overstuffed couch.

She curled one leg underneath her and turned toward me. "Well, I don't know what will happen after tonight, but I think some people were pretty happy." She let out the most adorable giggle.

"What's so funny?" Watching her blush was something I could get used to.

"Aubrey. I'm remembering her list of questions. But what's comical is how she answered some so she purposely wouldn't match with anyone. I was ready to kill her. It defeated the entire purpose of her being there."

"What would you have asked?" My heart beat wildly because I knew if she had participated, some man would have wanted her as much as I did. But I wouldn't rush whatever was happening between us—if anything was happening.

"Hmmm . . ." Her index finger tapped her chin as her eyes rolled up in thought. "Oh! I know!" She beamed, making my heart swell. She licked her lips and grinned. "If there was a contest, would you win funniest, most popular, best looking, or most likely to succeed?"

"Yes." I laughed at myself, and thankfully Julie did too, though she tossed in an eye roll. "Keep them coming, beautiful. I'll tell you anything you want to know." As soon as that remark flew out of my mouth, I knew it was a mistake. She didn't seem the type to hold back.

Her lips twisted into the cutest grin. "Well, if you want to play it that way, I do have a question for you."

Shit. I knew that would happen. "Okay, go."

"Between you, Alex, and Tyler, who gets hit on the most?" Her shoulders rolled back, and her chest rose as she waited for my response.

All I could do was stare at her. We all got propositioned every night, but for some reason, telling her that didn't make me feel proud or cocky. I almost felt embarrassed. Plus, she had witnessed it tonight. Even though we had just met, I didn't want to lose her before I had her. "I'd say we're pretty equal, but probably Alex because he's the primary owner, and women want a piece of him."

Her gaze lowered, and she nodded. I knew she had to be thinking of her friend. For Alex's sake, I hoped she kept that piece of information to herself.

"But don't worry. He looked at Aubrey differently than he's looked at any woman. What else do you want to know?"

She gave me a tight-lipped smile. "Do you always take a woman home with you?"

Boy, she didn't beat around the bush. "No, I don't." I omitted the part about sometimes going to their apartment or just fucked around in my car. Considering we were at her home now, she wasn't naïve to the fact that I wasn't a monk. "But I haven't met anyone like you."

Her face softened, and her lips curved up. "What's so different about me?"

"Everything." That was the God's honest truth.

"So we've established you're a smooth talker and get hit on a lot, but has a woman ever claimed you as her own?"

My body tensed. I could tell Julie noticed, and she stared at her hands, which twisted on her lap.

"Once. I'm divorced. I was young and stupid while she was smart and conniving."

The long lashes that shadowed her cheeks darted up. "Oh. What was her name?"

"Samantha and she was the biggest mistake of my life. Can we move on? I'd rather hear more about the sexy woman in front of me." That wasn't a line, but discussing my marriage wasn't what I wanted to do. It would definitely kill the mood—especially mine.

"Such a smooth talker." She smiled appreciatively, which made me relax. "What did you think when you first laid eyes on me?" Her voice was barely above a whisper.

For the first time, I saw vulnerability etched in her features, and it was sexy as hell. I could feel my cheeks rise as I recalled her ambling toward me. She was tall—I'd guess around five-foot-seven—slim but not skinny. Her hair, which resembled a golden haze, had rested on her ample sized breasts. The way she carried herself with such grace was a complete turn-on. Other men had had eyes on her, but if she was aware of it, she didn't let on. The self-assuredness in her stride made me want to be the one to capture her attention.

"I thought you were the most gorgeous woman I'd ever seen, and I was ready to take down anyone to have you to myself."

She swallowed hard. "Thank you."

All the air was sucked out of my lungs. This gorgeous woman actually thanked me for wanting to take her away from other men? She didn't even know me or them, but she'd chosen me.

"I think it's my turn to ask the questions now." I scooted closer to her so our knees were touching.

Her top lip curled under her teeth, and her fingers twirled the ends of her golden hair. I remembered how silky smooth it was and instantly wanted to pull her toward me, but I refrained.

Two could play at this game, so I asked, "What were you thinking when you first saw me?" I casually leaned back, awaiting her reply.

"Sex on the bar." She coolly smiled.

I thought I may have swallowed my tongue as I pictured her sprawled out naked on the mahogany, her pussy glistening as an invitation for me to bury myself inside her. "I could have arranged that." My eyebrows waggled.

She slapped my knee. "Down, boy. I was kidding."

"Can't blame a guy for trying." I winked. "Want to tell me the truth now?"

She let out a long breath. "It was an odd feeling." Her eyes penetrated mine. She was completely serious, and I was completely confused.

"Odd?"

"Yes." She shook her head. "It's too embarrassing, and I don't think you need me to boost your ego."

I took her hand and felt her pulse race as my thumb made circles on her wrist. "Please tell me." My heart craved her answer while my nerves frayed.

After what was probably only a few seconds but seemed like several minutes, she finally spoke. "It was as though time stood still. Everyone and everything in the room disappeared except for you." She tilted her head and shrugged one shoulder. "I don't know how to explain it."

She didn't have to go on, because I'd felt the same way about her.

But then her expression hardened. "Then I saw the other women at the bar come on to you, and I wanted to scratch their eyes out." Her face didn't falter. She was as serious as a heart attack.

"You would have gotten into a cat fight over me?" My lips twisted into a snarky smile. The thought of a woman fighting for me was totally hot, and envisioning Julie doing it was even better.

"No, I said I *wanted* to scratch their eyes out. There's no way I would have ruined my manicure on either of them." She had glanced at her nails before she flipped her hair in an over-exaggerated manner.

I burst into laughter. She would have fought to have me to herself. Once I caught my breath and realized what she had said, I continued my line of questioning. "Would you go out with me if I asked you?" I had a feeling I knew the answer, but I wanted to hear it from her. No, I needed to hear it.

"Are you asking me?"

I moved my index finger from side to side. "Tsk tsk. You can't answer a question with a question."

The sides of her lips rose into the sexiest smile. "Yes."

I'd expected her voice to be shy, but she answered with such definiteness that I could feel it in my pants. "Okay, if I wanted to kiss you again, would you let me?"

"Yes."

"Julie?"

"Yes?"

"I'm going to kiss you again." I pulled her onto my lap, and her hands rested on the back of my neck. Her fingers played with my hair. In a minute, she would feel how badly I wanted her.

"That's not a question."

"I know all I need to know." I smoothed her hair back and tucked it behind her ear.

"Then what are you waiting for?" She leaned in closer.

"Not a thing."

chapter 2

Julie

MY ARMS STRETCHED over my head as I woke up after a few hours of sleep. Spending time with Brett last night had been so unexpected. I wasn't sure if it was real or a dream. I rolled to my side, and my cheek sank into my pillow. A smile grew across my face. To think that I'd wanted Aubrey to find someone, and we both may have. Giddiness consumed me as though I were a teenager who'd just experienced her first kiss. I touched my lips and remembered how tender his lips were. Yes, it was definitely real, but the feelings that had soared through me were foreign. I wasn't one to fall head over heels for a guy, but I had a feeling Brett would be a different story.

I grabbed my cell off the nightstand and looked at the screensaver picture of Aubrey and me. I hoped she found the right man, and if it was Alex, I hoped he was good to her. She deserved nothing but the best. My finger swiped the screen and clicked on her name.

"Good morning, sunshine."

Aubrey's perky voice made me smile. Rather than wishing her the same, I let out a sigh.

"I take it you had a good night?" she said.

All of a sudden, I was a school girl describing her first crush. "Oh, Aubrey, Brett's amazing. We talked and danced and talked some more, and then we kissed. He's great. We're going out again today. We actually might meet up with you and Alex later for drinks. Now tell me all about Alex. What do you think?" I sat up in bed, praying that her night had gone as well as mine.

Aubrey exhaled. "Julie, first, I'm glad that you met Brett. You guys look great together, and I could tell that you both hit it off." She giggled and told me about all the women who had been vying for Alex's affections even though she was there when they did it.

That was exactly what I'd been afraid of. There were two women in particular that I was concerned about, and they were Leah and Nikki. Flaunting their asses and boobs around, they left little to be desired.

My phone beeped. When I looked at the screen, I saw Brett's name, and my heart rate accelerated. I was nervous that he might be canceling on our date. "Hey, chica, I gotta go. Brett's calling. Maybe we'll see you later."

I took a breath, calmed my nerves, and pressed the green button on my phone. I tried to keep an even voice. "Hello."

"Hello yourself, gorgeous."

I felt my smile grow. Brett's voice was like hot melted caramel, and I knew I'd crave and never tire of it. Rather than act as if I was crushing on him, I decided to have a bit of fun—not only to calm my shaking hands but to mess with his ego.

"Who is this?" My hand covered the phone as I tried to stifle a snicker.

"I'm wounded." He chuckled, and I grinned. "If you need a reminder, I'm the man who made you moan last night as my tongue tasted yours. The guy who held you close and felt your soft curves when we were chest to chest and sensed your pulse race as I tangled my hands in your hair." I was rendered speechless, and he continued. "You know, the one whose name you'll be screaming as I give you more pleasure than you've ever known."

My hand mindlessly rubbed the inside of my thigh. The joke was on me because I couldn't say anything more than his name, and I wasn't even sure if it was audible.

"Ahh, so you do remember me." His tenor voice reverberated through the phone and down to my girly parts. "How did you sleep?"

"Once I crawled into bed, I slept great."

He let out a ragged breath. "Next time . . . maybe I'll stay."

My eyelids fluttered closed at the thought of falling asleep in his strong arms. *What is going on with me?*

"I need to see you. I'll pick you up in an hour for lunch, and then we can come back here for drinks." He didn't bother asking, and he didn't need to.

I stood and walked into my bathroom. "Then I need to shower and get ready. I'll see you soon."

"Did you have to tell me you're going to get naked and wet?" He growled. "My mission is to get you like that all on my own."

Heat rose from my toes to the back of my neck. I stripped down and turned on the water so it would warm up, although I needed to cool off. "See you soon, Brett."

We hung up, and I stepped into the steam-filled shower. I squirted vanilla-scented body wash onto my hands and let them caress every inch of my skin. I thought of Brett's hands on me instead of my own. I licked my lips as I moved them slowly over my curves. The anticipation of spending the day with him made my heart soar. What would his hands feel like on my skin? I imagined they'd be soft and smooth rather than calloused and rough, but either way would be fine with me.

Brett

THE CITY'S HUSTLE and bustle couldn't distract me from thinking about Julie. I'd never experienced anything like this, not even when I was married to Samantha. After that relationship had gone south, I'd decided to go back to my old ways and play the field—a big field. Needless to say, when I met Julie, I couldn't wait to get her in bed, but sitting and talking to her had been fantastic. That was a rarity for me. Bringing a woman back to my place, or going to hers, to talk and get to know each other wasn't my norm.

I'd had my share of women. It was difficult not to while being a bartender. Women didn't need a lot of liquid courage to tell me about the horrible men in their lives or their lack of a love life in general. Shit, sometimes women would lean over the bar, crook their flawlessly manicured fingers, and tell me they wanted to fuck me. So my pickings weren't slim, and I'd acted on some of them, but none of those women had made me feel like Julie had without even saying a word. The sight of her strutting toward me, poised and confident, got me hot and hard. I needed to get to her place.

Even on a Sunday, the streets were crowded with traffic and a slew of pedestrians trying to get from point A to point B faster than the last person. I arrived at her apartment building, and naturally, parking sucked. I should've taken a cab, but the thought of having her scent in my car again made me want to drive. Once I found a spot, I looked at the clock. I was fifteen minutes early. Not wanting to seem overanxious, I called my brother Bentley.

"Hey, Brett. It's early, isn't it?" His voice was raspy as though I had woken him.

"It's almost lunchtime. Did you have a late night?" I chuckled, and he moaned in irritation.

"Yeah. I had a review to turn in, and it was one of those that needed to be written though I didn't want to write it. Not to mention I'm in a hotel in Jersey. I miss my bed."

Bentley was a highly acclaimed theater critic and known for being brutally honest. I'd gone to a show with him once, and when I told him that I thought it was good, he pointed out all the reasons it wasn't. After that, I was happy that I was a bartender. I obviously didn't know much about the theater world.

"So is this another one of your reviews that will make actresses cry?" I asked.

"It's not like that's my goal, but I won't write an untruth so they don't shed a tear."

"Wow, you're cranky this morning. Maybe you should go back to sleep." I laughed, but he didn't reciprocate.

"It's not that. I'm sorry, man. I'm drained, and there's this actress . . . let's say I know she can be better."

"Breaking hearts one review at a time. That should be your tagline."

He let out a ragged breath. "Whatever. What's going on with you? Is there a reason for this call?"

I looked at the clock then at Julie's door. "I met someone."

"Someone like . . ."

"A woman."

"You always meet women." He chuckled.

"This one's different." My fingers rubbed my forehead.

"I need coffee for this conversation." He groaned, and I heard him moving around.

My brother and I were close but didn't see enough of each other. Our work schedules were almost the same, but Bentley actually put in more hours than I did.

"Maybe I should call later."

"I'm up now. Tell me about her and what has you apparently tied up in knots."

"She's different."

"You said that already. What does that mean?"

"It isn't a single thing—it's everything." I looked out my window, imagining her inside and getting ready. My heart rate sped up at the mere thought of her. "I'm comfortable with her. I don't need to use my normal pick-up lines or entice her with the best martini in Manhattan. We just clicked." Those words sounded ridiculous to my ears. I shrugged even though he couldn't see me. "She's . . . Julie."

"Sounds like Julie has made quite an impression. When did you meet her?"

"Last night."

Bentley let out a hearty laugh. "You've known her less than twenty-four hours?"

"I know. That's why I'm saying she's different. We didn't even have sex—we talked."

"Hmm. So what are you going to do about it?" Bentley's voice teetered between excited and apprehensive.

"I'm going to try not to screw it up." I looked at my clock again. Enough time had passed. I needed to see her. "Thanks for listening."

"Anytime. Don't worry about screwing things up before you even get started. Enjoy each other, and everything else will fall into place."

We hung up, and I knew he was right. I pressed the buzzer to her apartment and was thankful she lived in a secure building. The thought of anyone being able to enter her building didn't sit well with me. The buzzer sounded, and I opened the door. She was standing in the hallway wearing a pair of light blue skinny jeans with a simple white low-cut T-shirt. Her hair was still damp, and she looked sexier than she had last night.

"Hey there." She smiled and opened her door wider for me to step in.

"How did you know it was me?" It bothered me that she hadn't verified who was at the door. Was she that trusting?

"What do you mean?" Her brows furrowed, creating the cutest vertical line slightly above her nose.

"You let me in and didn't ask who it was." I stalked up to her and placed my hands on her hips as hers went to my shoulders.

"I saw you walking up." She bit the corner of her lower lip and quirked a single eyebrow.

Shit. How long had she been watching me? Did she notice I'd gotten there early and waited for the time to pass? I pulled her close, and she let out a gasp. I studied her face and her soft blond curls. They cascaded over her shoulders and made my fingers want to grab on to them. "You're beautiful."

Our eyes locked, and an indescribable feeling passed through me as her cheeks turned pink. She was a natural beauty. I leaned in and gently kissed her. She smelled like vanilla icing. I wanted to lick and taste her until I'd had my fill, but something told me I'd never be completely satisfied and leave wanting more from her.

"Would you like something?" She started to head toward her kitchen, but I grabbed her hand and stopped her. She pivoted toward me and tilted her head.

"Only you." I yanked her back until we were chest to chest.

I placed my hands on the small of her back and pulled her close to me. It felt so natural, which was odd considering I generally had no desire to hold a woman while she was fully clothed. After my divorce, I'd decided to be a no-commitment guy. The women I met, generally at the club, were fine with that arrangement. We'd go to their place or my office. The thought of Julie spread across my desk or, better yet, in my bed made my dick come to life.

My hands rose from her waist to the center of her back. My embrace tightened as though I was afraid to let go. I needed to get a grip. I'd just met her, and she didn't appear to be looking for anything more than to have fun. Our first kiss had been in front of our friends in a crowded club, yet we'd kissed as if we were all alone. It was pure lust, and it stirred something in me that I couldn't quite pinpoint. It exhilarated me at the same time.

She leaned back and looked at me. "So what's the plan for today?"

"I thought we'd go grab lunch at this phenomenal Greek restaurant before we head back to my place for cocktails. We can have Alex and Aubrey over if you'd like." We? I was referring to my place as though it were ours or we were a couple.

She didn't flinch; instead she smiled and nodded. "Let me grab my purse, and we can head off."

I watched her delectable ass sway as she strolled away. I wouldn't make it too long without knowing what was under those jeans. Once she had her Gucci bag in hand, we were on our way.

The restaurant I wanted to take her to had a long waiting list. It was the best Greek food in the city, and my friend Pirro, who would have found a table for me regardless of the number of people waiting, wasn't working today. I laced my fingers with Julie's and walked outside without leaving my name on the list. We stood on the sidewalk and tried to think of what to do. When I turned to look at her, her eyes were closed, her head was tipped back as she soaked in the sun which hit her hair like a halo. She sighed, and I wanted nothing more than to tangle my hands in her soft waves and kiss her exposed neck.

She smiled, and her eyes popped open, almost catching me daydreaming. She bounced up and down on the balls of her feet, and I couldn't hide my smile at the sight of her tits bouncing in the V of her shirt. "I have an idea!"

"Oh yeah? What's that?" I chuckled.

"Let's go to the street vendor, grab a couple dogs, and have an impromptu picnic at the park." Her head turned toward the white-and-red hot dog cart on the corner.

I'd never pictured her as the street-food type, but I had a feeling she was the kind of woman who would keep surprising me at every turn. "If that's what you want, let's go."

We grabbed our food, and I retrieved a blanket I kept in my trunk. Then we headed toward the park. I held the food while she spread the blanket on the sun-coated grass. She knelt and held her hands out for the bag. I laughed when she unwrapped her chili dog and cheese fries.

After she had taken a bite, she blushed and looked at me before grabbing a napkin to wipe the corners of her plump lips. "Do I have food on me?"

"No, you surprise me. That's all." I took a bite of my food and washed it down with a sip of my soda. *Gucci bag and street food—this chick rocks!*

She bobbed her head as she popped a fry in her mouth. "Oh my God! These are so good they're practically orgasmic! Here, have one." She held one out to me, which I took from her delicate fingers. After she had licked her fingertips, she put another fry through her rose-colored lips, which glistened from the greasy food.

I nonchalantly adjusted myself and tried not to choke at her words. If she thought a fried potato smothered in cheddar was orgasmic, wait until I got her in bed.

After we were done, she texted Aubrey and asked them to meet us at my place. I tossed out our trash while Julie shook the blanket and folded it into a square. I was all for getting together with our friends, but I needed to be alone with her. Dating wasn't my thing, and Julie didn't seem too interested in it either. After our twenty questions game, I was fairly confident she wasn't looking for a long-term relationship. My chest tightened with jealousy of the men who'd had her before me and most likely those after me. I needed to get my shit in check before I started acting like a pussy.

We got in my car, and I couldn't resist tasting her. My body moved across my center console as I brought my lips to hers. Her hand cupped my cheek as mine went to her thigh. We moaned as our tongues twirled. She was amazing. I decided right then and there that if I needed to beg to have her, I'd check my man card at the door and do what needed to be done.

chapter 3

Julie

SO FAR, OUR day had been fantastic. Having an impromptu picnic was better than sitting in a crowded restaurant. At Brett's building, we took the elevator up to the fifteenth floor. His apartment was bigger than most others I had seen. It was comfortable and decorated in earth tones. The floors were a rich-colored hardwood and covered by a plush area rug in the living area, under the sofa and coffee table. The kitchen cabinets were dark and brightly lit by the recessed lights above them.

He went upstairs to change while we waited for Aubrey and Alex to come over. I was super anxious to see how they were together. I was oddly comfortable with Brett as if we'd known each other for longer than a day. As I stood in front of a gorgeous painting of a neighborhood street that hung on his wall, I thought about why. Why did we click so well? Was it because we didn't have any expectations? Were we both out to have a great time? Was I? Was that all I wanted?

"Penny for your thoughts." I looked up and saw Brett wearing a snug navy T-shirt and faded jeans. He sauntered over, wrapped his arms around my middle, and pulled me toward him, so we were both looking at the painting. "I had it commissioned. It's a rendering of my grandparents' brownstone."

"It's beautiful." I admired the warmth and hominess the artist had brought to his work. Flowers were in the boxes outside the windows. The obscure people on the sidewalk walking by had a natural movement. It almost looked alive.

"My brother, Bentley, lives there now." When I turned in his arms, he placed his hands on my lower back. "When my grandfather passed away, he left it to us. I preferred to live where there was more action, so Bentley bought me out, and I purchased this place."

My jaw dropped, and I felt my brows rise. "You own this place?"

"Yeah. Not bad for a bartender, huh?" His brilliant smile beamed with pride.

"No, not bad at all. You should be proud of yourself." We leaned toward each other. As I licked my upper lip in anticipation of a kiss, there was a knock on the door.

Brett rested his forehead on mine and let out a frustrated moan. "Later." He placed a chaste kiss on the top of my head. "Can you get that? That's probably Alex. Since he lives upstairs, he doesn't need to be buzzed in."

Brett walked into the kitchen while I headed for the door. When I opened it, Alex and Aubrey were hand in hand and laughing about something.

Before either of them could say anything, I grabbed Aubrey for a hug and whispered in her ear, "Brett's totally awesome! I really like him!" I squealed, and Aubrey giggled.

Brett came out to greet them. He shook Alex's hand and gave him a "bro" hug, then he kissed Aubrey's cheek. "I have drinks out on the terrace."

I watched my friend interact with the guys, and it was so natural as if we'd all been friends for years rather than hours. Aubrey was generally guarded and tended to have anxiety in certain situations, and I was thrilled at how relaxed she was. I stood and gestured for her to follow me after I excused us. I saw the guys watching us appreciatively.

We ended up in the kitchen, out of earshot of the guys. "How are things with Alex? Did you have a good lunch?"

"Everything's great. We talked about the women who seem to always be around since he was approached during our lunch date." She shrugged.

"No way!" I quickly covered my mouth as my eyes darted around the room.

"Shhh, really, Julie, lower your voice." Aubrey explained the situation.

Although I understood what she was telling me, I knew Alex was a player. I'd warned her about his bachelor status. Then she told me about how gorgeous the other women were and the fact that she didn't feel worthy of him.

Holding her hand, I smiled at her. "Aubrey, someday you'll look in the mirror and see what others do. You're beautiful and kind. Leah and the other women I've seen him with are fake and nasty. I can tell you like him, and he seems to like you. Maybe you should tell him about the book and forget about your research. He'd probably give you chapters of romantic notions." I winked and giggled, but Aubrey didn't.

She was adamant about keeping Alex in the dark. I wasn't completely on board with her decision, but it was hers to make. I prayed she would tell him before he found out on his own.

We walked back to the balcony to rejoin the guys. After a few more cocktails, Alex took Aubrey's hand, and the unspoken want in their expressions made me happy. Brett tossed me a wink. That was when I realized Brett was as close to Alex as I was to Aubrey.

I couldn't take my eyes off of Brett as we said goodbyes to Alex and Aubrey. He closed the door and turned until we were face to face, and I was busted for ogling him. His lips quirked up, and I felt the blood rise in my cheeks.

"Do you feel it too?" he asked.

I wasn't sure exactly what he was referring to, although I had a pretty good idea. I wasn't one to instantly fall for someone, and I had the feeling he wasn't either. But the pull I felt toward him was more than magnetic—that was so cliché and not us. *Us*. How could we be an "us" already? I shook my head to get rid of the thought of anything serious; we were having a good time.

"Why are you shaking your head? Don't tell me you don't feel the attraction too." Brett placed his hands on my neck while his thumbs stroked my jawbone. "I can feel your pulse, so you don't even have to give me an answer. I already have it."

I tilted my head and looked at his lips. "I feel it."

"I know." He brought his lips to mine.

Our kiss was simple and soft. Only our mouths moved in pure tenderness. The kiss continued for what seemed like forever, but it was probably only a minute or so.

"Let me show you around." He took my hand and led me through his spacious apartment.

If he hadn't told me how he'd gotten such an amazing place, I would have thought he was up to no good at the bar. Brett opened a glass-paned door to a stunning office. Why he needed one at home was beyond me, but it was gorgeous nonetheless.

We turned around. "You've already seen the kitchen, and the powder room is down that hall." He pointed at the opening next to the picture I'd admired earlier, and before I knew it, we were standing in front of it. "I have one guest room, and this is my bedroom." He pulled the brass handles and swung the double doors open.

His room complemented the rest of the apartment. It had deep tan walls and a navy bedspread on the king-size bed, which wasn't adorned with any fancy pillows—only two in matching pillowcases. It screamed "man," and the air was laced with his cologne. My insides quivered.

"It's stunning." I glanced at him, and he looked proud. "This room is quite large. You must get lonely being here all by yourself." Then it dawned on me—he wasn't the type to be alone.

The gold flecks in his hazel eyes sparkled in the light beaming through the slats on the window. "I'm not by myself. You're here with me, and I wouldn't want to be with anyone else right now."

Right now. I smiled and walked over to the window to take in a breathtaking view of the city's skyline. I was trying not to be "that girl" who was always worried about previous women who'd occupied his time. "Wow, now that's a view."

"I couldn't agree more."

His voice was low and gruff, which did odd things to my body, but when I peered over my shoulder to look at him, he was staring at me. The way his eyes perused me sent such heat through me that I was sure my thighs would burst into flames.

He strode over to me and wrapped his arms around my waist. "Don't leave tonight."

My pulse raced, and I cleared my mind of all the reasons why I should. It wasn't as though I was a virgin, but I didn't want to be like the others who'd come before me. I was assuming, of course, but he was a hard man to turn down.

"I can see the gears churning. What are you thinking about?" he asked.

"How this is only our first real date, and I don't want you to think I'm that kind of girl." Okay, I had been that type of girl in the past, but those had been one-night stands. I knew once Brett was inside me, I'd need him again. If holding off ensured me more time with him, then I'd wait.

"Julie, ever since I met you, I've wanted you. I want to give you the most intense pleasure you've ever felt."

Heat rose in my cheeks as I felt a wave of embarrassment laced with a hint of guilt.

"Stop overthinking this. I know this isn't your first time, nor is it mine, but right now it's us—our first time." His index finger stroked my cheekbone. "But if you'd rather not, I'll understand. I don't want this to be a one-night deal."

I nodded and rolled up onto my toes before placing my arms around his neck. "I don't want this to be one time either."

Our lips met, and his strong arms came under mine as he lifted me. My legs wrapped around his waist, which tightened as he moved us across the room to his bed. He laid me down on my back and took off his T-shirt. Every muscle on his torso flexed with each movement. He was impeccable, from each curve of his abs to the two beautiful lines that vanished into the waistband of his jeans. I couldn't help but notice his hardened length straining against the zipper.

He bent over, unfastened my pants, and pulled them off, taking my thong with them. I lay there completely exposed from the waist down.

His Adam's apple bobbed as he swallowed hard. "Stunning."

I smiled, reached for the hem of my shirt, and pulled it off. Before I knew it, my bra was on the floor, and I was completely bare. Brett didn't move. He stared at me, and if I hadn't known I was in great shape, I would have been self-conscious.

"Fuck me." The drawn out and seductive tone in his voice matched his dilated eyes.

"I'd like to, but you have your jeans on." I smiled and coyly bit my upper lip, wanting to see him as naked as I was.

He unbuttoned his jeans and glided the zipper down so gradually it was as if he was going tooth by tooth—it was pure torture. He hooked his thumbs in his waistband and shoved the denim down his long legs. My eyes went wide as I admired his hardened length as it sprung free from the confines of his black boxer briefs. I could feel my core throb in anticipation of Brett filling me like no other man had done. To feel him pulse inside me as he reached his climax while buried deep inside me.

I sat up and splayed my hands on his lower abs, feeling every curve and indentation. I ran my fingers along the edge of the wonderful V that was no longer hidden. My lips found the tip of his erection, which I gently kissed. I swirled my tongue around the ridge at the top and was ready to take him in my mouth until he stopped me.

His eyes darkened. "As much as I'd love to feel the heat of your tongue stroke me and to fill your mouth, I need to be inside you. I've been thinking about it since my lips first tasted yours."

All I could do was nod. Brett's words had me on the edge, and I knew it wouldn't take much more for me to have an orgasm. He hovered over me and caressed my breasts one at a time. I moaned, and my back arched off the bed. His hand trailed down my flat belly until he was between my legs. "You're so ready for me." He brought his thumb to his mouth and licked it. "Exactly as I thought . . . delicious."

His fingers rubbed me before he put two inside me, making me gasp as I could feel my insides tighten. "Yes, impeccable." He moved them in and out, and I raised my hips to mirror his movements. "I want to feel you come on my hand, Julie."

His palm pressed on my most sensitive spot, and my legs stiffened as I saw white sparks behind my eyelids. He moved faster and pressed down harder. I was on the verge of another orgasm.

"Oh God! I need you inside me. Please." I came down from the most euphoric high, and I knew I was on the precipice of another. I wanted to share it with him—I needed to share it with him.

He sheathed himself in a condom he'd taken out of his nightstand and brought the tip of his dick to my entrance. His hands were gentle as he held my head and lowered his mouth to mine with a fervor I'd never experienced before. A loud moan escaped me when his hardened length slid inside my wet core. His hips rolled while I wrapped my legs around his waist. Every nerve in my body sparked to life. My hands had minds of their own as they ran up and down his sculpted back before they tangled in his wavy hair.

Being connected with Brett felt so right it scared me. Not in a way that would send me running for the hills, but I knew this could be so much more, and I didn't know if that was what he wanted or even if I did. I'd been ruined for any other man. No one could compare to how Brett made me feel.

Brett

WE MOVED IN UNISON and picked up speed at the same time.

"Damn, babe, I'm so ready for you. Give me everything, Julie." I ran my tongue along her jawline, took her earlobe between my teeth, and gently nibbled it.

"Brett." My name was a plea accompanied by lust-shadowed eyes that made me feel like a king—her king.

Her hands ran up my back, caressing each groove between my muscles. She lifted her hips to meet my final thrust, making me come with such fury I saw stars.

I lay down beside her and sprinkled kisses on her forehead, the tip of her nose, each cheek, and down to her tender lips. "That was . . . I don't know what that was. Perfect?" I smoothed back her dampened hair and stared into her emerald eyes.

She quirked a single brow. "Are you asking me or telling me it was perfect?"

"Telling." My thumbs stroked her forehead, and she pushed a few stray strands of hair off her beautiful face. Our eyes locked. "Absolutely perfect."

"I think so too." She smiled and laid her head on my chest. She traced my pecs with her nails as she let out a gentle breath. "Good night, Brett."

I kissed the top of her head. "Sweet dreams, Julie."

Waking up with Julie in my arms felt natural and surreal. I didn't do sleepovers, and from what I knew of her, she didn't either. This was an anomaly, and it oddly felt right. We had a chemical connection, and time would tell if it fed into our hearts. I wasn't looking for true love, but a lover who made me feel alive, as Julie had, would be more than welcome.

I looked at her golden hair splayed across the pillow and the swell of her breasts peeking over the sheets—she was exquisite. Her phone beeped, and after she groaned, she stretched toward the nightstand to turn off her alarm. The sheet fell, and her flawless tits were exposed.

"I hate mornings." Her voice was raspy and sexy as hell. She rolled toward me. "Hi." She shyly smiled. "I need to get going."

As she swung her legs over the side of the bed before she could stand, I wrapped my arm around her waist and pulled her back to me. She laughed as she fell toward me.

"When can I see you again?" I asked.

"I don't know. Work has been busy. One of our copy editors is leaving, so I've been handling some of his workload." She kissed my cheek, and before I knew it, she was out of my arms. I watched her lean, toned body pick up her clothes, which were strewn around various areas in my room and she quickly got dressed.

"I'm working tonight, but if you want to get together afterward, we can do that."

She grabbed her phone. "I think I have an early meeting tomorrow, but I'll text you later." I moved to get out of bed, and she up put her hand. "I'll grab a cab and can see myself out. Thanks for a great night." She smiled, and just like that, she was gone, leaving me with rumpled sheets and the smell of her perfume.

There was no way I would be able to go back to sleep, so I got up and went to the gym. I always warmed up with a jog on the treadmill, but my jog turned into a full-blown run. Before I knew it, I'd run five miles.

I grabbed a towel and laid it on the bench before grabbing some free weights. My arms stretched to the sides then came together above my chest, working my arm and pectoral muscles. I couldn't stop thinking about the golden-haired beauty who'd invaded my brain—thoughts of how different she was from Samantha were refreshing. Eating a chili dog from a food truck rather than going to a traditional restaurant wasn't something my ex would have done.

My back rolled up, and I walked over to the racks to put the weights away. I wiped my forehead and neck with a small towel and grabbed my water bottle for a generous swig.

"I love when you're all sweaty."

Nails on a chalkboard.

"Hi, handsome."

I glanced over. Leah stood next to me. "Leah." I acknowledged her presence but was ready to leave.

"So, Julie Michaels . . ." She let out a catty laugh. "Really, Brett, you could do so much better."

I shook my head as I tossed the towel over my shoulder. "Why don't you worry about yourself, Leah? You're good at that."

"Geez, Brett, you don't need to be an asshole." She unzipped her jacket, revealing a purple sports bra with her boobs spilling out of it. "I'm late for my step class.

Catch you later." She strutted away, garnering stares from the muscleheads she passed.

I walked into the locker room and showered. Thoughts of Julie continued to flood my mind, including how she'd never flaunt herself the way some women did. One more thing to like about her.

chapter 4

Julie

WORK WAS INCREDIBLY busy. We were short-staffed, and my boss's assistant, Mark, and myself were doing the jobs of three people. On top of that, we were about to lose another copy editor. There was no way I'd be able to handle all the work. I was tasked with reviewing the job posting prior to it going to HR, and as I read it, I told Brian, my boss, that we didn't need to post it. I knew the right person for the position.

I grabbed my phone and called Aubrey. I told her our copy editor was leaving the company, and we needed to replace him. "If you're interested, Brian would like you to come into the office tomorrow afternoon at four o'clock for an interview."

"No way, that's awesome! Thank you so much! I'm definitely interested. I can't tell you how much this means to me. But I guess I won't be joining you tonight at the club. The last thing I need is to go into the interview hungover and dragging."

"Yeah, I don't know if I'm going out either. I'm exhausted. How about if we go tomorrow night to celebrate? It's ladies' night, and the drinks will be cheaper, not that Brett or Alex would let us buy our drinks."

"Sounds great," she said. "Hopefully we'll have a reason to celebrate. See you tomorrow. I have to go make sure I have something to wear to the interview and get my writing samples in order. Thanks again. I love you."

"I love you too. Bye."

The rest of my day went by in a flurry. Mark and I had a working lunch, which added to my exhaustion. I couldn't take anymore, so I packed up my things and went home for a much needed rest.

Aubrey nailed her interview. The three of us—Aubrey, Mark, and I—spent the next few weeks reviewing projects and upcoming pitches we needed to make. Brett and I also became closer as the days passed. We exchanged texts that ranged from a simple "hi" to "I can't wait to touch you again"—those were my favorites. We took occasional lunch breaks, grabbing a quick bite at various food trucks.

But today, we were finally having lunch at Fao's, the Greek restaurant where Brett had been itching to take me. The décor was old-fashioned, classic, and tasteful. I was engulfed by delicious aromas. I couldn't wait to enjoy our lunch.

A handsome dark-haired Mediterranean man greeted us. He gave me a wink and a sexy smile. "Brett, it's good to see you." They shook hands, then he looked at me. "Who is this beautiful woman?" He extended his hand, and when I put mine in his, he brought it to his lips and kissed the back of it.

Brett put his arm around me, so there was no question we weren't there as friends—he'd staked his claim on me. "Julie, this is my friend Pirro."

"Welcome to Fao's." Pirro grabbed two menus and led us to a quiet table in the back of the restaurant.

Once he left, Brett held my hand across the table. "Thank you for being with me today."

"It's my pleasure, Mr. Chambers."

Our waitress brought water to our table. When she noticed Brett, she smiled. "Hi, Brett." Her fake eyelashes fluttered as she turned her back to me and faced Brett.

Was I invisible, or did this woman not care that he wasn't alone?

"Hi, Daria." He smiled, and my eyes rolled.

"Can I get you your usual, or are you in the mood for something different today?"

An innocent question, but there was an underlying message. I suddenly felt like the third wheel and was instantly reminded why I didn't do relationships or jealousy. Aubrey had had a similar experience when she went out with Alex. I remembered her telling me how she'd felt, and I could relate. Daria's behavior shouldn't have bothered me though so I wouldn't let it. Instead, I let Brett take the lead.

"Daria, this is my girlfriend, Julie."

Wait. Did he introduce me as his girlfriend?

She turned and gave me a half smirk "Do you know what you'd like?"

His eyes never left mine, and he smiled.

"I'll have whatever Brett's having." I grinned.

He placed our order, and she walked away.

Brett took my hands. "So, will you?"

I coyly replied, "Will I what?"

He shook his head. "Be mine."

"Brett Chambers, are you asking me to be your girlfriend?" I felt my lips curl up, and my cheeks rise.

"Yes. Julie Michaels, I'd be honored if you would be my girlfriend."

"I'd love to." I leaned across the table and brought my lips to his.

We enjoyed the most delicious Greek food I'd ever tasted. Daria remained professional and even told me to come back. Something told me she'd said it so Brett would come back, but I didn't make a big deal about it. I gave her my best smile and left. Once we were outside, Brett pulled me into his arms and held me tight.

"What are you doing?" I asked.

"Hugging my girl. Is that okay?"

"Completely."

The warm sun beat down on us as we made our way back to my office. Brett had to work that night, and I was beat, so I told him I'd see him tomorrow. He tried to talk me into coming to see him at the club, but I did one better.

"How about I go home and rest, and you come over after work?" I asked.

"It'll be late. I won't get to your place until three in the morning. I don't want you to wait up for me." He placed his hands on the small of my back.

"Call me when you're done. If I don't answer, I'll see you tomorrow." I rolled onto the balls of my feet and placed a quick kiss on his lips. "Have a good night, and thank you for lunch."

"You're welcome. Now go to work before I take you home and make love to you until you forget your own name."

I felt a twinge of excitement between my legs. "Well, that's not a great incentive for me to go into the office." I snickered. "I'll talk to you later."

Thank God my office was air-conditioned because I felt as though I would melt into the sidewalk—and not because it was hot. I had a boyfriend. Holy shit. Me, Julie Michaels, actually had a boyfriend.

Brett

THE CLUB WAS extremely busy, which was great because time went by quickly. I wanted to get to Julie. It was funny how I'd never noticed how many phone numbers I received on cocktail napkins until I didn't want them anymore. Tonight I'd received six, and it was the middle of the week. It should have been a slow night, but there was a bachelorette party, so several of the bride-to-be's friends wanted a man for themselves. Turning down their advances was new for me, but at the same time, I didn't hate it.

Alex and Tyler left after last call, but I stayed to reconcile the till and make sure everything was ready for tomorrow. By the time I finished, it was a slightly after 3:30. I didn't want to wake Julie, so I didn't call.

But at home, I was wired and couldn't sleep. I lay in bed, wide awake, and thought about how different Julie was. She could have lost her shit today at the restaurant or asked me a thousand questions about Daria, but she didn't. I knew if the tables were turned, my blood would boil at the thought of her with another man. I sent her a text to let her know I was thinking about her.

Me: I got home too late and didn't want to call. I hope you're dreaming of me.

I didn't expect a text back, but it didn't take long for my phone to ding.

Julie: I was until my phone woke me. It's a shame too because I was having a really good dream.

Me: Want to tell me what it was about?

Julie: Nope, I'd rather make it come true. Good night, Brett.

That woman would be the death of me.

Me: Sweet dreams.

Julie: You have no idea.

Me: OK, you can't leave me like this.

Julie: Like what?

I needed to hear her voice. She was obviously awake, so I called her.

"Hey." Her voice was sleepy and sexy as hell.

"Tell me."

"I don't know what you're referring to." She giggled, and my dick stiffened.

"Jules, cut a guy some slack."

She sighed and let out a breath that I swore I could feel on my cheek. "Fine, if you must know, we were having hot sex."

My body came alive. "Where?"

"In an airplane hangar." She was so nonchalant about it, which made her words sexier than they already were.

Note to self: rent an airplane hangar.

"So you want to have sex in an airplane hangar?"

"I didn't say that. I said we were having sex in an airplane hangar."

"So you don't want to have sex in an airplane hangar?" I strained not to laugh. I just wanted to keep her on the phone.

"You're ridiculous." She giggled again, then in true Julie fashion, she flipped it on me. "It's a shame you aren't here because we could pretend we were there, but now I'll have to satisfy myself." Her sensual groan and teasing tone set me off.

Holy shit. "I'll be there in twenty minutes." Who needed sleep when I knew my girlfriend was priming herself for me? "Don't hang up. I'm going to talk to you until I get to your place." I slid on my shoes, grabbed my keys, and headed out the door.

"Are you serious?"

I started my SUV, and my Bluetooth kicked in. "You still with me?"

"Yes." She exhaled, and I adjusted my pants.

"What are you wearing?" I asked.

"Nothing."

"Jesus Christ, Julie. I'm going to get in an accident."

"Did you want me to lie to you?"

"No." Traffic was moving, but I felt as though I caught every light. I finally pulled up to her apartment building. "Buzz me in."

"Okay."

I heard her shuffling around. Once I was inside, I took the stairs two at a time and got to her door. I knocked once and looked around to make sure no one was in the hallway. The last thing I wanted was for someone to see her naked. She opened the door, and I walked in and saw the most beautiful woman standing completely naked except for a pair of black patent leather stilettos.

I closed the door and clicked the deadbolt. My eyes took their time drinking her in from head to toe. "I thought you said you were naked?"

She glanced at her feet. "I threw these on because they make my ass look better. See?"

Julie slowly spun on the balls of her feet, giving me a three-hundred-sixty-degree view of her fantastic body. Her toned abs, beautifully formed legs that led up to her glorious ass, and her bare pussy made me lose all composure. I stalked toward her, and she rested her hands on her hips.

"You like?" She tossed in a wink.

"No, I love."

I placed my hands on hers right before I scooped her up, carried her to her room and laid her on the bed. My clothes landed on the floor in record speed, and she perused my body with her gorgeous bright green eyes.

I hovered over her. "So, about that dream."

Our lips melded together, and our tongues made love to each other. I skimmed my finger down the center of her breasts until I slid it inside her. She moved her hips up, and I added another finger and then another.

She broke our kiss. "I need you, Brett." Her hand found my stiff shaft, and she stroked it.

I grabbed a condom out of my pocket.

"Can I?" she asked. I gave her the condom, and she rolled it on, letting her hand linger and rub me.

"I'm not going to last long if you keep doing that."

My left arm supported me as my right hand pulled her leg around me. I noticed that she'd never taken off her shoes, and I about came on the spot. I easily slid in and arched my back. I moved my hips, meeting hers with each thrust.

"Is this what your dream felt like?"

She shook her head, "No, this feels better . . . much better."

Her slender neck arched. I needed to taste it. My tongue swept from the base to the tip of her chin. Julie's fingers gripped my back as we picked up the pace.

I wanted this to last longer, but I wasn't about to stop. "You're ready, aren't you?"

I watched her cheeks color as she tilted her head back. She tightened around me, and her legs shook. I increased my speed with each thrust until she screamed my name. My release hit me quick, and I grunted as I plunged as deep as I could into her core.

"Oh my God, Brett!" Her heels grazed my lower back.

I collapsed on her chest and kissed her hard. My hands held the sides of her face. "Next time you dream, that's what I want it to be—what we just did."

Her lips curled into a sexy smile. "That's what it was—except for the airplane hangar." She snickered then said with all sincerity, "But this was much better . . . much, much better."

I pulled her into my arms and held her back to my chest. "Good night, Julie." I kissed the back of her head.

She sighed and wiggled closer to me. Our legs were bent together, and her ass was pressed against my abs. "Sweet dreams, Brett."

chapter 5

Julie

OVER THE LAST few months, my days had been fantastic and my nights even better. When I was with Brett, something inside me was different. I couldn't pinpoint it, but it was there. Each kiss and embrace had become more and more important to me. It was as if he awoke a side of me that had been dormant or maybe didn't even exist.

The smell of coffee made my senses wake and my stomach rumble as I waited for the barista to create my morning indulgence. While I sat in the coffee shop with my latte and scone, I watched the people walking down the busy city streets. They all blended into a sea of hurry-up-and-go. I wondered if I had always been the same way. Maybe that was what Brett was changing in me—making me stop and take time to enjoy other things in life rather than just my job.

I picked apart my pastry, put a bite in my mouth, and savored the juicy blueberry explosion. Once I was done, I headed to the office again, becoming one in a sea of many.

Brian had decided to try to expand into the international market, which meant long nights trying to figure out which companies would be viable for us to approach. I disliked that part of marketing and advertising. Multiple agencies pitched their services to one company on the same day—cattle calls if you will. I didn't know what the agency before or after me said to the potential clients, and it was nerve-racking.

I stared at all of the work on my desk. Brian needed to hire more people. I loved my job, but when the end of the day came, I was exhausted. For the past few weeks, Mark and I had been trying to get the job done. Aubrey and Alex's relationship had hit a major bump in the road, the thought of which broke my heart. Alex ended up finding out about Aubrey's secret journal she kept for her novel. It listed romantic gestures Alex had made throughout their relationship and how she could use them in her book.

When they'd first started dating, Aubrey hadn't expected to fall in love, but she did. What started out as research turned into a diary of sorts. However, Alex didn't ask her about what the journal meant. He assumed she'd been using him. He was hurt and angry.

That night, Alex went to his club and drowned his aggravation in liquor. Aubrey rushed to the club to try to explain, but when Alex spotted her, he grabbed Leah who was passing by and kissed her.

I had just arrived at the club when Aubrey ran by me. The next thing I knew, Brett was yelling for someone to call 9-1-1 because Aubrey was lying unconscious on the sidewalk. Apparently, when she ran out of the club, she was accidentally shoved to the ground and sustained a horrible concussion when her head hit the concrete.

At the hospital, Aubrey woke to darkness. My best friend was blind, and I was terrified for her. Not only did she lose Alex, but she had lost her sight.

There wasn't anything the doctors could do. She received the standard, "In time, your vision may return," prognosis. Looking back, I supposed they didn't have the necessary information to tell her more than that, but for Aubrey, their prognosis was enough for her to realize her life was forever changed.

When she'd decided to move to Paris to be with her parents, I went with her to help her while her mom and dad made their home handicapped accessible for her. When she was settled, and I came back to the States, I was heartbroken for my friend. She was lost and confused. Alex did everything in his power to stay by her side, even though she fought him every step of the way.

All Aubrey had wanted was to be a writer, and although she taught herself, Braille, it wasn't the same. She was a pen-to-paper writer, and that was no longer an option for her. I prayed that my best friend would have the strength to go on living a completely different way of life.

My heart ached for her. Aubrey had been working on overcoming her anxiety, but this was a major setback. I didn't know if she'd recover—emotionally or physically.

Brett and I did our best not to let our friends' breakup affect us, and for the most part, we succeeded. We didn't take sides, but it was a difficult time. Although my thoughts were with Aubrey, I was plagued with guilt for feeling happy. I couldn't help but appreciate what I had—especially, Brett.

I looked at the clock. It was already after six. I wanted to leave, but before I left, Brian called me into his office to discuss a new client that wanted a marketing plan for his vineyard in Italy. Brian had heard this vineyard wanted to market their wine in the States but wanted to partner with an upscale club, and the White Orchid would be an ideal fit. And since it was my client, giving me the project was a no-brainer since I was the lead on the White Orchid's account.

He filled me in on the details of the family-owned vineyard, what they desired and their budget, which would be easy to work with. I told Brian I'd come up with something brilliant. Thankfully I had about a month to give him my preliminary draft.

I walked back to my office, looked at the mounds of paperwork and storyboards, and decided I'd had enough. I grabbed my purse, turned off the light, and closed my door. My body screamed at me to go home and soak away my day in a lavender bubble bath, but I wanted to surprise Brett at the club. I needed a drink and, more importantly, a hug. We hadn't seen each other in a couple of days due to my many business dinners and his schedule at the club.

I hopped in my car, dropped it off at my apartment building, and called a cab. I didn't want to deal with city traffic when I was this tired—it was bad enough when I was wide awake. The yellow sedan dropped me in front of the club and knowing Brett was beyond the double doors sparked enough adrenaline in my body to wake me up a bit. I couldn't wait to see his smile and how sultry his eyes became when he looked at me.

As usual, the club was hopping, and the energy inside was powerful. Young professionals, with their ties loosened, were at one end of the bar, unwinding over a pitcher of beer. At the other end, a party was going on. Women were hooting and hollering, and one even wore a small white veil and a sash that said "Bride." It must have been her bachelorette party.

I saw Brett's back. I'd have known his form and the effortless way his body moved as he mixed cocktails anywhere. I couldn't help the sense of want and belonging I felt when I was around him. The closer I got, the more my body came to life. The tension in my muscles fell away, and contentment washed over me.

As I rounded the corner, my feet stopped moving. A stunning brunette was leaning across the bar, and her sultry round breasts protruded from her blouse. She was laughing with Brett at something he'd said, and I watched like a smarmy voyeur as he tossed her a wink and gave her his award-winning smile—as he had when we'd first met. He poured two shots, one for her, and one for himself. They clinked glasses. She never took her eyes off him as she tossed it back. He wiped the bar and continued their conversation.

Never once had I felt jealous, not once had I felt possessive, but at that very moment, I did. I didn't care for it. A small part of me wondered if this was a common occurrence when he worked. What a ridiculous thought—of course, it was. He was a sexy bartender with a reputation as long as the mahogany wood that was his workplace.

The pounding bass of the music mimicked the pounding in my ears as I slowly walked toward them. But I didn't feel like dealing with it, so instead, I turned toward the door without paying attention to anyone around me. My brain felt foggy, and my heart ached.

"Julie?"

I blinked and looked to my left.

Tyler chuckled. "Damn, I've been calling your name."

A fake grin appeared on my face. "Sorry, I didn't hear you. It's busy here tonight."

"Yeah, every night has been like this lately." He beamed with pride.

Every night is like this. Every night is like this. Every night. Like this.

Tyler asked, "Can I get you a drink?"

I tried to blink away the haze that had formed in my brain. "No, thank you. I think I'm going to head out."

"Are you okay?"

"Yes, I'm fine. Just a bit tired." The confusion that had washed over me, not to mention the jealousy that had infiltrated my heart, drained me of any spark of energy I'd had. Numbness took over.

"Let me get Brett for you." His face softened, and his voice was laced with worry.

I panicked a bit and put up my hand. "No, it's fine. I don't want to bother him. I'm just exhausted."

He tightly smiled. "Okay, if you're sure."

"I am. Thank you, Tyler."

"Take care of yourself."

I nodded, and he shifted to his side and brought the business guys another pitcher of beer. I chanced one more glance at Brett. He was back in front of his new friend. Maybe it was because I was worn out, but I felt so defeated. What irritated me the most was that I'd let a man make me feel that way. This situation was getting ridiculous. I was ridiculous, but what was worse . . . I was jealous.

I heard my name and stopped dead in my tracks. I turned. Brett was behind me.

"Hey, did you just get here?" He leaned in and gave me a kiss on the cheek.

I relished the tenderness of his action. "No, actually, I was about to . . ."

He glanced at the doors. "Were you going to leave?" Worry lines formed above his eyes.

Before I could answer, I lowered my head and did my best to conjure up the appropriate word. Instead, I went for an honest one. "Yes."

"Without saying hello? Why?" His brows drew together in a confused expression.

"I didn't appreciate seeing you flirt." God, I hated how I felt. I wasn't the lovesick-fool type, and that was how I sounded.

Loud laughter that sounded like cackling took my attention. Brett looked back to where it came from, then with a tilt of his head, he looked at me. He took my hand and led me to a quieter spot in the club. "Was it the bachelorette party? Was that it? There's no reason to be jealous or angry."

"I'm neither jealous nor angry." Okay, I was a tad jealous. "I saw you having a great time with Miss Boobs Galore flirting with you, and I was too tired to deal with it. All I wanted was to see you, and there you were laughing and having a great time, so I was going to leave you to your . . . business. As I said, I didn't want to interrupt, and that's exactly what I would have done." My blood pumped hard. I was so irritated that I sounded immature.

"It was nothing. We make more money and sell more drinks when we toss in some flirtation here and there." He was so nonchalant about it that my skin crawled, and my stomach rolled.

"This is why I don't do boyfriends. I don't want my man giving another woman the wrong impression. One day, that's going to backfire on you, and you're going to break a heart." Pressure built beneath my eyes and my face began to tingle. The realization hit me that the heart he would break could be mine.

He placed both hands on my shoulders and looked into my eyes. "I'm sorry." His voice sounded an infinitely compassionate. "Your heart is the one I care about, and I didn't mean to hurt you." He wrapped me in his strong arms. "That's the last thing I'd want to do, but please don't doubt what I feel for you. If something bothers you, I want to know about it so we don't have misunderstandings." His arms loosened, and he lifted my chin so our eyes met. "Okay?"

I nodded. "Okay."

"Now, can I get you something to drink?"

"No, I really am tired and want to go home." That was the God's honest truth.

"I'll call you later." He pulled me close and kissed me. "Just you, Jules."

His killer smile and those three words made me feel better as I left the club.

I padded across my living room into my kitchen and poured myself a glass of chardonnay. A bath would have been too much effort at that point, so I put on my pajamas and sat on the couch with my wine and a movie. Why I decided on a sappy love story was beyond me. I set down my glass and rested my head on a pillow as I watched a couple kissing under an oak tree. Enough of that crap. I grabbed the remote and flipped to a *Law & Order* marathon. Better.

My mind drifted to Brett. Love. Was I . . . ? I let out a sigh, rolled to my back, grabbed a throw pillow, and held it to my chest as if it were a shield that could protect my heart. I had a feeling it was too late. Brett had taken down the walls that I'd built over the years, and I hadn't even realized it. Had he? Did he know he'd penetrated a barrier I had erected?

When I woke on the couch, I cursed myself for not going to bed. I needed to get to work when I could have used more sleep.

Mark was in the break room when I got to the office.

"Good morning," I said.

"Hey, Jules. Are you ready to clear off some of our workload?"

"Sounds great, thank you." I poured myself a cup of coffee.

His brows lowered as he studied me. "Are you okay?"

"Sure. Want to come to my office so we can sift through the files and prioritize accordingly?"

Mark stood and followed me in. He closed the door, and I sat in my chair and opened my laptop.

He sat in the chair opposite mine. "Spill it. What's bothering you? Don't tell me nothing, because I know you, and you're acting strange."

I slumped back in my chair. "I don't know how to explain it." I exhaled. "Being in a relationship is new to me, and most of the time, I love the way it makes me feel. I never even think about it, because it's so effortless, and then *bam,* I'm hit over the head with reality, and it makes me feel vulnerable."

Mark nodded. "I'm not the best when it comes to relationships. When I was with Jessica, I thought we had it all and we were great together, but then she decided to study in London. I was hit with the harsh reality that she didn't want me the way I wanted her." He shrugged. "But everything happens for a reason. Now I have Val, and she's great."

I remembered how upset he had been when Jessica moved. It prompted me to ask, "Are you happy?"

"Yes." His smile was genuine. "Val's fantastic and everything Jess wasn't."

"But you loved Jessica." That was the part of relationships that confused me. Love didn't come with a switch, so how did one turn it off? It was hard enough for me to turn it on.

"I thought I did." Mark rubbed his temples. "No, I did love her. I thought she was it for me, but she was so quick to dismiss what we had. That's not love." He shrugged in defeat.

My head bobbed as I tried to figure out what my heart was telling me.

"Jules, did something happen with Brett?" His voice softened.

"No, not really. I don't know." I dropped my head in my hands. "I'm not sure how to deal with the reality of having someone consume my thoughts." *Not to mention my heart.*

"You're in love with him, aren't you?"

My head snapped up. "Why would you say that?"

"I don't know what happened between you two, and I will kick his ass if he hurt you, but I've never seen you like this. The Julie I know and love doesn't get hung up on a guy, so my only conclusion is during the past few months, you fell for him and you fell hard. Now you don't know what to do about it."

"Maybe. Yes." I grabbed some files and handed them to Mark. "Let's get to work and put a dent in this."

He stood and took the files. "Jules, I'm here if you need me. I wasn't kidding when I said I'd kick his ass. If he hurts you, it'll be my pleasure to wipe the floor with him."

I smiled. "Thank you, but that won't be necessary."

Mark walked out, and I tried to dive into my work. Instead, I nibbled on the tip of my pen as I recalled my past. I'd lost my parents when I was a teenager and lived with my grandmother until she'd passed away my junior year in college. Then it was just me, and I'd been fine with that. I didn't need to rely on anyone or fear losing someone if they weren't close to me. My motto was, "You can't miss what you never had." So I kept people, especially men, at bay, and it had worked for me until last night. The possibility of Brett being with someone else gnawed at me.

I grabbed a storyboard and placed it on an easel. I moved pictures around until they looked like an incredible ad. Storyboarding may have been the old-school way, but I liked it. There was something real about touching the images. Nothing was computer-generated. My work was honest, tangible, and pure.

As I perused the ad I'd created, I realized storyboarding was like my relationship with Brett. The pieces may have been scattered, but once in place, they came together and worked.

Brett

WORK WASN'T THE same after my talk with Julie. She hadn't come by in the past couple of days, and I missed her. The sound of her voice over the phone wasn't the same as having her in my arms or tasting her. Julie wasn't the jealous, possessive type. I needed to figure things out with her, so when I left work early, I made my way to her place.

My shaky finger pressed the button to her apartment. Once I was buzzed in and made it to her door, I was sure my blood pressure was at an all-time high. When I saw her standing in her doorway, the urge to pull her into my arms was fierce.

I stopped myself and just said, "Hi."

"Come in." Julie looked beautiful, as usual. Her gorgeous blond hair had been pulled into a ponytail, and even in jeans and a T-shirt, she was the most stunning woman I'd ever seen. She looked over her shoulder as she crossed to the kitchen. "Beer?"

"Yeah, sure. But then I want to talk." I couldn't take my eyes off her.

She handed me my beer and sat on the couch, and I did follow suit. It didn't escape me that she hadn't hugged or kissed me hello, not that I had pulled her into my arms either. I let her guide me. The tension in the air grated on me.

She grabbed a glass of wine she'd left on the coffee table. "How was traffic?"

"I don't want to discuss traffic. I want to talk about us."

"Brett, look, I know you said we were exclusive, but if you said that because you thought it was what I wanted to hear, then don't worry about it. Honestly, it's forgotten if you want it to be."

My brows furrowed. I was shocked to hear her speak those words. "What the hell are you talking about? Julie . . ." I stood and paced in front of the sofa.

"Look, I didn't want this. I don't want to worry about losing what I have."

"What? You didn't want what? Me? Us? Give me a bit more to go on here." My jaw ticked, and I felt my shirt tighten with each rise of my chest.

"I want you more than anything I've ever wanted in my life. I'm not used to that feeling." She shrugged.

I sat back down, took her hand, and squeezed it.

I was about to say something when she continued. "Then I started thinking I don't know much about you. I know you have a brother, but that's it."

I nodded. "I guess we never talked about our families when we played our question-and-answer game."

She tentatively smiled, which gave me an uneasy feeling. "No, we didn't."

"Then I'll go first. My parents are wonderful people. You know I have one brother, Bentley, and he's a theater critic, so I don't see him too often even though he doesn't live too far away. I have several cousins, and we're a pretty close family. My parents have a home in the Hamptons and stay there year-round, so I don't see them as much as I'd like. That's why I haven't brought you to their home so I could introduce you to them, but I assure you, they know all about you."

"They do?" Her nose crinkled, and a tiny crease formed between her eyebrows as they drew inward.

"Do you honestly think I wouldn't tell the people I love about you?" Her eyes became watery as she looked into mine. "Did you tell your parents about me?"

She shook her head, and my heart fell. "My parents passed away. It's just me."

She shrugged, and my feelings for her multiplied. One of the strongest women I knew was alone. Maybe that was why she had that strength. Another reason why she never relied on others—she'd only had herself until me.

"I'm so sorry. I didn't know."

"It's okay. It was a long time ago. But I know they would have loved you." She sniffled.

I placed my hand on her cheek and wiped a stray tear with my thumb. "I'm sure I would have loved them too, just like I do their daughter."

Her lids opened, and her lashes glistened with moisture. "What?"

"I'm falling in love with you, Julie. We may not have known each other for a long time, but who's to say there's a right or wrong amount of time to fall for someone? What I felt for you started as a deep physical attraction, maybe even lust, but I think you're perfect for me."

She didn't say anything for a bit, as though she was processing everything I'd said. "I think I'm falling for you too, Brett. I'm sorry for acting like a jealous girlfriend. It wasn't what was happening in the bar as much as how it made me feel. I don't let people into my heart for fear I'll lose them. Aubrey is the exception. But I've never been as close to a man as I am to you. I'm happy being your girlfriend, and if you could forgive my temporary bout of insanity, I'd appreciate it." Her hand rested on my leg. She leaned in closer and placed her head on my chest.

I held her tight. I couldn't believe she'd told me she was falling in love with me. Shit, I couldn't believe I'd said it to her. It had been years since I said those words to a woman. Oddly, I'd thought I'd meant them then, but compared to now, I didn't know that I had.

"You're forgiven on one condition."

She leaned back and smiled. "What's that?"

"Friday night, it's me and you. I have plans for us."

"Okay, I'd like that."

"Great, then you're forgiven."

We laughed and held each other. She told me more about her parents, and I told her about mine. I also found out how busy her office had been. I couldn't wait to spend Friday with her. She didn't know it, but

I'd called her boss and asked him to give her the day off. Hopefully, she wouldn't get mad at me or think I was going all caveman on her, but I needed her for more than a few hours. More than anything, I wanted her all to myself.

Friday morning, I picked Julie up for work using the excuse that I would be in the area since I was going to the gym. I dropped her off at the office and kissed her good-bye.

Before she left, she mentioned how excited she was for our date. Her smile broadened as she opened the car door. "See you later." Julie winked.

She didn't know I was only going to drive around the corner and park to wait for our day together to begin. I'd traded nights with the new bartender, Mike so I could relax with her all day. I stood on the corner and waited a bit before going inside.

Mark greeted me at the door and shook my hand. "I don't know what you have up your sleeve, but I'm glad she's happy. I was ready to come kick your ass."

"I'm glad she has you for a friend," I said, trying not to laugh at the idea of him kicking my ass. Mark was a fit guy, but when it came to Julie, I'd fight for her no matter what.

Brian caught me in the hall on the way to Julie's office, and I thanked him for giving her a day off. He said he was more than pleased to do it because she'd been working too hard and needed a break.

Julie was tapping away on her laptop when I knocked on her open office door. Her face lit up. "Hi, what are you doing here? Did I forget something in your car?"

"Nope, grab your things. We're leaving." I smiled and held out my hand.

"Brett, don't be ridiculous. I have a ton of work to do, and I have meetings today."

"No, you don't." Mark walked into her office and placed his hands on her shoulders. "You have the day off. I'm covering your meetings." Julie opened her mouth to say something, but Mark stopped her. "It's a done deal." He cocked his head toward me. "Your boyfriend here planned it all. Now leave and go enjoy yourself."

Mark looked at Julie, then he looked at me as if he was giving me a silent warning of some sort. I took it as a good friend concerned for another.

"Really?" She closed her laptop and didn't hesitate to pack her things.

I took her bag and grabbed her hand, lacing her fingers with mine.

"Thanks, Mark."

We walked out, and she was practically bouncing. "Are you a bit excited there, Skippy?"

She giggled. "Skippy?"

"Yeah, you bounce like a kangaroo. They're sometimes referred to as Skippy."

"Oh, haha, I guess I do." She shrugged. "So what are we doing today?"

"It's a surprise." We stopped in front of my SUV, and I opened the door for her.

Before she got in, she kissed me. "Thank you for today. It means a lot to me."

"You don't even know what we're doing yet."

"It doesn't matter what it is. You took the time to plan whatever it is, and we could do absolutely nothing, and I'd be happy because I'm with you." She slid into my car and fastened her seatbelt.

I stood there dumbfounded as I stared at her.

"Well, are we going or what?" She winked, and we were on our way.

chapter 6

Julie

BRETT NAVIGATED THE traffic with ease, and before I knew it, we were in the Hamptons. I stared, in awe of the homes and the beautiful landscape. We didn't have all of this foliage in the city.

I rolled down my window and inhaled the smell of freshly cut lawns, flowers, and the salty essence of the ocean. "Wow, it's so serene. I could get used to a place like this even though I'd miss the sound of car horns and the hustle and bustle." My hair blew in the breeze, and I relaxed. "It's beautiful here."

"I think you're the beautiful one." Brett picked up my hand and kissed it. He didn't let go but rested it on his thigh and held on tight. He turned down a long driveway and stopped in front of a gorgeous home.

"Who lives here?"

"My parents."

My throat may have closed at his reply. He gave my hand a quick squeeze before he released it and turned off the car. He hopped out, and my heart hammered. I rubbed my thumbs on my palms, which were now coated in a thin sheen of sweat. I wiped them on my pants to get rid of any evidence of my nerves.

Brett opened my door. "I can't wait for you to meet my mom."

I shyly smiled, trying not to let my uneasiness show.

"I'm her favorite." He chuckled and closed the door.

"Does your brother know that?" I giggled as he pulled me close in a reassuring hug.

"Yes, but he's in denial." He kissed the top of my head and held my hand. "Let's go."

He opened the front door, and I was once again in awe. The foyer was grand, and I loved the décor. I could tell it was a home full of love and not a showcase. The pictures on the walls weren't painted by famous artists; they were family portraits and some candid shots of Brett's family having fun. I couldn't help but smile as I looked at a photo of two young boys and an extremely handsome man on a boat. The man held up a fishing line with a good-sized fish on it. I wasn't sure who had caught it. Both boys looked as though they had, and the man beamed with pride.

"Is that your dad?"

He chuckled. "Yes, that was a great day. Bentley and I were competing, as usual, to see who would have the biggest catch of the day, and it ended up being my father." We walked toward the back of the house. "My mom's probably in the garden. She may be a tad miffed."

I stopped dead in my tracks. "What? Why? Does she not want to meet me?" Heat rose up the back of my neck.

He tugged me forward, and I stumbled as I followed him. "No, silly, I didn't tell her we were coming. So not only will she be surprised that her favorite child is here, she'll be shocked to finally meet you. But don't worry. She'll love you."

I swallowed hard.

The backyard was stunning. There was a beautiful patio with what looked like comfortable and expensive furniture, a grill, bar, and a large table that was just right for a family.

As Brett had guessed, his mom was kneeling on a cushion in front of a flower garden. She was clipping and gathering the most stunning bouquet.

"Hey, Mom."

Her hand went to her chest as she looked at us. She stood, laid the flowers down, and took off her gardening gloves. "Hi, honey, I didn't know you were coming over. I'm a mess."

He let go of my hand and gave her a hug. She looked at me then at Brett.

"Mom, this is my girlfriend, Julie. Julie, this is my mom, Madeline Chambers."

"Hi, Mrs. Chambers." I held out my hand.

"Please, call me Madeline. It's wonderful to finally meet you." She pulled me into a hug.

I looked at Brett over her shoulder, and he gave me a thumbs-up, which made me smile. Madeline exuded the same tenderness as her son—he must have gotten it from her.

"Brett, grab those flowers for me, will you?" He did as she asked, and she said, "Come with me, Julie. Would you like some iced tea?"

"Yes, thank you. That sounds wonderful." I followed her into the kitchen.

Brett wasn't far behind us. He opened a cabinet and pulled out a large Mason jar, filled it with water, and put the flowers in it.

"Thank you, sweetheart." She took the flowers and put them in the center of the dining table before getting us each a glass of iced tea. We sat at the table, and Brett held my hand.

His mom looked at us. "So where did you two meet?"

Brett spoke first. "I met her at the club."

My heart sank. I wondered what she must think of us meeting in a bar. "I was working an event at the club that evening, and my friend met Alex when I met your son." I took a sip of my tea.

"It's funny how things happen." She smiled. "When you least expect it, right? Are you two hungry?"

"No, thank you, mom. I just wanted to bring Julie here to meet you." He kissed my hand, and my stomach fluttered.

"Well, I'm glad you did. Between you and your brother, I was beginning to lose hope. You're both so busy and don't take time for yourselves to find happiness for more than a few hours."

I snickered. I loved this woman. She called it like she saw it, and she was right. Brett was all about one-night stands. Okay, we both had been before we met each other, but she didn't need to know my relationship history.

"Mom, really." Brett shook his head and laughed. "Keep talking that way, and I won't have a girlfriend for very long."

"Oh, Julie seems like a smart young woman. I don't think I'm giving her any new information." She waved dismissively. "So, Julie, you said you were working when you met Brett?"

"Yes, I work for a marketing firm, and the White Orchid is one of my accounts. That evening, I was managing a speed dating event. Alex was kind enough to let us use the club."

"Speed dating? Does that work?" Her nose crinkled.

"That's what I asked," Brett interjected. "How can you find someone within minutes and know they're the one? It seems more like a hook-up party." He laughed, and I raised my brows at him. "What?" He shrugged. "It did."

I shook my head. Didn't he realize that even though we weren't part of the event, it hadn't taken much longer than several minutes for him to kiss me, and now I was his girlfriend? Men and their selective memories.

"Julie, do your parents live in the city?"

I hated answering questions about my parents. Not because of the way it made me feel—I'd accepted that—but for the way the other person seemed affected by the information. I put on a happy face to reassure her that it was okay before I replied. "My parents passed away."

"Oh, honey"—his mom placed her hand on my forearm—"I'm so sorry for your loss."

"Thank you." I needed to change the topic. "Your home is beautiful."

She looked around, pride etched in her features. "Thank you. Hopefully the next time you're here, you can meet Brett's father and maybe his brother if I can ever get him to take a break."

"I'd love that."

She patted my arm, and a feeling of calm and happiness coursed through me. It was as if I were home. Brett stood and held his hand out for me. I took it and stood.

"We need to get going, but I promise you we'll be back. I kind of kidnapped her today, and I have some other places we need to be." He kissed his mom and gave her a hug. "Tell Dad I said hi."

"Will do, sweetie." She embraced me. "It was so nice to meet you. You're welcome here anytime."

"Thank you, Madeline."

Brett

"WELL, THAT WENT well." We were back in my car and ready to get on with our day. Seeing the two women I cared about the most together made me feel as though everything was in place and as it should be. But every time I heard Julie say her parents had died hurt.

"She's wonderful. You're extremely lucky to have her in your life."

My heart went out to her. I couldn't imagine not having my family. We may not have seen each other all the time, but I had no doubt they'd be there for me if I needed them.

"You've made me very happy today," she said.

"The day has just begun." I shot her a wink, and she bit her bottom lip as her shoulders rose.

We went to lunch at an outdoor bistro, then we spent most of the day going to quaint antique stores and fresh markets. I loved how she took the time to enjoy everything around us, but the gorgeous scenery didn't hold a candle to Julie's beauty. The way the sun shone down on her head reminded me of the first time I'd laid eyes on her under the club lights. She had an indescribable aura that was almost mysterious and definitely intriguing. I looked forward to getting to know more and more about her. I tossed my arm around her shoulder, and her hand slid into my back pocket.

"You're a pretty great boyfriend to go to all this trouble."

"It wasn't any trouble, and I'm glad you're happy." I was thrilled to have her with me and that my day had gone off without a hitch. If anyone had told me I'd have a woman I could love and who would love me back without expecting a ring, I never would have believed them. But there I was with someone who fits that bill.

When we hopped in my SUV and started heading out of town, she said, "Okay, Chambers, where are we going now?"

A broad smile grew across my face. "A very special place."

We drove down quiet roads and through serene neighborhoods until we got to my next destination, The Point. I loved it there. The lighthouse was still active, and at night, the beacon could be seen for miles. Families were taking pictures, and couples relaxed in each other's arms.

Boats sailed by, creating picture-perfect ripples in the water. I remembered going out on my grandfather's boat when we were younger. I loved my time out there, away from it all—even as a kid. Although back then, I hadn't appreciated it as I did today. My life was fulfilling, especially since I'd bought into the club and become a co-owner of the White Orchid, but at that moment, there wasn't any other place I'd have rather been or anyone I'd have rather been with.

"Wow, this is gorgeous!" Julie's eyes brightened with pleasure as she took in the beauty of Montauk and pulled me out of my thoughts.

"This was where we'd come as kids when we went on vacation. My grandparents loved it here and wanted my brother and me to appreciate life outside the hustle and bustle of the city." I parked and breathed in the ocean air.

She placed her hand in mine, and I took in her beauty as her head tilted back to look at the top of the lighthouse.

"Come on," I said.

We walked around the museum then stood on the edge of the rocky cliff, watching the waves lap at the shore. I positioned her in front of me and rested my chin on her shoulder as my arms snaked around her waist.

She rested her head on my chest. "Your grandparents were right. It's peaceful here." She sighed.

I took her into the gift shop and bought her some salt water taffy. Julie bounced on the balls of her feet as she held the box of sweet morsels. I also bought a print of the lighthouse, a small replica statue, and a baseball hat with a logo on it. So basically all of the touristy stuff.

She opened the box of candy and unwrapped a pink piece. “Do you want one?”

“No, thanks.”

She bit the taffy and let out a moan that drew my attention to her mouth. Once she was finished, she licked her lips, making my pants a bit tighter. The content look on her face filled my heart with a joy I’d never experienced.

“Let’s go back to my place. We could order in and relax.”

She threaded her fingers in my hair. “I think that would be the best ending to this day.”

I held her face and claimed her mouth. She tasted like cherries, and I couldn’t get enough of her. I needed more.

Once we were back at my apartment, we were both exhausted. We decided on pizza and a movie. Being together was easy, comfortable, but not complacent. After we had finished our dinner, we sat on the couch, and Julie curled up next to me. I’d given her one of my T-shirts to put on since she didn’t have any of her things with her.

She let out a yawn with a tiny squeak at the end. “I’m so sorry.” She giggled. “I guess I’m more tired than I thought.”

“Let’s go to bed. I don’t want us falling asleep on the couch.”

She stood to walk toward my bedroom, but I scooped her up so her legs hung over my arms and carried her upstairs.

“Mmmm, who said chivalry was dead?” She sighed and grinned.

"Someone who had an asshole for a boyfriend." She laughed, and a confident warmth ran through my veins. "See how lucky you are?"

"Yes, I'm the luckiest girl in the world."

chapter 7

Julie

AUBREY AND ALEX wanted us all to get together for lunch, and I was excited to see her. She had been in Paris for the past few months, and I'd felt as if part of me were missing. The time difference had thrown us off, and our girl talk was reduced to text messages and emails. But today, everything was as it should be. She was back together with Alex, and I was with Brett. I wished the horrible day that had taken part of her were nothing but a nightmare, but it wasn't, and it was something I'd never forget.

We met them at an Italian restaurant that a family friend of Alex's owned. Mark happened to be dating the owner's daughter, Val, so we frequented the restaurant. The familiar scent of tomatoes and garlic made my stomach growl. Brett laughed, and I blushed.

"Is someone hungry?" he asked.

I punched his arm when I really felt like laughing. The playful look in his eyes when he teased me, turned my insides to Jell-O.

"Ow! Shit, no one can say you hit like a girl." He chuckled, and my eyes narrowed. "What did I say now?"

"A girl? Listen to me, Chambers, girls can do anything boys can do—maybe even better."

He put his hands up in surrender. "Yes, okay, okay. Geez, settle down, Rocky, I was kidding."

My lips curled up, and he threw his arm over my shoulders. We made our way to the table where Aubrey's parents and Val were already sitting. We exchanged hellos, then I saw Aubrey walk in, hand in hand with Alex. She walked slowly as he guided her to her seat.

We ordered our meals, and I noticed Alex had a weird look on his face. All of a sudden, he turned Aubrey in her chair and took her hands, and I think I stopped breathing for a moment.

"I'm looking into your eyes, and I know you can't see me, but soon you will. I'll repeat this to you then." The sincerity in Alex's deep voice rendered us speechless.

We all looked at them, not knowing what he was going to tell her. Then he continued.

"You're the love of my life, Aubrey Ryan. I don't know how or why, but you were brought into my life, and I've never been more thankful for anything. You're my best friend, my lover, and I don't want to be without you ever. I want to travel the world with you, have a family with you, and grow old with you. You're my life, my reason, and my world. My heart beats stronger when we're together. You give me hope. Aubrey, will you marry me and be my wife so we can start our future?" His smile was wide and his eyes soft as he regarded her.

I wished she could see him. I was so happy for her—for them. I grabbed Brett's hand and squeezed it, waiting for Aubrey to reply.

"Alex, I love you more each day. You're the love of my life too."

I took a deep breath as I watched the romantic scene unfold in front of us.

"Yes, I'll marry you. I'd love nothing more than to be Mrs. Alex Logan." My friend radiated happiness as she accepted his ring.

The entire restaurant erupted in hoots and hollers as Alex slid the ring onto her finger. I jumped up and hugged Aubrey.

"I'm so excited for you!" I turned and kissed Alex.

After our congratulations were done and our food had arrived, we sat down to one of the most memorable lunches I'd ever had.

Aubrey and I spent the next few weeks talking about how much had changed in our lives—especially when it came to relationships. It made me wonder about my future. Was marriage something I wanted too? I'd never thought I did, but I could see it now. But what was more exciting was that the doctor had diagnosed her vision loss as hysterical blindness. After intense therapy sessions, her sight had returned. There was always the chance of it temporarily diminishing, but she'd become a stronger, more self-assured woman and knew how to cope with situations.

Our friends were meeting for lunch—Alex, Aubrey, Mark, Val and Tyler. The whole group was coupled off, except for Tyler, but I doubted he was lonely. Brett may have said that they all got hit on equally, but Tyler was in a class all his own. With his model looks and confident charm, women didn't stand a chance.

I looked around the restaurant and wondered where Alex and Aubrey were. They should have been there already. The rest of us chatted until Alex and Aubrey finally showed up. I could tell by the look on her face that she had just rocked Alex's world.

"Where did you and Aubrey run off to? I turned, and you were gone." Brett said with a grin.

I stifled a giggle as Aubrey's cheeks went from flushed to red in an instant. I raised my brow at her. "Really? You don't have the JFL. Were you standing?"

Everyone laughed except for Brett, who looked confused, and Aubrey, who buried her head in Alex's chest.

"What the hell is JFL?" Brett said, very matter-of-fact.

I whispered in his ear, "Just fucked look."

He erupted in laughter as he decided to clue in the rest of the table. "You're a lucky man!" Brett lifted his hand to high-five Alex, but Alex just shook his head.

Mark whispered something to Val before he said to the table, "On that note, we're outta here." Mark and Val stood—obviously foregoing food.

"Hold on a minute. Aubrey and I have an announcement." Alex cleared his throat as pride washed over his face. "We're getting married on December twenty-first."

I knew that was the day his mom had passed away, so it was important. However, it wasn't far away. I squealed and clapped while I bounced in my seat. "Yay! When are we going gown shopping? I'm in the wedding, right?" Pure joy and happiness filled my entire heart.

After a silent exchange between her and Alex, Aubrey said, "Yes, you're my maid of honor, and Val, I'd love for you to be my bridesmaid."

The three of us had a group hug as we spun in a circle like school girls.

Alex looked at the guys. "Brett, you're the closest thing I have to a brother, and I'd like you to be my best man. Ty and Mark, I'd be honored if you would also stand up for me as groomsmen."

My excitement tripled! I'd be standing up with Brett. Then I looked at Aubrey and our friends and realized she was short a bridesmaid. "Don't worry, Aubrey, I can handle two at once." I shot her a wink and smiled.

Tyler looked at me then at Brett. "Right on!" They high-fived and threw their arms around me.

Then Brett said to Tyler, "You better remember she's mine."

The possessiveness in his voice shot through me like a lightning bolt. His eyes consumed me as if he was telling me that he would never share me, which was fine with me. I wouldn't have wanted him to.

"Yeah, I know. You don't have to take all the fun out of it." Tyler quirked his lips and shook his head.

I was sure he could find a single guest to dance with.

Brett

I DIDN'T KNOW WHAT it was, but when I saw the look on Tyler's face when he looked at Julie, my blood ran cold. They would never have stepped out on me, but Julie was a fine-looking woman. Tyler had been approached by modeling agents, so it wouldn't have been a huge stretch to think that she might be interested in him. All I could think was, *Thank God I got to her first.*

My girl and I went back to her place.

"I'm so psyched about their wedding!" Julie threw her arms around me when we got in the door. "It's going to be so much fun!" She shrieked, and I chuckled. "Let's celebrate!" She walked into the kitchen to get us some drinks.

We were both ecstatic for our friends, but Julie's excitement went beyond that. Since I'd met her, she'd made me look at relationships differently. I'd never thought I could love someone after what my ex-wife had put me through, but Julie was nothing like Samantha. Julie never brought up the subject of money. Between her job and the money she had received when her parents passed away, she had enough to give her a comfortable life.

Even better, she'd never brought up the subject of marriage. It was refreshing to know that exchanging vows wasn't on Julie's mind. I didn't need a document stating we belonged to the each other, but I needed her.

She was in her kitchen, pouring herself a glass of wine, and I couldn't stop staring at her. I stalked up behind her, took the bottle out of her hand, and set it on the counter next to her glass.

As she turned her head to look at me, I grabbed her face and pulled her lips to mine. Our mouths molded together as our tongues glided across each other's in a fury of passion. She tasted of the red wine she'd sipped and her natural sweetness—it was intoxicating.

I ran my hands down her sides until I got to the tops of her thighs. I picked her up, forcing her legs to wrap around my waist. She broke our kiss and made me gasp as she brought her mouth to my neck and gently sucked on my pulse point. My dick stirred, and I carried her into her bedroom and laid her on her bed.

I unbuttoned her faded jeans and slid them off before stripping her of her top. I stepped back and admired her beauty. Her white lace bra which didn't do much to hide her pebbled nipples. Her taut abs and beautifully contoured hips brought my eyes to her tiny white thong. I slid my fingers under the sides and removed it.

She adjusted herself on the center of the bed and nestled her cheek on the pillow. Her emerald eyes darkened with desire as she arched her back. I quickly stripped and lowered myself to hover over her. Julie dropped her knees to each side, giving me ample access.

I lowered my head and ran my tongue up her inner thigh, tasting her skin that was prickled with goose bumps. I kissed her clit before I wrapped my lips around her folds. My tongue went to work, lapping and savoring every ounce of her until she squirmed.

"Brett . . ."

My name came out as a plea, and I glanced up at her.

"I need you now." Her fingers slid down the backs of my arms to my back. The tenderness she exuded made me feel more desired than any words she could have spoken.

"You have me, Jules."

She reached into her side table and grabbed a condom. Once I was sheathed, I glided into her. The way she felt around me was like no other. I felt her wetness and heat through the rubber and wished we were skin to skin. I'd never gone bare, not even with

Samantha. Even though she had been on the pill, she'd never wanted to risk getting pregnant.

We moved in unison, slowing down and picking up our pace at the same time. I brought my lips to her breasts, which were still covered in white. I pulled the cups of her bra down with my teeth before I stroked her breasts with my tongue. I gently bit her nipple.

She bowed her back and moved her hands behind herself to unfasten the bra. As soon as she'd pulled it off, I gave each of her tits the attention they deserved.

Julie ran her fingers through my hair as her hips bucked up to meet mine. Our lips crashed together. She tightened around me as I pulsed into her. We were amazing together.

"You're stunning." I pushed her hair back from her face, which had a sheen of sweat and peppered her with kisses.

She sighed, and I rolled us to our sides. We were still connected, and at that very moment, everything in the world was as it should be. Being with her was comfortable and peaceful. When I'd told Bentley she was different, I wasn't kidding. Little did I know how different she was. The more time we spent together, the more she surprised me. My heart opened up more to her each day.

The difficult part of our relationship was our schedules. She'd leave in the morning, and I'd be at work when she was headed home. I enjoyed my job, and the nights used to fly by, but not so much anymore.

Happy hour was a bitch tonight. I spotted my ex-wife with a group of women who looked as though they were on the prowl for their next hook-up. I hadn't even realized Samantha was in the city. My lawyer took care of ensuring she received her monthly alimony checks, so I had no idea where she even was, nor did I want to.

The sight of her made my skin crawl. She still looked good, but she worked as a personal trainer, so she should have. She'd been working at the gym I belonged to, one push-up led to another, and we'd hooked up. We were young, and she had a body that wouldn't quit. Her chestnut hair paired with her deep brown eyes and olive skin was a heady combination, and no twenty-year-old man with a pulse would have passed her up. But now I was almost a decade older and had better sense.

Things with us weren't all bad until I heard I was getting part of my grandparents' estate. That was when her true colors came to life. All of a sudden, she wanted designer clothes and fancy cars. When I told her the money was in a separate account that had been set up so she couldn't get her hands on it, she turned into the bride of Frankenstein, and I was poor Frank.

I went to my parents and told them not to give me the money yet. There was no way in hell she was getting her hands on that account. It was bad enough that after we had split up, I found out she'd been banging some musclehead while we were married. Unfortunately, I couldn't prove it, so she still got a nice monthly check.

When Alex made Tyler and me co-owners in the club, I made sure she didn't know about it. My lawyer had said according to our divorce agreement, she couldn't go after my future income, but I knew Samantha. She'd make my life a living hell until she got what she wanted.

"Well, I see you're still bartending." Samantha's voice was like nails on a chalkboard and sent shivers down my spine.

"Samantha." That was all. No cordial banter. I didn't want to spend any more time with her than I needed to.

I wanted her out of the club. God forbid Julie walked in—I couldn't imagine what type of scene my ex would create. Aubrey was upstairs with Alex, and I knew she had plans with Julie to look at wedding stuff tonight. My girl was set on being the best maid of honor a bride had ever seen—her words, not mine.

"Brett." She eyed me up and down. "You're looking good," she practically purred.

Is she coming on to me? I nodded. "Did you want a drink?"

She was about to order when I heard a commotion in the corner of the bar that stole my attention. Two female patrons were arguing and yelling at our fairly new bartender, Mike.

Samantha clucked her tongue. "Some people don't have any class at all." She turned her nose up at the women talking to Mike.

When I heard one of them tell Mike they wanted to talk to the owner, my eyes closed. I quickly prayed that he'd call Alex, but he didn't. He put his index finger up to the women and walked over to me. I glanced at Samantha.

"Brett, can you help me out? They want an owner, and you're the only one available." He looked at Samantha, not knowing who she was, and politely apologized for his interruption.

Her eyes went wide as she realized what Mike had said. I nodded and followed him to the complainants.

I straightened out their tab and gave them a drink on the house for the confusion.

By the time I got back to Samantha, she was on her phone. "That's right—an owner." Her eyes shot darts at me. "The agreement states if he got a new job, not a promotion." She nodded, said something I couldn't hear, tossed her phone in her purse. She tucked her purse under her arm. "You owe me, you bastard! You'll be hearing from my attorney."

I told Mike to cover for me so I could deal with this nonsense. Samantha followed me outside.

"You have absolutely no right to any more money. You get enough from me as it is." I paced the sidewalk and tossed my hands in the air as frustration took over. "Jesus Christ, Samantha, can't you give it a rest?"

"No. Our divorce agreement states that when you get a raise, so do I. You owe me." Her impeccably manicured hand went to her hip, which jutted to the side.

"The fuck I do!" My heart was beating so fast, it sounded as if I had a drumline in my ears. This was why marriage was a bad idea.

Her entourage of friends exited the club and told her they were headed to the next club.

She glared daggers at me. "Get your checkbook ready." Her finger tapped my chest before she spun on her heel and walked away with her clique.

My hand balled into a fist. I was about to pound the brick wall but leaned up against it instead. I needed to get it together and worry about my ex-bitch on Monday. I didn't want Alex or Aubrey to know what had transpired. They were happy, and just because marriage wasn't for me didn't mean I wanted to rain on their happiness parade.

After Samantha was out of sight, and I cooled down, I headed back in. The DJ had started playing, so many of the customers who had been at the bar were now dancing.

Mike came over to me. "Is everything okay, man? I'm sorry about my mistake. I'll cover the free drinks."

I smiled. Mike was young and a good guy. "Don't worry about it. We've all made a mistake here and there. As long as we learn from them, that's all that matters."

Alex and Aubrey were talking at the end of the bar, and I heard something about who was paying for the wedding. He wanted to pay for it, and she said she needed to talk to her parents, but she wanted to pay too. Money was nothing but a nightmare.

I interrupted them. "Hey, Aubrey, make sure Julie doesn't get any ideas while you're gown shopping."

Alex shot me a look, and Aubrey's eyes narrowed. She kissed Alex good-bye and left without a word to me.

"What was that about?" Alex crossed his arms and shook his head.

"That was about my greedy fucking bitch of an ex-wife who wants more money from me." I swallowed hard. "I'm happy for you and Aubrey, I truly am, but hell if I'll ever go through that again." I rubbed the back of my neck. "Sorry, man. Not everyone is meant to take those vows."

Alex nodded, and that was the end of the marriage conversation. My energy was drained, and I was infuriated. I had an entire night ahead of me, so I would do what I needed to and push through with a smile, but all I wanted to do was go to sleep and pretend Samantha Chambers had never existed.

chapter 8

Julie

I WAS SO EXCITED to help Aubrey pick out her wedding dress. It was funny how things happened. Several months ago, she had been looking for a muse, and we'd both ended up finding the loves of our lives. For once in my life, I was thinking about sharing the rest of my days with someone.

When Brett had first told me he was falling in love with me, my heart almost ejected from my chest. When I said it to him, I was certain I was floating like a feather on a gentle breeze. Now there we were, my best friend and I, in love with two men who were as close to each other as we were.

Once I had purchased every bridal magazine at the corner newsstand, I headed to Aubrey's apartment. In the cab, I glanced at the beautiful gown on one of the covers. I would have loved to wear that one day. To think I'd never wanted anything permanent, but now I was in love, and marriage seemed like the next natural step for us too.

The cab jerked to a stop, taking me out of my bridal-induced daze. I swiped my card in the payment machine, exited the car, and made my way up to Aubrey's apartment.

"Your maid of honor is reporting for duty," I said into the box by the door. I was beyond excited for her and Alex, but especially for Aubrey. Her wedding was something she'd always dreamed of. When she opened the door, I threw my arms around her and squealed, "You're getting married!"

Aubrey giggled and squeezed me. "Yes, I am. Are you hungry?" She walked into the kitchen and came back with wine and snacks.

"Ta-da!" I pointed at her coffee table, which I had covered in bridal magazines.

"Oh my God, Julie, did you buy out the store?" She sifted through the publications, and her eyes went wide.

"No, I stopped at the newsstand on my way here. I wanted to make sure you had all your options. Look at this one. The gowns featured in here have been worn by celebrities. Aren't they incredible?" I flipped through pages while explaining the different gown styles: princess, mermaid, A-line, and so on.

Aubrey looked at me with wide eyes.

"Do you know what style you like? I mean, you have a kick-ass body, so I'd go with something straight, strapless, and hot. Alex will pop something when he sees you in something like this." I pointed at the dress on the cover. "That's what I'm going to get when I get married. When I was a little girl, I thought I wanted to be a princess, but I don't know about all that fluff. Maybe I'll get a gown that can be converted from poufy to short and sassy."

"How about we have dinner before we start checking off which ones I like?" Aubrey smiled and grabbed my hand.

"Lead the way! Let's eat. I can't wait to get started!"

We sat at the table, and when I looked at Aubrey, worry lines were etched across her forehead. I hoped this wasn't too much on her. Then it dawned on me that she and Alex had had a meeting with his dad about the wedding.

"Oh hell! I totally forgot—how did it go with Alex's dad?" I asked.

She put a forkful of crisp lettuce in her mouth and looked at me. "Well, my future father-in-law had a lot to say. Let's see, what should I start with? The part where Jack told us Mr. Pierce was upset because his beloved daughter, Leah, had been exiled from the White Orchid, or the fact that Leah was expected to be Mrs. Alex Logan, or that Alex should have me sign a prenuptial agreement?" She took a bite of her bruschetta and looked at me with tear filled eyes. "How's that for a 'welcome to the Logan family'?"

"Are you shitting me? What did Alex say?"

"To which part?"

"To all of it. Who does that? What an arrogant prick." I was so infuriated with Alex's father. Aubrey didn't need that. With all of her anxiety issues, his words could have sent her over the edge again.

"Well, Alex told his dad that if he wanted Leah to be a Logan, then he should marry her." She snickered. "Then he told him to stick the prenup up his ass."

I swallowed a big sip of wine, trying to squelch the desire to go kick his ass. "Thank God. I'm telling you, if Brett asked me to sign anything like that, I'd tell him to go to hell."

She nodded and put down her fork. When she looked at me, her eyes softened, and sadness flashed across them.

"What's wrong, Aubrey? I'm sure dealing with his dad isn't easy, but Alex is all about making you happy. You don't have anything to worry about."

"It's not that. How do I say this?"

"Okay, spill it. What the hell is going on?"

She was fidgeting, and something was off. She must have opened and closed her mouth a half a dozen times before she spoke.

"Do you and Brett talk about getting married?"

"No, not really. I mean, we love each other, so it's inevitable, right?" I smiled at the thought of being Mrs. Brett Chambers, but when she looked as though that would be the worst thing that could happen, my skin prickled. I had a sick feeling in the pit of my stomach. Brett and I had been seeing each other for months. Was he hiding something? I mentally slapped myself—that couldn't be it. "What? What aren't you telling me?"

She cleared her throat. "I think you should talk to him about it."

"About getting married? Why?" My chest felt heavy, and fear coursed through me.

"When I saw the guys earlier, Brett said . . ."

"Brett said what?" I braced myself for what she was about to say.

Aubrey whispered, "Brett said to make sure you didn't get any ideas."

"He did?" I felt my hands tremble. What did that mean?

"Yeah. Jules, I'm sorry. Maybe he was kidding. I mean, Brett is the comedian of the bunch." Aubrey was struggling to tell me this, and that saddened me as well. I was there to help her, not to bring her down.

"No, it's fine. If he doesn't want to marry me, that's fine. But he won't have me either. When it comes to Brett, I don't want a boyfriend. I want everything." My voice rose with anger laced with frustration. He owned both my heart and soul and I wanted a future with him. I'd thought he wanted one with me. I hated the person I'd become, and I had him to blame.

"Please don't do anything without talking to him first."

I knew she was thinking of her experience with Alex. Suddenly all of the bright hues decorating Aubrey's apartment looked bland. "Oh, I will talk to him, don't worry about that. Now let's grab more wine and look at gowns for you."

We went back to the couch, and I picked up a magazine. "Oh, look at this one. It's beautiful, and it's a Vera Wang. I think you would look gorgeous in a sheath style. It's a great silhouette for you."

"Isn't Vera Wang expensive? I mean, it's a stunning gown, but I don't know." Aubrey's shaky finger traced the outline of the picture.

I had a feeling she wanted to be frugal because of Alex's father. "Yes, Vera Wang is expensive, but I'm sure your parents or Alex would buy it for you. Take a look at the intricate beading, and the chiffon is to die for. Did you guys pick a venue?"

"Yes, we're getting married in the small chapel next to Creekside Park, and the reception will be at Anthony's." She beamed as though she had told me she was having her wedding at the Four Seasons.

My mouth dropped as I stared at her.

"What?" she asked.

"You're marrying one of New York's most eligible bachelors, and you're getting married in a chapel and having a small reception at a restaurant?"

"Yes. Since the guest list is small, Anthony is rearranging the restaurant to include enough tables and a small dance floor. It will be intimate. What's wrong with that?"

"Nothing, I guess. I'm surprised. This is society news. If you're going to do that, then you need to have a gorgeous gown."

She shrugged. "Okay, we can go look at them, and I'll try them on, but if it's too expensive, I'm not buying it."

I tagged pictures with pink Post-It notes.

"Are you okay?" she asked.

I felt completely deflated, and I should have been feeling the complete opposite. I closed the magazine, tossed it on the table, and flopped back on the couch. All of the times Brett and I had been together and told each other we loved one another, never once had he mentioned that he'd never want to get married. Granted, we'd never discussed the topic, but he must have known at some point I'd want it all.

"I'm sorry I told you what Brett said. I wanted you to know. Maybe what he said doesn't have anything to do with you. Maybe because he was married before, he doesn't want a big wedding. I bet that's it. He probably wants to get married but doesn't want all the hoopla."

"Yeah, maybe you're right. I'm still going to ask him about it. I should go. It's getting late." I pushed myself off the comfortable cushions and gave Aubrey the best smile I could.

"You're okay, right?" Aubrey placed her hand on my shoulder.

Although I should have felt comforted, my nerves were on edge. “Yes, I’m fine.”

I kissed her cheek, grabbed my purse, and walked out the door. My head spun, and tears pricked my eyes. Maybe he didn’t want to marry me since he had been married once before. There was only one way to find out, and that was by going to the source.

I called a cab and decided to wait for Brett at his apartment. The doorman, Jim, greeted me and told me that Brett wasn’t home yet, so I waited for him in the lobby. I watched residents and a pizza delivery man come and go, and I stared at the door, willing Brett to come through. All the while, I prayed that Aubrey had misunderstood him.

Looking at my hands twisted in my lap, I heard Jim say, “Good evening, Mr. Chambers.”

My head snapped up.

Brett smiled at me. “Hey, I thought you were having girls’ night at Aubrey’s?” He gave me a chaste kiss.

“I was there, but I wanted to come and talk to you.” I heard the tremor in my voice.

Brett grabbed my hand and led me to the elevator. Once the doors were closed, he pulled me into his arms. I rested my ear on his chest, listening to his heartbeat.

“I wish you would have called me. I would have had Jim let you in.” The warmth of his voice penetrated my skin, and I had second thoughts about my visit.

Nothing seems wrong. Maybe Aubrey misunderstood what he said.

We walked into his apartment, and he crashed his lips on mine. I savored every bit of him, praying my tears would stay unshed. Deep down, I had a feeling Aubrey hadn’t misunderstood anything, and to say that I was terrified this would all come to a screeching halt would have been a pure understatement.

"Do you want a drink?" He walked into the kitchen.

I studied my glorious boyfriend as he reached into his refrigerator to grab a beer. "No, thank you." I gingerly padded toward him.

"Okay, what's wrong? You look like you lost your best friend. Did something happen at Aubrey's?" He took a draw of his beer. "Did you two argue?" Sympathy flashed across his face, but something was off.

"No, of course not!" I crinkled my nose at that ridiculous comment, then I shook my head and swallowed hard.

"My night didn't go as planned either. It actually sucked, but I know how to make us feel better." He slammed back the rest of his beer and pulled me into his arms.

"I want you." His mouth devoured mine, and he thrust his tongue into my mouth, tangling it with mine. His hands grabbed my ass as he lifted me. My legs instinctively wrapped around his taut waist, and he pushed his erection against my core. He groaned, and I froze. I broke our kiss and turned my head.

Leaning back, he looked into my eyes, his eyes darkened with lust. "What's wrong, Jules?"

"We need to talk." I loosened my grip, and he set me down. He pulled away, and I had an aching feeling that that might have been our last kiss.

His hand raked through his hair, and he let out a frustrated breath. "Now? Let me have you first, and then we can talk. I've had a long night and my share of talking. I want to fuck and go to sleep."

He pulled me close, but I splayed my hands on his muscular chest and pushed him away.

"What's your deal tonight?"

All I could do was stare at him. Did he say he wanted to fuck? I had never been so insulted or felt so cheap. He'd never spoken to me like that. Shock ran through me. My world tipped off its axis, and our love dangled off the edge.

"Seriously, Julie, what's your problem?" When he crossed his arms, his biceps bulged under the sleeves.

I was nervous. "First, I'm not your fuck buddy, Brett."

His head jerked back, and his eyebrows arched.

"I love you, and I'm in this for the long haul." I placed my hand on his forearm, which tightened under my touch as if I were burning him. "Don't you want that too? To build a life together?"

"Obviously we're together. You're my girlfriend, and we have a good thing, and that's enough for me. Isn't it for you?"

His chiseled face remained stoic, and I realized Aubrey hadn't misunderstood a thing. "No, it isn't. I never wanted forever until you. But now I do, and I want it with you."

"Unbelievable." His voice stayed steady, but there was a determination and an assuredness in his tone that scared me. "Sorry, but I'm not that guy. If that's what you really want, then maybe we should end this so you can find someone else. That isn't in the cards for us." He shook his head, and sobs crawled up my throat. "I can't do it again. Sorry, but if you're talking marriage, that's not going to happen. You should never expect a proposal from me because there won't be one."

My heart shattered. The room spun, and I was sure I was going to be sick or pass out. My chest ached as if I'd been stabbed by his cold and piercing eyes. As I turned to walk away, he grabbed my arm, which I tore from his grasp. I let time pass silently. We didn't speak or move for what felt like an eternity. It was as if we were strangers, and I became more depressed and hurt with each tick of the clock.

Brett finally broke the silence. "Is this because you're feeling left out? Did you get caught up in all wedding shit with Aubrey? Is that what this is?"

I slowly shook my head. Not once did his voice waver; it stayed steady, and I felt like a fool.

"I've been there before. You know that." He walked into the kitchen and grabbed another beer. The bottle cap landed on the counter as he took a long pull from the bottle. Annoyance crossed his face as he gritted his teeth. "Goddammit! Why, Jules? Why ruin a great thing?"

"Because I love you and we are a great thing. I didn't go into this relationship thinking we'd walk down the aisle, but I also didn't plan on falling in love with you. I thought you loved me too." I grabbed my purse and choked back tears. "But I guess I was wrong about that. Seems as though I've been mistaken about a lot of things. And I'm not the one ruining a great thing—you are."

"I do love you, but that doesn't mean we need to get married." He placed the bottle on the kitchen island and sauntered over to me. "Come on, let's go to bed."

Was he kidding? Tears poured down my cheeks as a tremor ran through my body. I swept the moisture away with trembling fingers, mustered up whatever self-esteem I had left and tried to keep my voice steady as I said, "No, I'm leaving."

"So it's all or nothing? Is that how you're going to play this?" He sat on the couch and glared at me. "Seriously, Jules, I've had the night from hell. Can you just lay off?" The aloofness in his tone mirrored the hardening of his eyes.

I thought I'd try a different tactic. I softened my voice while trying to stop the tremors running through my body. "Tell me what happened. What can I do to help?"

His expression turned to stone, doing absolutely nothing to ease my fears and pain. "Help?" He snorted. "That's rich. I told you what I wanted, and you shot me down." He shook his head and tugged on his hair. "What is it with women tonight? Is there a full moon or some shit? Jesus Christ!"

Women? What was he talking about? His curt tone made me cringe. I placed my hand on the front doorknob and braced myself for what I was about to say. I took a steady breath and peered over my shoulder at him. "You won't have to worry about this woman anymore because I'm leaving." More tears threatened, but I refused to let them fall as we made eye contact. Before I stepped out, knowing I'd never be back, I said, "I honestly can't believe this is happening. I'm sorry that my love for you wasn't enough to make you want a future with me. I'm sorry I let myself think you wanted a commitment. I'm sorry for wanting you more than you wanted me. I'm sorry for not knowing how to help you, but you won't tell me what happened tonight, and that's on you. I'm sorry that you don't understand how deep my love runs for you." My breath hitched as his eyes never left mine. "But what I'm truly sorry for is giving you my heart. You did what I thought you never would—you broke it."

I shut the door gently behind me, and once I was in the small elevator, I let the dam break. Every tear I had flowed freely as I wailed. I didn't care who was in the lobby or what Jim thought when the doors opened. Nothing mattered anymore because we were over.

I'd lost Brett.

I'd lost my heart.

I'd lost the love of my life.

Brett

WHAT THE FUCK just happened? I stared at the door and couldn't believe she was gone. Maybe it was for the best—no, that was a lie. Goddammit!

I tossed my head back on the couch. I couldn't believe I'd lost my girlfriend. After what felt like forever, I got up and went to bed. I didn't bother getting undressed or even under the covers. I crossed my arms under my head and replayed what had transpired. How had we gone from laughter to this? I was sure we wanted the same things. Julie was so free and fun. She wasn't the serious type, and that was why we were so right for each other. We'd figured that out the first night we met. Neither of us had ever talked about marriage or forever. Sure, we were exclusive, but I'd never planned on making our relationship legal. Fuck!

My brain replayed our conversations and moments together in an effort to figure out what signal I had missed. How did I not see that she would be like every other woman and expect marriage? *Because she was different.* I grabbed my phone out of my pocket and tossed it on the nightstand.

Her words replayed in my mind. I'd broken her heart. How could I live with that? I told her I'd been married before and how awful it was. That should have been an indication of how I felt about the institution. What a joke. Fucking Samantha. No wonder marriage was called an institution—people went crazy once they entered into it.

I balled my fist and struck my pillow; there was no way I was getting comfortable tonight. I grabbed the remote and turned on the TV, but every blonde I saw reminded me of Julie. I thought of the way her hair bounced when she walked, her laugh when I told a funny joke—which was different when she really didn't think my joke was funny but didn't want to hurt my feelings. Would she ever bounce up and down again in excitement? Would I?

After I woke from a short and fitful night's sleep, I called Alex to see if he had any indication of what was going on. I didn't want him to spy on her or anything, but I needed some help. Even if I wasn't her forever, I still wanted to be her friend. *Is there a waiting period for this?*

"Hey, Brett." Even over the phone, he sounded agitated.

"Hey. I need to know if you spoke to Julie after she left here last night."

"No, but Aubrey feels horrible that she said anything to Julie."

Fantastic. Just when I'd thought I couldn't feel worse, I did. "Tell Aubrey not to worry about it. It wasn't her fault—it's mine and Julie's. I shoulder the blame for never telling her that I never want to get married again, but she never indicated that she was hoping for a proposal. I guess it's better that it happened now rather than later."

"Seriously, Brett?" His disappointment rang clear. "I thought you two were perfect for each other."

"So did I until we weren't." The more I thought about it, the more aggravated I got. "I'll see you later."

"Do you plan on coming to the Orchid tonight? I know it's your night off."

"I could use a few dozen drinks, so yeah, probably."

"Maybe Julie will be there and the two of you can work this out."

My man was whipped. He needed to realize that not every couple had a happily ever after.

"Doubtful. I'll talk to you later." I disconnected the call and stared at my ceiling.

chapter 9

Julie

I LEFT HIM.

He let me go.

How did this happen?

We broke up.

This hurts.

My eyes literally ached with each blink as I gripped my steering wheel. I hadn't slept, and I was sure I'd lost a pound in water weight. I needed to talk to Aubrey, so I grabbed my phone and dialed her number. As soon as I heard her voice, I completely lost it.

"Aub . . . rey . . . it's . . . o . . . ver." I couldn't catch my breath and thought I would hyperventilate at any minute.

"Sweetie, what are you talking about?" Her voice was the opposite of mine.

I was pretty sure I'd woken her and prayed Alex wasn't there. All I needed was for him to tell Brett I was an emotional wreck. I sobbed. Talking wasn't working very well. "It's Brett . . . We . . . b-bro-broke . . . up . . . We . . ."

"Julie, honey, where are you? Are you home?"

I shook my head. "N-no, I'm in my c-car."

"Pull over, and I'll come to you. Where are you?" Her words were laced with worry, making me feel worse, but I needed her.

"I was on my . . . on my way to your place."

"Please be careful. I'll put coffee on, okay?"

I sniffed and heard her sigh. "Will Alex be there?"

"No, he's leaving. Don't worry about it."

We said good-bye, and I made it to her apartment unscathed, which was a shock. I felt as if I were driving under the influence because my vision was completely blurred with tears. When Aubrey opened the door, she looked at me with such sympathy that my heart ached more. This should have been one of the happiest times of her life, and I was a complete mess.

I was sure I looked exactly as I felt—like shit. I'd gone to bed in yoga pants and a hoodie to try to warm the ice coursing through my veins, and I hadn't changed. I wasn't even sure that I'd looked in the mirror before leaving my apartment. I was just glad I'd called in sick and didn't need to go to work until tomorrow.

Aubrey took my hand, and I followed her inside. "I can't believe this. I didn't know he didn't want to get married again. How could he not tell me?" I shook my head and sat on the couch.

She had baked muffins, which made me smile. Aubrey was anything but a baker, but I appreciated her wanting me to have comfort food. She handed me a cup of coffee.

"Jules, I'm sorry. Maybe he was just tired?"

"If he wasn't tired then, he's probably tired now. It was horrible." The thought of him being able to relax while I couldn't was unsettling.

Her fingers tensed in her lap. "I'm so sorry. I shouldn't have said anything."

Great, now she felt guilty. With all of her health issues, I needed to get my shit together, if not for myself, then for her. "No, I'm glad you told me. It's better to know than not to. I didn't expect us to end. I thought he was my forever. I pictured me and you, our gorgeous husbands, and our children growing up together. I guess I was way off base."

I couldn't stop myself. All of the magazines I'd brought over were still on the table, and I picked up one. "I'm supposed to stand up with him at your wedding, and your engagement party is soon. I'm never going to be able to avoid him. You're my best friend, and he's Alex's. If I want to avoid him, I need to avoid you, and I can't do that."

The thought of losing Aubrey was enough to give me the kick in the ass I needed. I wiped my hands over my face and forced a smile as something inside me snapped. This isn't me. No. I wouldn't do this. The pre-Brett Julie would have bitch-slapped this sappy version. She'd tell her that no man was worth such agony and grief. Maybe I'd found the on/off switch after all, or perhaps my mind had snapped.

On impulse, I decided shopping and a night out was the remedy—even if it was for temporary relief. Aubrey hesitantly agreed to go shopping with me to pick out a "look how hot your ex-girlfriend is" outfit to wear to the club later. Screw Brett Chambers and his non-marrying ass. If he didn't want me, then I was sure I could find someone who did. Deep down, I knew I didn't want to, but wallowing wasn't my style. This was how I coped with my feelings.

After our shopping spree, girl time, and the countless times Aubrey asked me if I was okay, we got ready and headed to the club. I never did answer her question. The truth was, I didn't know if I'd ever be okay, but I couldn't think about that. I put on a brave face and my big girl panties and tried to block out everything else. Because of what had happened with my parents, I attacked life as if it could all be over in the blink of an eye because the reality was that it could—like my relationship with Brett.

I wasn't sure how tonight would pan out, but there were enough men at the White Orchid to assure me that finding someone to dance with wouldn't be an issue. Alex had told Aubrey that Brett would be there, and I couldn't wait to show him what he'd miss. I could flirt as well as, if not better than, he could. I hated mind games, but right then, I didn't care. I wanted him to hurt as much as I did. *Maybe he'll come back to me.*

We arrived at the club and my sight landed on an attractive blond, and when I sauntered by him, he asked me to dance. I didn't introduce myself, and I didn't care what his name was. I wasn't going to sleep with him—he was just a dance and a distraction. We moved together, and I did my best to hide any hint of misery that I was feeling.

Then I saw Brett grinding against Nikki. Was he drunk? I immediately stopped, and my legs felt like dead weight. My dance partner tried to shift my body, but my feet were rooted to the floor. I took one more look at Brett and Nikki. His hands were all over her body. But when she looked over his shoulder and smiled at me with confidence, I left the dance floor and my partner. A lump formed in my throat as my heart broke more than I'd ever thought it could. *This was a stupid idea.*

Once I finally got my bearings, and after I made a pit stop in the ladies' room, I headed to the bar. Brett and Nikki were there, talking to Alex and Aubrey, who looked beyond uncomfortable. As soon as I made eye contact with Brett, my insides turned to mush. This had been a horrible mistake. I had no idea why I'd thought jealousy games would make me feel better because I felt worse.

Tyler said, "Hey, Julie, what can I get you?"

I attempted to steady my resolve and at least sound like the old me. "Hey, Tyler, can I have a Jack and Coke?" I repeated to myself, *Don't look at them. Don't look at them.* I decided to focus on Alex and Aubrey instead. "So are you guys ready for your engagement party? Is there anything I can do to help?"

"Julie." Brett's voice was curt and a bit slurred.

I rigidly held my sadness at bay. I glanced at him as he knocked back a shot of golden liquor. When he put the glass down, I noticed a handful of others empty beside it.

"Brett." I tried to remain as impassive as I could. My attention went back to Aubrey. "So, your party—"

"This is Nikki," Brett interjected.

I wanted to disappear and be anywhere else. Did he just introduce me to her? Is he that wasted? He knows I know her. What the hell is he trying to prove? I get it—we're over, and he's moving on with someone I despise. At least I danced with a stranger. How did we get here so quickly? Not even an entire day has passed. "Yes, I know who she is, but thanks for the introduction."

"Weren't you two together, like, yesterday?" Nikki giggled and flipped her hair. Her Botoxed lips twisted in a sarcastic grin. "I told you not to get your hopes up."

It took every ounce of my strength not to rip that overly dyed auburn hair out of her brainless head. Aubrey suggested we head upstairs, which was a wonderful idea.

As we walked away, Brett called out to me, "Hey, Julie."

My eyes scrunched together. I opened them and turned to look at him.

"See you 'round." He shot me a wink, and I continued on my way.

My body was numb, and I was sure my heart had died somewhere along the way. I felt my chest attempting to take in air, but it was useless.

The rest of the night consisted of me seeing Nikki and Brett sucking on each other's faces and sharing tequila shots the way she'd always wanted to do them—with him licking her neck and snagging the lime from her lips with his. I couldn't take it anymore. Alex told me that Brett was hurting too and was obviously drunk, but that wasn't a good enough excuse. Alex attempted to break them up on the dance floor and talk some sense into him, but that was futile.

Brett was out to prove a point, and he did so in spades. I'd concede—he'd won. I had wanted to make him jealous and maybe see what he'd miss, but that had been an immature and stupid thing to do. Now the joke was on me.

When I asked Alex if he thought Brett would sleep with Nikki tonight, and he didn't give me a definitive no, I knew it was over. We were done. I was completely devastated. My life had changed overnight. How had that happened?

I spent the night at Aubrey's, but I couldn't sleep. Every time my eyes closed, I saw Brett and Nikki making out as if they were starved for each other. But I didn't cry. My tear ducts had turned into the Sahara Desert. I didn't have any tears left.

Did he take her to his apartment? Are they having sex right this minute? I flew off the couch, wrote Aubrey a note, and went to Brett's to see for myself. But once I got to his place, I couldn't do it. Staring at his building was like torture. The thought of them tainting the bed we'd made love in was enough for me to go home.

Brett

MY LIFE WAS officially fucked up. I'd woken up in Nikki's bed with a foggy memory. Once I got the hell out of there, I tried to remember everything about the night before. I remembered seeing Julie dancing with some guy who wanted in her pants. After a few shots of tequila, I'd allowed Nikki drag me onto the dance floor. After more cocktails, we left the club. Now I was in a taxi and wondering what the fuck had happened.

After the cab dropped me off at home, I read a text from Alex about some meeting I needed to get to, so I hopped in the shower.

I tried to think of ways to make this right with Julie, but I'd let the wrong head make a decision, and I knew I'd messed up any chance of getting Julie back. Who knew I could miss someone so quickly? But then, everything with us had been fast, from our first kiss to our breakup. When we did something, we attacked it. When I saw her dancing with that guy, all I'd wanted to do was fight fire with fire, not end up in Nikki's bed. How could I have been so stupid? Julie would never forgive me.

I grabbed a cab and headed to Walker-Stone for Alex's emergency meeting. What could be so dire about marketing? The last thing I needed was to look into the eyes of the woman I loved while knowing she hated me—with good reason. What an asshole I had been. Not to mention I had the mother of all hangovers.

I was the last one to arrive. Alex, Aubrey, and Julie were already sitting at the conference table. I took the seat across from Julie, who looked beautiful. Her hair was pulled back into a low ponytail, and she was wearing a white blouse which was unbuttoned just enough to alter the rhythm of my breathing.

She pulled out her notepad and pen. "So, Alex, what can we do for you?"

Her professional tone, lack of friendliness, and the sadness etched in her eyes was painful. This wasn't my fun and exuberant Julie. Knowing her transformation was all my fault made me sick to my stomach.

Alex cleared his throat, stood, and walked around the table. "Nothing. I'm sorry to have deceived you all, but I don't have any marketing needs at this time."

Her eyes narrowed in confusion. "Why are you here?"

"I'm here because this is the only place I could think of where you and Brett could talk without killing each other. Aubrey and I are getting married soon, and I'd like both of you to get along. Our engagement party is coming up, and I don't need you two taking aim at each other. Aubrey doesn't need the stress. If you two can't find a common ground, then I'll take Aubrey away and elope."

"Alex! You can't force them to talk." Aubrey's voice was so loud it made me balk.

Julie shifted in her chair and sat straight up. "No, it's okay." She looked at me, and every nerve ending in my body stood at attention. The natural light in her eyes wasn't there, and it was because of me. "This is good. I have a question for Brett, and his hopefully honest answer will clear all this up."

I leaned back in my chair and prayed she didn't ask me what I knew she wanted to. After our twenty questions session, I knew she didn't hold back. "Okay, what do you want to know? Do you want to know if I love you? Because the answer is yes. If you want to know if I already miss you, that answer is yes too." That wasn't what I'd intended to say, but I meant every word. My head throbbed and was ready to explode.

A look of disgust crossed her features, but Julie calmly ran her hand over her hair. "No, actually. I need to know if you slept with Nikki last night."

"What? Why do you need to know that?" *Fuck!*

"Tell me." Her features hardened, and her voice had a finality in it. There was no way out of this.

I let out a deep breath and took a moment before I looked into her eyes. Lying wasn't an option. I knew if I didn't tell her, Nikki would be more than happy to. Better to hear it from me. The entire situation pissed me off. This would all have been a non-issue if the topic of marriage hadn't come up, and that wasn't my doing. Granted, I could have handled it better. On any other night, I would have, but she'd caught me at the wrong time. I thought of Samantha, and my anger returned in force.

"Yeah, I did. Feel better now?" That came out a bit harsher than I'd intended.

Julie picked up her notepad and pen and stood. The room was completely silent. I was sure Aubrey was in shock, and Alex undoubtedly wanted to punch me.

Julie's sweet voice broke the silence. "No, I don't, but thank you for your honesty." She walked toward the door, but before she left, she turned toward us. "Alex, I appreciate what you tried to do here. Although I doubt this is the way you wanted it to go, I'm glad you brought us together. This way, everyone knows how my ex-boyfriend, who claims to love me, shows his love. I promise your engagement party will be beautiful and won't be dampened by our issues. Same goes for your wedding." She looked at Aubrey, whose eyes were glistening with unshed tears. "I'll be your maid of honor, Aubrey. I wouldn't miss that for anything in the world."

Then she looked at me. Although I knew she was doing her best to be strong, I wasn't fooled. "Don't worry, Brett. When you and I walk down the aisle that day, we'll be walking away from the altar, not toward it."

That was it. She was gone.

Alex's eyes narrowed. "What the fuck, Brett!" He shook his head, making me feel worse than I already did. "You need to make this right."

"I don't think I can. I fucked up."

When I left the office building, I felt as if I'd left my heart and soul inside. I was hollow, and the space could only be filled by the one person who hated me and had every reason to.

Over the next month or so, my life felt robotic. Aside from working, I didn't do much of anything. I didn't even go to the gym.

The one time I went to the club when I wasn't working, I ran into Julie and Aubrey. Julie asked me where my girlfriend was, and when I told her I didn't have one, she reminded me that all I wanted was fuck buddies, so she wasn't surprised I wasn't dating. Truth be told, I hadn't been with anyone since my awful mistake with Nikki.

With every fiber of my being, I wanted to pull Julie into my arms and tell her how much I missed her and needed her in my life, but she was getting stronger. She didn't cry when she saw me, and for that I was thankful. I'd always known Julie was a strong woman. She was exquisite, confident, and every man's dream, but her strength made her who she was. So I put my hands in my pockets and walked away, leaving my heart with the beautiful blonde who had once been mine.

As soon as I made my way outside, my phone rang, and it was my brother. I wasn't going to answer, but I wasn't sure if he needed me, so I picked up. "Hey, Bentley."

"Hi, Brett. Are you at work?"

"Nope, I'm getting into my car to head home."

"I've been thinking about you. How's everything going? How's your girl?"

"You always know, don't you?" I had decided not to tell my family about my break-up with Julie in hopes I wouldn't need to, but ever since we were kids, he'd known when something was up. I could never hide anything from him.

"Know what? I just called to shoot the shit before intermission was over."

"You're at the theater?"

"Well, I stepped out for a bit, but yes. So I only have a few minutes—give me the Cliff's Notes version."

"I ran into Samantha a while ago."

"Oh shit," he said.

"Yeah. Anyway, we fought—no surprise there. That same night, Julie came over because I may have mentioned to her friend that I never wanted to get married. So Julie confronted me, and I was so pissed off at my situation with my ex-wife that Julie and I broke up."

"Jesus, Brett." His voice had a vague hint of disapproval.

"Yes, I know. But there's more because your brother is an asshole. I decided to get back at Julie by sleeping with someone else the following night."

"So let me get this straight. This started with your ex-wife and ended up with you gaining an ex-girlfriend?"

"Don't forget the part about me fucking someone else. I mean, when your brother sets out to prove a point, he does so with gusto." I arrived at my apartment building, and Nikki was standing out front. *Son of a bitch.* "I need to go. I'm sorry I dumped this on you. We'll talk soon."

I clicked the phone off and looked at Nikki. "What are you doing here?" If she was there for sex, she shouldn't have bothered. It had been a several weeks since our tryst, and I wasn't interested in a repeat performance.

"We need to talk. Can I come upstairs?"

"No, here is fine." I wasn't going to bring her up to my apartment.

She shrugged. "Fine, have it your way. I'm pregnant."

Am I asleep and having a nightmare? Did I die and end up in hell? "What did you say?"

Her hand went to her stomach. "I'm pregnant with your baby."

Nope. I'm wide awake and alive, but definitely in hell. "How do you know it's mine?"

Her jaw dropped. "Because I've been away on a modeling shoot since the last time I saw you, and I haven't been with anyone since you and I made love. You're the only man I've slept with in the past two months." Her lips turned up into a sinister grin that could rival the Joker's. "Plus, we didn't use a condom."

What the fuck? Made love? We fucked! And I always used a condom. I'd never gone unprotected, not even with Julie or Samantha. "You're lying. I always wear one."

She shook her head. "Well, accidents happen."

"You need to leave and figure out who the real father is."

She shrugged. "You'll know later this summer. It was confirmed this morning."

I couldn't look at her anymore. The only thing I could do was walk away, so I did. When I opened my door to my apartment, I lost it. I grabbed a small vase that was on the entry table and hurled it across the room.

What the hell was I going to do? Could Nikki have been telling the truth? I flopped on the couch and dropped my head into my hands. I searched my brain, struggling to remember that night. How could I have not been careful? If only I had a rewind button and could go back in time, I'd change everything.

The following weekend was the engagement party, and if it weren't for Alex being my best friend, I'd have skipped it. I sat at the bar alone, sipping a whiskey and tried to be cordial. I couldn't help but be in awe of Julie. She said hello to people and laughed as if everything in her life were normal—maybe it was.

Aubrey came up to me, and I glanced at her. "Hi, Aubrey, nice party."

"Thank you. Are you okay? No offense, but you don't look great."

I sat up straighter. "I'm sorry, I just have a lot on my mind. Don't be offended, but I can't talk to you about it."

"It's about Julie, right? Look, Brett, I know she's my—"

"It's not Julie. Well, in a way it is, but not entirely." I swallowed another sip of my drink, relishing the burn as it slid down my throat.

Aubrey's eyes widened. "This is about Nikki, right? You broke it off with her and she's upset?"

"I don't want to talk about it."

"That's fine. You don't have to tell me. Can I say just one thing?"

I turned toward her and saw her arms were crossed over her chest. "Am I going to be able to stop you?"

She shook her head. "No, probably not. I'm just surprised you're this upset. When you stopped seeing Julie, who you claim to love, you moved on. Are you telling me you're more broken up over Nikki than Julie? Because if that's the case then—"

I couldn't take it anymore. "She's pregnant."

She opened her mouth in dismay. "Nikki's pregnant?"

Aubrey's voice was full of sorrow. Not disgust, because that wasn't the type of woman she was, but she sounded so sad I ached.

"So she says." I dropped my head and looked at Aubrey, who had turned pale. "Ironic, isn't it? Julie left me because I didn't want to get married, and now I may have a kid on the way and I'll probably end up married to someone I don't even love." My eyes found Julie, and what was left of my heart broke. "And the love of my life will hate me forever because of it. I'm stupid. That's all there is to it."

"How do you know it's yours? She's not a one-guy type of girl."

"Yeah, I know. That's what I said to her, and she got pissed and said that she's only been with me. I've always used protection, but like she said, things happen sometimes." I looked at Julie again, who was still mingling with guests. "She's going to hate me forever, but I need to tell her." I shook my head and tossed my crumpled napkin across the bar. "I'm an asshole. I let her go. What the hell was I thinking?"

Alex came up to us. "Trying to steal the bride-to-be?" He slid his arms around Aubrey's waist.

I was consumed with jealousy for the love they had and how much smarter than me he was. I threw the rest of my drink in my mouth and swallowed hard. "No, but never let her go. Don't do what I did and totally screw up your life because you got scared. I lost the one person I truly loved, and I'll never get her back."

"You were scared?" The hopeful tone in Julie's voice was like a bullet to my chest.

"Jules, I need to go to the ladies' room. Want to come?" Aubrey gently tugged on Julie's arm, but she pulled it away.

"No, I want to hear this."

"You look beautiful, Julie." I couldn't help it. She was a gorgeous woman.

Julie tilted her head in confusion. "Thank you. What did you mean when you said you were scared?"

"Babe, let's leave them to talk." Alex took Aubrey's hand, but she didn't budge.

"No, I think we should hang with our friends."

Alex looked at her and chuckled. "I think they'll be fine. Let's dance." Alex pulled her to the dance floor, and once again it was just me and Julie.

"I don't understand. What do you mean you were scared?" Her green eyes didn't sparkle, but I saw a flicker of hopefulness in them, and I couldn't do it.

Defeat coursed through me as I slowly shook my head. "Just the thought of a legally binding commitment scared me because of what happened before, but that doesn't matter now."

She lowered her brows. "Why? Why doesn't it matter now?"

God, how I missed her sweet voice. I braced myself and decided I needed to rip off the bandage. "Because Nikki told me she's pregnant and claims it's mine."

The force of her hand against my flesh made my ears ring, and I completely deserved it. She ran off before I could tell her that I thought Nikki was lying. My eyes trailed her as she ran toward the ladies' room. I saw Alex and Aubrey go after her. All I could do was hope she was okay because I knew I was anything but.

I went home alone that night and each that followed. I had no desire to do anything other than wallow in my grief. Granted, no one died, but it felt as though part of me had. When the flicker of hope dimmed in Julie's eyes after she heard about Nikki, wounded me so deeply, I knew it would haunt me forever. I did that to her—to us. If only we could get past it—if only she understood how sorry I was and how much I loved her.

The next time I saw her, Alex, Tyler, and I had just wrapped up a meeting at the White Orchid and as we made our way toward the bar, my heart stopped as I watched Aubrey, Val, and Julie laughing and hugging each other. *She was here.*

"What'd I miss?" Alex asked as we approached the happy trio. "Why is my fiancée jumping around? I hope you guys haven't been doing shots."

Julie slapped his arm. "No, we haven't been doing shots. You know Aubrey can't drink while she's taking her medication."

Alex rubbed his arm. "Damn, Julie, you didn't have to hit me so hard."

"She has quite the right hook," I deadpanned.

The women stopped laughing, and Julie glared at me. "You deserved it. You deserve everything you have coming to you." Her voice grew colder with each word.

My frustration came to a head. "Okay, I'm done with this. Let's go, Julie. You want to lay into me? Go ahead. You want to punch, kick, or scream at me? Here I am. Let me have it. Get it all out. Will that make you feel better?" I stretched out my arms and stood stock still and egged her on. "Come on, I'm waiting. We're all waiting."

The group went silent.

She stepped forward until we were chest to chest. I held my breath as Julie raised her hand as if she would slap me again, but instead, she gently placed it on my cheek. The warmth of her skin on mine made it hard for me to breathe. "I don't want to fight with you or scream at you. What's done is done." She removed her hand, and I immediately felt the loss.

Nikki, who was sitting at a nearby table, glared at us. Julie gave her a glance and then returned her attention to me. "Brett, I don't forgive you for being with Nikki, but for the sake of our friends, I'll forget it for now. I won't be the dark cloud at their wedding. So . . . that's it."

I couldn't help it or stop myself, I pulled her into my chest and held her. I softly said, "I love you, Julie." When I felt her body flinch, I raised my voice for all to hear. "Did everyone hear that? Did you hear that, Nikki? I love Julie! This woman right here! I will always love Julie!"

Nikki got up and stalked toward us, but instead of coming all the way over, she turned and walked out of the club. Julie didn't say a word.

Julie stayed stock-still until Aubrey came up to her and placed her hand on her back. She looked at me with the same confidence she always possessed and I missed. "Yes, okay. We can be friends, Brett, but that's it. I just can't be here right now, I need to leave." I watched as she walked out not realizing it would be one of the last times I saw her for months.

A heart that loves is
stronger after a loss.
A heart that endures loss
realizes what true love is.
– Julie Michaels

~Part Two~

chapter 10

Julie

THE LAST TIME I had spoken to Brett was at Aubrey's wedding.

Aubrey had been a stunning bride, and Alex's love for her oozed from his pores. She deserved all of the happiness in the world, so I knew I needed to step up and be civil to Brett even though I gave my other groomsman, Tyler, most of my attention. I'd promised I wouldn't do anything to ruin her day, and I would stick to that. But being with Brett wasn't easy; it was physically painful.

When I'd linked my arm with Brett's to walk down the aisle at their wedding, I felt nothing but hurt, loss, and the jolt of electricity that used to make my stomach flutter made my nerves spike. My heart ached when I saw him, which was funny, since seeing him also made me feel alive.

I blew off the bridal party dance and blamed it on a headache. Brett looked as lost as I felt. It was as if we both had amnesia and couldn't recall the good times, friendship, and love we'd shared. Every once in a while, I thought I saw a flash of remorse or love in his eyes, but then it was gone. It didn't matter anyway. The thought of him not only sleeping with Nikki but having a child with her was too much to bear. Once the wedding was over, Brett and I had no reason to coexist—except for the fact that I still loved him and our best friends were married to each other.

Some said that in time, pain subsided and loss got easier to cope with. Well, not in my case. Getting over Brett was neither easy nor had time helped. I even added distance and that didn't help. It had been over two months since I'd spoken to him, and the pain and hurt were still raw.

My personal life was shit. I'd tried dating, but that didn't work. I felt bad for my dates since I compared them all to Brett, and they didn't come close. It didn't help that I still wasn't over him. Maybe if my heart had an on/off switch, life would have been easier, but it didn't.

My professional life, on the other hand, had blossomed. Not too long after the wedding, Brian had sent me to Italy to land a new account. He was over the moon because, if I could pull it off, we'd be an international company. The only downside was the account, Calabrese Vineyards, would be tying into Amoreaux, the wine room at the White Orchid.

Thankfully, despite my personal issues, I secured the account, which took a couple of months. But now I was tasked with getting Alex and Brett on board. Who knew if Brett would still want to work with me? Aubrey had told me he asked about me every time he saw her, but per my request, she didn't tell him much except I was still out of the country.

My arm stretched to my nightstand to hit snooze on my alarm. Once the beeping ended, I rolled over and pulled the covers up to my neck. I hated getting out of bed, but I had a meeting with Alex about spotlighting Calabrese Vineyards in the club's wine room. Roberto Calabrese was a traditional Italian winemaker. He'd loved keeping personal barrels of wine in his basement, where his business had started, but once his son and grandsons had taken over due to Roberto's age, things changed. The old manual presses were retired, making it easier to fulfill more orders. Because of Roberto's children and grandchildren, Calabrese Vineyards was one of the largest wineries in Southern Italy.

One of Roberto's grandsons, Luca Calabrese, had traveled back to the States with me. When I first agreed to go to Italy for our firm, Brian had connected me with Luca because he spoke fluent English thanks to his time studying in London. Listening to him speak as if he was from the UK with an Italian accent was funny. I had been picturing an older man when I went to meet him, but he was in his early thirties—only a few years older than I was—and one of the most gorgeous men I'd ever met.

The thought of good looks and laughter reminded me of Brett, the man who would always own a large piece of my heart. Life without him had been difficult, and I'd forced myself not to ask Aubrey about him. But the day had come to see the man I'd once thought would be my forever.

I got out of bed, looked out my window, and was greeted by sunshine and blasting car horns—there wasn't anywhere I'd rather be. Italy was beautiful, and the Finger Lakes region was lush, green, and picturesque, but it had been too quiet. New York City was my home, and I was glad to be back—sirens and all.

After my shower, I grabbed a cab and headed over to the W Hotel to pick up Luca. I sent him a text and told him to meet me outside. We pulled up, and I couldn't help but smile when Luca walked through the brass door being held open by the doorman.

He wore pale blue jeans, a light gray V-neck sweater with the sleeves pushed up to his elbows, a gold chain that picked up the rays of the sun, and his Dolce & Gabbana brown crocodile loafers that he had purchased on one of our shopping days in Capri. The man had impeccable taste. His deep chestnut hair rested on his shoulders, and he had a smile that could stop traffic.

The cab door opened, and he slid in. "*Buon giorno, bella.*" He leaned over and kissed each cheek once, as Europeans did.

I giggled. "Good morning, Luca. You can save your sexy Italian ways for the women who don't know you speak English." I winked and readjusted myself in the seat. I was so nervous. I'd decided to wear my fitted black pants, a red camisole with black lace trim that rested perfectly on my chest, and my short black blazer. Naturally, I had on a gorgeous pair of Prada pumps—I've always loved shoes.

"You are so funny, bella. Not many women don't like it when a man says, 'Good morning, beautiful,' in the most romantic language." He winked.

All I could do was shake my head and smile. "I'm so sorry. Did I bruise your ego?" I laughed, and he followed suit with a hearty chuckle.

"No, no, my ego is fine. How could it not be? I'm with my gorgeous friend in one of the most exciting cities ever." He looked out the window as his gaze rose, stretching his neck. "*Mamma mia,* those buildings are beautiful."

I leaned over to look out his window and was engulfed in his scent. It was clean and light. I loved it. "That's the Chrysler Building."

My heart dropped knowing we weren't far from Brett's apartment building. I forced down the lump that had formed in my throat. I needed to focus since I'd be seeing him soon.

"All the people are in such a hurry. The women even have tennis shoes on with suits. Do they ever stop and take a look around? They're missing so much. This is why we Italians are more relaxed. We work, rest, and take time to enjoy life." He shook his head and looked at me curiously. "Are you thinking about our meeting? Your face . . ." He waggled his fingers between my eyes. "You are tense? No?"

Professional, Julie, be professional. Yes, Luca is your friend, but rein in your emotions. "It's been a while since I've been back home. That's all. I'm fine." I had told Luca all about my failed relationship over a couple of bottles of cabernet, and he'd told me Brett was crazy.

He grabbed my hand. "It's him, isn't it?"

"Him?" I tried to sound oblivious, but that was a lost cause.

"Brett. The man you told me about in *Italia.*"

His voice was smooth and comforting, but I still felt out of sorts. However, there was no hiding my feelings. I figured better to explain in case things got weird during the meeting. "Yes. As you know, he's a co-owner of the club. Before I came to Italy, I avoided him as much as possible, which wasn't easy."

I thought of all the times I'd blown off going to parties at Aubrey and Alex's because I knew he'd be there. Then Aubrey would tell me that he hadn't gone and was spending more time with his brother, whom I hadn't met. Maybe Brett and I hadn't been as close as I'd believed. My lips quirked as I shook my head. No, we were close. I let out a breath.

"Julie, if this makes you uncomfortable, I can meet with them alone. After seeing you in action at the wine room in the Finger Lakes, I think I can handle this." He squeezed my hand.

I gave him a reassuring nod. "No, I'm fine. Thank you for understanding, but this is my job, and I'm here to help both you and the White Orchid. I think Calabrese Vineyards and the club are an ideal match. Even more so than the wine bar in the Finger Lakes." I smiled as the cab came to a halt in front of the White Orchid. I saw Alex's Maserati and Brett's black Range Rover parked in front, and my heart jumped into my throat. Truth be told, I was almost looking forward to seeing Brett . . . almost.

Luca swiped his credit card in the reader before I could pay the fare. He got out and opened my door. "We're good, yes?"

"Yes. Thank you." I smiled. "Let's do this."

He opened the club door, and my eyes met Tyler's, who was wiping down the bar. His model-worthy smile hadn't changed. I thought his blond hair was bit longer, but as always, it was impeccably styled. Luca placed his hand on my back as we walked toward Ty.

"Julie." Tyler engulfed me in his arms. "You're a sight for sore eyes. It's been too long." He let me go and looked at Luca.

"Hi, Ty, it's good seeing you too. This is Luca Calabrese, from Calabrese Vineyards. Luca, this is Tyler. He's another owner of the bar."

Luca extended his arm and offered Tyler his hand. "Good to meet you."

Tyler's eyebrows rose. "Good meeting you too. I didn't expect you to speak English." He chuckled. "Welcome to the White Orchid." He was so laid-back I wished my skin was a sponge that could absorb his vibe.

"Thank you." Luca smiled as his eyes grazed the room.

"So we're scheduled to meet Alex. Is he in his office?"

Tyler's expression changed. His eyelids softened to a slow blink before he looked at me again. "Yes, they're expecting you." He looked as though he wanted to say more, but he didn't.

They. I nodded. "Thank you."

"Aren't you coming?" Luca asked Tyler.

"No, I'm more of the bar man. I try to leave the wine room to Alex and Brett."

My chest rose, and my heart rate sped up at the sound of his name. "Thank you, Tyler."

We made our way upstairs, and my nerves spiked with each step I took. So much time had passed, and so much had happened. I wasn't sure what waited for me on the other side of the closed door. I knocked and said a silent prayer that I could keep my composure. It had been so long since I'd seen or even talked to Brett. The door swung open, and I was greeted by Alex.

A natural smile grew across my face, and relief washed through me as I looked at him. "Alex." I couldn't help throwing my arms around his torso and resting my cheek on his chest.

He kissed the top of my head as he held me close. "Jules, I'm so glad you're back. Aubrey has missed you. Your FaceTime chats aren't cutting it, and her hormones are out of whack." He chuckled.

I pulled back. Wow, he looked so happy. I knew it wasn't because I was back but because of Aubrey and their baby on the way. The thought of spending time with Aubrey filled me with utter joy. "How about I come over this weekend?"

"Great, we'll have a barbecue."

I gestured toward Luca. "Alex, I'd like you to meet Luca Calabrese. Luca, this is Alex." The two men shook hands.

"Come in, please." Alex motioned toward the small table in his office.

Just as Luca's hand went to the small of my back, I heard the legs of a chair scrape on the floor. For what seemed to be the first time in a lifetime, my eyes met Brett's. I swallowed hard as I tried to keep on a brave face. His lips curled into a small smile that didn't quite reach his eyes.

"Julie, it's good to see you."

Even after all this time, my skin still tingled at the sound of his voice. *Keep it together, Julie.* That needed to be my mantra. His eyes shifted between Luca and me.

"Hi, Brett." I turned to Luca, who was now at my side. "Luca Calabrese, this is Brett Chambers."

"*Ciao,* Brett." Luca put out his hand. "It's good to meet you."

Brett took his hand and briefly shook it. "Thank you, nice to meet you too."

"Ahem. Shall we sit and discuss your ideas?" Alex motioned for us to sit at the small table.

I had no idea how I would get through this meeting. I made sure to sit between Luca and Alex so I wouldn't be next to Brett, but then I had him directly in my sight.

I steadied my nerves as best I could and began my presentation. "When I was in Italy at Calabrese Wineries, owned by Luca's family, I was impressed. We had wine shipped here. Did you receive it?" I shifted in my seat. I should have asked that before we scheduled the meeting. I was so uncomfortable. I'd have given anything for Aubrey to be there to break some of the tension that filled the room.

"We did. The white is chilled, and the red is breathing." Brett said before he went to retrieve the bottles from the wet bar in Alex's office.

My eyes betrayed me as I drank the sight of the man I was once in love with. His charcoal gray slacks and black shirt, which hugged his muscular form, made my mouth water.

Brett brought the bottles to the table, along with two glasses for each of us. I couldn't help but notice the corded muscles in his forearm as he decanted the red wine. I stared at him as he expertly poured the burgundy liquid. When he looked at me, I quickly shifted my eyes away and prayed he hadn't seen me gawking at him.

Luca took the glass by the stem and made the wine swirl up the sides of the glass. He brought it to his nose and inhaled the essence. "*Perfetto.*" He softly nudged me with his elbow, taking me out of my daze. "Julie, this was your favorite, no?"

I mimicked what he did. Once I inhaled the wonderful scent, I smiled. "Yes, it is. It has just the right blend of oak and fruit."

Alex raised his glass. "Cheers."

"*Salute.*" Luca clinked his glass against Alex's, mine, and finally Brett's.

I looked across the table at my ex-boyfriend's face. Something was missing. His features weren't light and playful; they bordered on confusion and sadness. My body was beginning to react to him, but I couldn't give in. I couldn't go to him and hold him. So I softly tapped my glass against his and took a sip.

"This is wonderful, Luca." Alex smiled, then he tasted the chardonnay after he had a water cracker to cleanse his palate "This is just as good." He placed the glass down. "So, Julie, what idea do you have about these bottles?"

"Well . . ." I cleared my throat and glanced at Luca before I brought my attention back to Alex. "When Luca and I discussed what could benefit both the club and the vineyard, I thought about having a special label made especially for the club. Something like, 'Made exclusively for Amoreaux by Calabrese Vineyards.' The label can have a muted white orchid on it and, naturally, the name of the wine." My eyes shifted between Brett's and Alex's.

Alex raised his eyebrows as he bobbed his head, while Brett remained stoic.

"This press will only be for you so it will be exclusive." Luca chimed in. "Exclusively made for Amoreaux by Calabrese Vineyards."

"Right. No one else will have this press, and you have to admit it's refined and easy on the palate. We can schedule private tastings for the elite." I turned slightly toward Alex. "What do you think? Having your own wine label would draw in the aficionados, which means more revenue. Calabrese Vineyards is a wonderful name to be tied to." I smiled at Luca. His pride in his family's business was so apparent it made me proud, and I was an outsider.

"*Grazie,* Julie. Yes, I think that we could both benefit from this." His Italian accent came through and made me swoon.

I wasn't completely unaffected by Luca. This was business, but the man was fine. All the men in the room were beautiful specimens, but only one made my soul burn.

"So let me see if I understand this." Brett's tone verged on annoyance and I wasn't entirely sure why. "Your vineyard will have a special press of grapes solely for us? Who will be overseeing the project on your end here in the states? I wouldn't expect Julie to fly to Italy every time we needed something."

The possessiveness in his voice made me draw my thighs together. But I wasn't his anymore. I wasn't anyone's.

Luca answered before I could. "Me. I will be, as you say, your liaison. I will travel back and forth overseas. Bella just brought us together." He looked at me and smiled, making me do the same.

"It's Julie."

Brett's deep voice made my head jolt in his direction. My jaw dropped in embarrassment.

"I'm sorry, yes, Julie." Luca leaned toward me and whispered, "I didn't mean any disrespect."

I waved him off because it was no big deal. I scowled at Brett, who had his eyes on me. Warmth crept into my body.

"I like the idea." Alex stood. "Luca, let me show you the wine room."

I pushed my chair back to follow them, but Alex told me to stay. *Dammit.* I knew what he was doing, and I didn't like it one bit. But it was too late. Luca had followed Alex out, and the room was so silent you could hear a cork drop.

"Jules . . . please, can we talk? It's been months." Brett moved to where Alex had been sitting.

The smell of his cologne made me sad. I remembered having that scent on my sheets, my pillow, and on me. "About this idea?"

"No. I want to talk about us, not business." Brett moved his hand to mine, which I swiftly pulled away as I stood.

My feet somehow moved me to the window. I saw Brett's reflection as he came up behind me. He caged me in with his arms and stared at me.

I slowly turned. "There is no us."

He looked as if someone had given him a blow to the stomach. "Please, Jules, I haven't seen you in so long. Talk to me. Please."

His pained voice mirrored the hurt in my heart, but I couldn't do much about it. The feeling of his warm breath on my neck, as he spoke, reminded me of what we'd had, but I couldn't go there. Not anymore.

"What do you want to know?" My voice was soft, but I knew he'd heard me. I was uncomfortable between his arms, so I glanced at the right one, and he lowered both of them. I crossed mine. My eyes met his, and I raised my eyebrows. "Okay, what?"

"How have you been?" His eyes panned over me from head to toe, and I did my best not to do the same to him. "You look gorgeous, but you always did." He smiled, still without the spark in his eye that usually accompanied it.

"I'm doing well, thank you. I've been busy working and traveling." I shrugged one shoulder. "It's been a great experience. How are you?"

He chuckled. "How am I? Let's see, how am I? Well, I'm not that great actually. I've missed you so much that it hurts to breathe. I think of you, and the world stops revolving. I wonder where you are, if you're safe and happy . . ." He cupped my neck, and a surge of loss filled my pores. "If you've thought about me or us. I just want to talk to you."

"Brett, don't." I started to walk away from him, but he placed his hand on my forearm. My head fell back. I closed my eyes and let out a shaky defeated breath.

"Hear me out, please." His voice cracked.

I knew he was sad, but I couldn't have this conversation. "Brett, I'm here on business. That's it. I don't think we need to rehash the past. It's over."

Before he could say anything else, Alex and Luca came back.

I moved around Brett and headed toward them. "So what do you think? It's a beautiful room, isn't it?" I tried to regain some composure on the outside because my insides were a twisted into a knot.

"It's perfect." Luca smiled and looked at Alex.

Alex clapped. "Well, it looks like we have a partnership. Let me go over some figures with the team, and I'll get back to you."

Luca shook Alex's hand and turned to me. "Are you ready?"

"Yes, thank you." I gave Luca the best smile I could muster before turning to Alex. "I'll draw up the marketing proposal and email it to you."

"That's great, Jules. I'll see you this weekend." He hugged me.

"Brett, it was nice to meet you." Luca extended his hand to Brett.

"Yeah, same here. Thanks." Brett took Luca's hand, but he was curt, and his eyes never left mine. Brett's mouth opened, and the vein in his neck throbbed as he attempted to say something but didn't.

I couldn't handle it. "Bye, guys." My voice was boisterous, and I left the office the way I'd walked in: head held high, Luca's hand on my back, and my heart riddled with pain.

Once we were in a cab, Luca turned to me. "I'm sorry if that was uncomfortable for you. Are you sure you don't want me to handle this on my own? Your beautiful eyes aren't smiling."

He knew me better than I'd thought. Either that or I hadn't concealed my feelings well. I wondered if Brett had seen through my façade. "No, but thank you. This is my job, and I'll take care of it."

I looked out the window as the cab zig-zagged through the city. The mass of people hustling on the sidewalk caught my attention. I wondered how many of them had a broken heart that matched mine.

"My flight is in a few days, so I'm going to spend time wandering around the city. Would you like to join me? I know you've been away, so I understand if you can't."

"I should spend some time in the office, but I'll definitely see you before you leave." I would have loved nothing more than to show Luca the sights, but I had work to do. After our meeting at the White Orchid, I needed to regroup and get it together.

The car pulled up to Walker-Stone. I opened the door, paid for my share of the fare—which Luca didn't appreciate—and told the cabbie to take him to the Empire State Building. I knew Luca would want to see it.

"Thank you, Julie. You have my number, so if you change your mind, call me."

"Yes, I do, and if you need anything, please let me know."

He kissed the top of my hand, and I exited the cab, ready to get my life in order. I wasn't sure what role, if any, Luca would play in it, but it was nice having him around—even if it was temporary.

Brett

WELL, HELL, THAT didn't go as I expected. She'd looked beautiful, not that I'd thought she wouldn't. I wondered about her and Luca though I could have sworn she had been affected by my presence. The way her skin flushed and the goosebumps that formed on her skin used to be telltale signs that she wanted me. But maybe I only saw what I wanted to.

"So what do you think?" Alex asked nonchalantly.

"About what?"

His forehead creased. "About the partnership with Calabrese Vineyards?" He shook his head. "What did you think I meant?"

Completely drained, I sat in the chair across from the desk he sat behind. "Oh, yeah. I guess it'll be fine."

"Fine?" Alex leaned back in his leather chair. "Are you okay? I know seeing her threw you off your game today, but we stand to make a good profit with this partnership."

I scrubbed my hands over my face. "It's cool, man. I knew she'd still affect me the way she always had, but it was harder than I thought it would be." I picked an invisible piece of lint off my pant leg. "Would you mind taking point on this? I know we're partners and we started the wine room together, but I don't know, Alex. This hurts." Admitting that to him wasn't as difficult as admitting it to myself. I ached for her to love me again, to touch her soft skin and kiss her tender lips. Would there ever be a day when I didn't feel that way? I shook my head to pull myself out of my Julie-induced daze.

"Whatever you need, you know that. But once Aubrey has the baby, we'll need to reevaluate our schedules."

Baby. What if I have a baby? A chill ran through me. "Yeah, okay. We may be in the same boat, except you'll be a family. Nikki and I won't be."

"I think you need to wait and see what happens. This baby may not be yours, so you could be worrying for no reason, but if it is, then I know you'll find a way to make it right." He spoke with such assuredness. I only wished I felt the same.

"There's just no way I didn't use protection." I was still struggling to remember even a hint of that fateful night. Then in a flash, it hit me—*an ill attempt to open the foil wrapper*. "Fuck!" *Purple!* "I did wear a condom! I remember Nikki handing it to me."

Alex's eyes widened like a cartoon character as he leaned forward. "You used a condom that she gave you? Don't you think she's the type to fuck with it beforehand? She's been wanting to land one of us since the first day she walked into the club. She's a gold-digger."

Bile churned in my stomach as Alex's words penetrated my brain. "Son of a bitch. She trapped me." It was official—I was in hell.

He stood. "Let's go to the bar. I think you could use a drink."

We sat down, and Tyler brought us a couple beers. I felt numb, and I hadn't even taken a sip yet. How could I have let her do this? How could I have been so stupid? I wanted to run to Julie and tell her what I thought had happened. I couldn't prove it, but it would at least show I'd taken precautions. She'd looked so good today and, for the most part, happy. If I told her this, would it just remind her even though I wore a condom, it didn't change the fact that I slept with someone else the night after we broke up? I didn't want to bring her down further than I already had, so I needed to gauge where she was in her life.

"How much do you know about what Julie's been doing?" I asked. "I don't mean to break any husband-wife confidentiality pact, but I'm worried about her."

"She's, you know . . . Julie." Alex shrugged.

"What do you mean she's Julie? Toss me a bone or something." I was concerned for her. She'd seemed okay, but I thought she was almost too okay. Maybe she'd been putting on a strong front so I wouldn't know she was hurt. I knew I'd broken her heart, and when I thought of that, mine broke more.

"Julie seems to be doing well. You saw how she was." Alex shrugged and turned toward Tyler, obviously trying to avoid the topic.

I grabbed his arm and turned him back toward me. "Do you think she's with Luca?" My heart leapt to my throat. When they were there, Luca had looked at her as if she were a fine wine. He drank in everything she said and seemed mesmerized by her.

"Look, man, I don't know the details. Aubrey said she was happy Julie was back. She got all teary-eyed, and I figured it was hormones or whatever. Then she said that she was glad Julie didn't travel back alone and would have company for a while. What did you want her to do?"

My tongue raked over my teeth. "I want her to come back to me. I don't want to lose any shot of getting her back to some slick-talking Roman Romeo." My muscles tensed. "Man, I didn't want to lose her at all." I drained my beer. I wished I could have a shot of tequila, but I needed to get out of there.

He lowered his brows and let out a breath. "Brett . . ."

"Yeah." I stood. "I know, I know. I've already lost her."

chapter 11

Julie

I WAS WEAVING THROUGH traffic when my cell rang. Using my hands-free device, I answered. "Hello."

"Bella! It's Luca." His sexy voice reverberated through my car, and I smiled.

"Hi, Luca. What are you doing?"

"I'm still sight-seeing. Papa called and would like pictures of the wine room at the White Orchid so he can see how the bottles will be displayed."

I thought about what pictures I had at the office that I could send to him. I was closer to the club though. "Okay, I'll go to the club, take some, and send them to you. Will that be okay?"

"*Si, si.* I mean, yes. Thank you. Is it okay if you go there? I hope it's not too far."

His worried tone made me realize he was thinking about Brett. His broken English told me he was nervous—probably for me.

"It's fine. I'm right around the corner. I'll text you in a few minutes. Did you have fun sight-seeing?"

"This city is amazing. I went to Times Square after I saw the Empire State Building. My feet are killing me. I shouldn't have worn my new loafers." Luca let out a hearty laugh.

"No, probably not. But I'm sure your style is appreciated." I was sure people had thought he was a model or an actor.

"Yes, well, I don't know about that. No one pays attention to anyone."

I pulled up in front of the club and was relieved Brett's car wasn't there. I wanted to get in and out quickly. This day was never-ending. "Okay, well, I'm here already, so I'll send you the pictures soon."

"Thank you, Julie."

"Have fun. I can't wait to hear more about your day." I hung up and took a deep cleansing breath before exiting my car.

The club was quiet except for the music they piped in. I missed this place. Yes, I had just been there for a meeting, but I missed hanging out, having fun with my friends—the beat of the music pulsing through the air—and dancing. I quirked my lips to the side and sighed. Maybe someday I'd be able to be there without feeling as though I didn't belong. Knowing the virile man Brett was, I'd have been shocked if he wasn't hooking up now and again, even if it didn't mean anything. Maybe Nikki was the safest play since she was already knocked up. I shook my head to get rid of that picture and walked toward the wine room.

"Jules?" Alex called from the stairs.

"Hey. I'm sorry I didn't call, but I wasn't far. I need to get some pictures of the wine room for Luca so he can show his father. Is that okay? I didn't want to disturb anyone, and I figured I could sneak in." I smiled.

He strutted toward me. "Yes, of course, it's fine. You can come here anytime you want."

I grinned. "Thanks, I'll be out of here in no time." I hustled into Amoreaux.

Alex followed me in. "Jules, can we talk?" He pulled out a stool at one of the wine-tasting tables and motioned for me to sit. "I want to ask Brett to come over for the barbecue on Sunday, but I wanted to make sure you'd be okay with it."

"Alex, I don't want to make you feel as though you can't have Brett over when you want to just because I'll be there." That was the truth. Maybe if Brett and I could move past the awkwardness, we could be friends again. "We were together earlier, and it was okay."

"Was it? Were you okay? Because he wasn't." He shook his head. "Maybe I shouldn't have said that, but he's so torn up."

I opened my mouth to say Brett had made his bed and needed to lie in it, but I didn't, even though his remark grated on me. Alex had always been the fixer. Telling him not to bother wasn't an option, so I changed my approach. "I'm sorry he feels that way. I truly am. But I think our breakup is trivial in comparison to everything else he has going on. So if you want him there, then please invite him."

Laugh lines formed around the corners of his mouth as he nodded. "You're the best, Jules, and you're right. Brett hasn't been himself since you guys broke up. I want him to have fun and relax. I'd never thought I'd say it, but I miss his jokes." He chuckled.

Hearing Alex tell me about Brett made my heart ache and me wonder if we could all be friends. I mustered up the most sincere smile I could. "Then I guess I'll see you all on Sunday."

"Thanks, Jules. I appreciate it."

"You got it."

He kissed me on the cheek and walked out.

My phone snapped away like a professional camera. I took panoramas and some close-ups. I walked backward to get a full shot of the back wall, and hands on my shoulders startled me. I spun around. Brett was staring at me.

"Shit!" I brought my hand to my chest. I was lucky I didn't drop my phone.

"Sorry, I didn't mean to scare you." Brett stared into my eyes, and I couldn't look away. My hand was shaking, and it caught his eye. He took the phone out of my hand and set it on the table. "I didn't know you were in here."

The air around us stilled, and the music I'd heard before was muffled. I looked behind him and saw that the door was closed. My brows lowered. "Why did you close the door?"

He slid his hands into the pockets of his slacks. My eyes betrayed me and stared at his stomach. I knew what rested under his black shirt, and I'd have been lying if I said I didn't miss it.

"I don't know why I closed it. I saw you in here, and it was automatic. Jules, I was just invited to Alex's place on Sunday. He told me you would be there. If I make you this uncomfortable, I won't go."

I exhaled and did my best to let go of some resentment. "He told me, and I'm fine with it. Like I told him, his guest list isn't up to me." His hazel eyes still didn't sparkle, and my chest clenched. "We're not together anymore, but I know you have a lot going on. I won't add to it." All I could think was, in a few months, he could have a family that wouldn't include me. Given our connections, I couldn't avoid him, or his family, forever.

He raked his hand through his hair. "I want you to know, regardless of the test results, I won't be with Nikki. She's not the one I love."

I gasped. "You'd walk away from your child?" I was appalled. Who was this person standing in front of me? He wasn't my Brett. But that rang true on several levels. He wasn't mine—not anymore.

He huffed. "No! Of course I won't walk away from the baby. You think I'd do that? I'll be there for the baby if it's mine, but that's it."

I shook my head. "Look, this isn't any of my business. We're just friends, so what you do and who you do it with doesn't concern me." I grabbed my phone off the table. "I have to go. I need to get these to Luca."

"Are we, Jules?"

I looked at him and furrowed my brows.

"Friends, I mean . . . are we?"

I closed my eyes and tried to gather my wits while my nerves frayed. "I don't know. Could you handle it if we were? I told you months ago I'd be your friend." That was the truth, but that hadn't seemed to be enough for him then. I wasn't sure it was now.

"Yes, I'll take what I can get. I miss you so much. There isn't a day that goes by I don't think about you. I need you in my life, and if being your friend is the way for that to happen, then yeah. What I can't handle is not being close to you and feeling on edge all the time. I don't want every conversation to be full of *I'm sorrys*." He stepped closer to me. "Friends?"

I closed the gap and extended my hand. "Yes, friends."

We shook hands, and a chill ran up my arm. He could still make every ounce of me come alive. Dammit. I knew he'd noticed because his eyes widened. I'd concealed it well enough during our meeting, but being alone with him was a completely different experience.

"You still feel it too, don't you." Not a question—a statement.

All of a sudden, I was drowning in everything Brett: the smell of his cologne, his sexy smile, his strong yet gentle hands . . . everything. He pulled me into a hug. Every bone in my body told me to let go and step away, but I couldn't. The feeling of his chest against mine and the pulse of his heart made me warm from the inside out.

He released me and cupped my cheek with his right hand while his left went to my hip. His eyes met mine, and I lost the ability to blink. My blood rushed up to my ears as we stared at each other.

Then my phone beeped and brought me back to life. With a shaky voice, I said, "Excuse me."

I turned away and looked at my phone. It was a text from Luca telling me he was with Rachel at Madame Tussauds Wax Museum. I wasn't sure who Rachel was. I thought maybe he'd met a friend until he sent me a picture of himself standing next to Jennifer Aniston's wax figure. I giggled and sent him a quick text.

Glad you're having fun.

I continued snickering until Brett cleared his throat.

"Oh, sorry. That was Luca." I smiled as I pictured Luca sending that picture to his friends.

Brett exhaled. "So, you and Luca . . ."

"What about us?"

"Nevermind. It isn't any of my business." He shoved his hands in his pockets. "I should go. So I'll see you on Sunday?"

"Yes. Sunday." I swallowed the lump that had formed in my throat as he turned to leave. "Hey, Brett?"

He pivoted to face me. The disappointment etched in the creases on his forehead wounded me.

"There isn't anything going on with me and Luca. It's business." There was no reason for him to think otherwise. My days of playing games and making him jealous were over. Not a day went by when I didn't wonder if that night would have been different if I'd never started flirting with other guys.

He nodded and gave me a tight grin. "I'll catch you later."

"Okay." After he left, I let out the longest sigh. I sat at the small circular table, looked at the pictures I'd taken of the room, and sent them to Luca.

Then my finger grew a mind of its own and started scrolling through my photos, automatically stopping at a selfie of Brett and me. It had been my phone's wallpaper. I thought about deleting it, but I couldn't bring myself to do it. He'd been the funniest, most loving man until we fell apart. I sighed, tucked my cell away, and left to go to my office.

Luca called from a cab, speaking broken English, which he tended to do when he was excited. "Julie, I got a photo with Leonardo DiCaprio." He chuckled, making me laugh.

"I'm so glad you're enjoying the city. Did you see the pictures I sent you?"

"*Si,* they are wonderful. I spoke to my father, and I'll be returning to Italia on Saturday."

I was sad about him leaving. Luca was a great distraction, and we'd become friends. "Okay. I'll give you a ride to the airport."

"Are you sure?"

His sweet voice made me smile. "Yes, I'm sure. Text me your information."

After I finished up my day at the office, I went home to relax with a nice glass of wine and a chick flick on the Hallmark Channel.

Brett

SEEING JULIE YESTERDAY made me dread today more than I already had been. The need to tell her about my revelation about my night with Nikki plagued me, but that would have been selfish. I didn't want to hurt her more just to ease my guilt.

The summer air was blanketed in humidity, and the cabbie needed to replace the small paper pine tree hanging from the rearview mirror because the odor surrounding me was vile. I had him drop me off four blocks away from the club just to get out of his disgusting sedan.

It didn't help that I was exhausted. Nikki had called me the night before to ask me—no, tell me—I needed to go with her to her ultrasound appointment. She was seven months pregnant, and this was her final attempt to find out the sex of the baby. All I could remember was her saccharin voice saying on the phone, "Don't you want to know if we're having a boy or girl?" I'd missed the original ultrasound since I hadn't answered the phone when Nikki called to tell me about it. Apparently, the baby was out of position that day, and the sex couldn't be determined.

All I wanted to know if it was my baby, but she refused to have the in-utero test because it could harm the fetus. Well, I didn't want the baby hurt, but I needed to know if it was mine. Anytime I asked her about that night, she tried to make me feel like a louse.

"Brett, we created a beautiful life. What if you're having a son? Don't you want to teach him things? You'll be a great father."

It had been months and months of the same tactics. I knew she wanted me to be happy about this—and not many nights had passed without her trying to get me into bed—but I just didn't feel the same way she did. Now I needed to go to her appointment, so I didn't look like a screw-up in case the kid was mine.

The air conditioning hit me as soon as I opened the club door. Thank God. I'd have sworn I was going to melt, and it wasn't even noon yet. My white shirt stuck to my body, and I was happy I kept a change of clothes in my office.

Alex was sitting at the bar, sipping a glass of water and going over inventory with Tyler. Alex looked at me as I plopped my ass on the stool next to him, and I asked Ty to grab me a beer.

"A bit early, isn't it, partner? You look like shit. Did you walk here?" Alex handed me a bar towel and swiveled to face me.

Tyler slid a beer in front of me.

"Thanks, man," I said.

Tyler nodded and went back to counting bottles.

Alex waited for me to swallow a long draw off of my bottle. "So what gives?"

I ran the towel over my face. "I didn't walk the entire way here, but the damn cab reeked, so I got the hell out." I took another swig and started peeling the label off the dark bottle. "I need some time off. Nikki has an ultrasound today, and I told her I'd go with her. I wish I knew if I was the father. What if I'm not and the real father isn't there for this?" I looked up at the luckiest guy I knew.

Alex nodded. "I get it. Yes, whatever you need. So she still won't have the paternity test?"

"Nope. She said it could be damaging and will stress her out, which wasn't good for the baby." I shook my head. "I don't know what to do. My head isn't in the game, and if this baby is mine, it isn't fair." I drained my beer. "I don't know, man. I still can't get Julie out of my head." I pulled the rest of the label off before Tyler replaced the bottle with a fresh one. I nodded in appreciation and took a swig.

"You want me to have the kitchen make you something to eat, or are you on a barley and hops diet today?" Alex asked. "You don't want to go to the appointment buzzed."

"I ate before I got here, but thanks. I need to go. I'll be back soon." I didn't even bother changing my shirt. I walked out of the club feeling worse than I did when I arrived.

Julie ran through my mind as a cab took me to the doctor's office. I leaned my elbow on the frame of the door and chewed the side of my nail. What if the baby was mine? Guilt washed over me for the way I'd been feeling about him or her. What type of role model would I be, knocking up a woman and not giving her my name? If the child was mine, they would be a Chambers—that I was sure of. Nikki on the other hand was a different story.

The cab pulled up to the office building. Before I walked in, I paused to collect my thoughts. Like pieces of a new puzzle, they were scattered and in no order whatsoever. I wondered what the picture would be once the pieces fell into place.

Nikki smiled as soon as I entered the office. "I knew you'd come!"

She stood to kiss me, and I pulled my head back, earning sneers from the other women in the waiting room. Nikki and I sat next to each other, and I'd never felt so out of place in my life. Pictures of happy families graced the walls, and the tables held a slew of parenting magazines.

The couple sitting across from us were clearly in love, and another woman was reading a brochure on what appeared to be breastfeeding. I glanced at Nikki, who had her hands on her stomach. All of a sudden, she smiled and grabbed my hand.

"Feel this, Brett! Our baby is kicking." She moved my hand to the right side of her belly.

I felt the sensation under my palm and was stunned by the overwhelming feeling that filled my heart. If this child was mine, I vowed right then and there to be the best dad I could—even if we weren't a family.

"He must know his dad is here." She squeezed my hand.

"He?" I pulled my hand away. "Did you already find out?"

She giggled. "No, a mom just knows, I guess. I bet he's going to be gorgeous like you. That's all I want. A miniature Brett." Her smile was wide as she rubbed her belly.

"Why don't we wait and see what the doctor says." I leaned back in the wooden chair and contemplated telling her I knew I'd worn protection. My thoughts were interrupted when the door opened.

"Nikki Chambers?" the nurse called.

Bile rose in my throat as Nikki bounced out of her chair. Nikki *Chambers?* What the hell? She looked back at me and winked. The nurse was old enough to be my mother, so rather than correcting her, I followed her into the small office. I'd take care of the name issue later.

The office was dimly lit. Aside from the bed, a couple of chairs and the ultrasound machine, it was rather bleak for such a happy place. I supposed not all of the news that came from these rooms was jovial, but the décor could have assisted with the atmosphere. I shook my head, ridding it of negative thoughts.

"Nikki, please change into this." She handed Nikki a light blue hospital gown made of paper. "Opening in the front, please. You can leave your bra and underwear on."

The nurse left, and Nikki began taking off her top. I turned to walk out.

"Brett, you can stay. It's not like you haven't seen me take off my clothes."

Again with that sickly sweet voice. My stomach rolled, but I turned around and waited for her to get under the paper sheet on the bed. Didn't the place have linens?

There was a knock on the door, and Nikki said, "We're ready."

Another woman walked in. She was younger than the other woman. "Hi, I'm Veronica, the technician. I'll be performing the ultrasound."

I held out my hand. "Brett Chambers."

She shook my hand. "Pleasure to meet you." She turned to Nikki, who only had her lower half covered with the sheet. "You must be Mrs. Chambers?"

Nikki opened her mouth to answer, but I did it for her. "Actually, she's Nikki Webster. We're not married." I looked at Nikki and shook my head. This needed to stop. We weren't getting married, and pretending we were wasn't an option.

"Well, it's a pleasure to meet you both." Veronica sat on the stool as I stood at the end of the bed. She flicked on the machine and grabbed a bottle off the cart. "This will be a tad cold." She squirted gel on a handheld device and placed it on Nikki's stomach, making Nikki flinch.

"Yes, it is cold." Nikki laughed. Her eyes met mine. "Come closer, Brett, don't you want to see him?"

I stepped around to the side of the bed so I was facing the small monitor attached to the ultrasound machine.

"Do you already know the gender of the baby?" Veronica asked.

"No, but I know it's a boy." Nikki smiled and took my hand.

I didn't pull away, but I didn't close my fingers around her hand either. I was sure Veronica didn't think much of me as it was. No need for her to think I was a horrible person.

A sound came out of the speaker, making my eyes dart toward the screen. It sounded like swishing or something underwater. A white arrow pointed at an image that was moving around.

"That's your baby's heartbeat," Veronica said. "Strong and steady."

Nikki squeezed my hand. I was in awe. Never in my life had I heard anything like it. The beat was fast, and my eyes fixated on the lines Veronica was making on the screen. She informed us she was taking measurements and everything looked good.

"Ah, there we go." Veronica smiled. "I know the gender of the baby. Are you sure you want to know?" She looked at Nikki then at me.

"Yes, of course we do. Right, honey?" Nikki looked at me and smiled.

Honey? I nodded.

"Well, congratulations, Mom and Dad, you're having a girl."

Nikki gasped. I smiled as her theory of "Mommy knows best" quickly turned into "Mommy knew nothing."

Nikki became snippy. "Are you sure? I'm telling you he feels like a boy. Check again."

I laughed. All I could think was if that were my son, there'd be no doubt. He'd be well hung like his father. She was most certainly having a girl.

"I'm 99.9% sure it's a girl. There's always a slim chance the results are wrong and the baby is hiding something, but I don't think that's the case here. But if you feel strongly about it, then don't paint the room pink yet."

Veronica stood and handed Nikki tissues to clean off her belly. She wheeled out the cart and told us she'd pass the images along to the doctor. Before she left, she handed Nikki a few pictures of the baby. Nikki gave me one.

After Veronica left, Nikki tore off the paper gown and got off the bed in a huff. "She's wrong!"

Seeing Nikki in her bra and underwear made me cover my eyes.

"Brett, stop being a jerk and hand me my clothes."

I picked up her shorts and top and held them out to her.

She snatched them from my hands and shrugged them on. "I can't believe it." She pulled her long hair out of the back of her shirt and shook her head in disbelief.

"Nik, what the hell is your problem? She said the baby's heart was strong and everything looked good. Isn't that the most important thing?" Seriously, the chick was crazy.

"Whatever. I don't want a girl. I want your son." She huffed and grabbed her purse.

"Excuse me? What did you say?" My son? What was the difference?

"You heard me—I want your son. Don't you want your name carried over for another generation? That's what I want to give to you—your heir."

I glared at her. My heir? She'd truly lost it. It wasn't as if I was the King of England. "We don't even know the paternity yet, just chill out and be happy. Shit, I'm happy, and I don't even know if I'm the dad. You should be thankful everything is okay."

The doctor came in and told us the baby looked wonderful. All the measurements were where they should have been. He told Nikki he'd see her next month.

I walked out and went to the front desk. If I stayed in that room any longer, I would lose it.

Once we checked out—and I addressed the Nikki Chambers issue. Thankfully, she had just checked in using my last name. We made our way outside. I grabbed my cell to call a cab.

"Brett, I'm sorry." Nikki placed her hand on my arm. "You're right. I was thrown. But you didn't have to announce I wasn't a Chambers. Pretty soon I will be Nikki Chambers." She smiled sweetly at me.

My head snapped toward her as my eyes widened. What was she talking about? The chick was delusional, and I hoped the baby didn't inherit that trait. "Pardon me?"

"It's the right thing to do, don't you think?" She batted her eyes at me and tilted her head as if she were a puppy.

"No, I don't think." I took her hand off my arm. "Look, Nikki, I told you from the start that wasn't going to happen. If she is mine, then I'll support her and we'll figure out custody, but that's it. I'll be the best dad to our daughter, and I'll love her with everything I have, but that doesn't mean I'll love you. I'll never love you."

"You're kidding me, right?" She crossed her arms, and her eyes narrowed.

"No, I'm not kidding. I don't love you, and I won't raise a child in a loveless house. Not happening." The heat in the air was nothing compared to the heat building in my body. "I think we should ask the doctor to perform a paternity test before the birth. It's been done before."

"So you want them to stick a giant needle through my abdomen and get close to the baby? I told you that puts too much stress on her. Stop being so selfish. I told you she's yours." She shook her head in disgust.

"You can't blame me for having my doubts, Nikki. But I suppose I can wait. I'd feel terrible if something happened to her."

You would think that in this day and age, there'd be a different way to find out paternity. I needed to do some research. Come to think of it, I should have asked the doctor about it.

The cab pulled up.

"Can I drop you home?" I asked. Her place was on the way to the club, so why not?

She didn't reply, but she got into the cab and slid to the other side. Once I was in, I gave the driver her address. I stared at the passing cars and wondered what would happen the day this little girl was born.

"Brett?" Her saccharin-coated voice was back, but it sounded like nails on a chalkboard.

I looked at her. She was practically pouting. I was done with her today. "What?"

"I'm sorry. You're right. But please don't close yourself off to the idea that we will never happen. Never is a long time. You've wanted me before; it could happen again." Her lips curled into a smile that made me want to frown.

My hand raked through my hair, but I wanted to tug on it. I turned and stared into her doe eyes. "Try to understand. This"—my hand waved between us—"was never supposed to be more than a good time." I shook my head, trying to figure out the best way to tell her she wasn't the marrying type. "I don't love you, and as far as wanting you, yeah, I wanted you that night, but not to sound like an asshole, what I wanted was to get back at Julie. You were . . . convenient." As soon as the last word left my lips, I knew Nikki would flip out.

"Keep telling yourself that, but once our baby is born, you'll see. You'll want me." She crossed her legs and faced forward.

"Drop me off at the White Orchid first."

The cabbie nodded. When we arrived at the club, I tossed him an extra twenty on top of our fares.

I opened my door. "Oh, by the way, I know I wore protection that night. Purple, Nikki? Really? Do you honestly think I'd buy purple condoms?"

A panicked look flashed across her face but was replaced with a look that resembled pride. Was she proud of herself?

"Sometimes they fail. It says so right on the box." She grinned.

"So I did wear one, and you've been lying this entire time?"

Her expression bordered on mockery. I couldn't wait to get the hell out of that car and away from her.

"Hey, Brett?" she called, making my head drop back in exhaustion.

I turned and glared at her.

"Thanks for coming today." She rubbed her belly and smiled. "We appreciated it."

I shut the door and ambled into the club. I looked at Alex, who was sitting at the bar, but I bypassed him and walked upstairs to the office. I still needed to change. I didn't want to think about Nikki, but I couldn't help thinking about the baby girl who could possibly be my daughter.

Alex met me at the bottom of the stairs as I came down. "How'd it go?"

"I have to say, hearing the baby's heartbeat made it real." I rubbed the back of my neck. "It's a girl. Nikki could be carrying my daughter. I got her to admit we didn't have unprotected sex."

"I'm surprised she didn't lie again."

"She probably doesn't feel the need to anymore."

"But wow, a daughter. That's great!" Alex smiled. "Aubrey wants to be surprised, so we don't know what we're having. Can you imagine if she turns out to be yours? Our kids will grow up together."

Suddenly, the concept of being a father wasn't terrifying. Alex was right—our kids would be right around the same age.

"Yeah, but you love your baby's mother. Aubrey is nothing like Nikki. I can't even picture Nikki being nurturing." I exhaled. "How do I do this, man? I fell in love with that baby today. What do I do if she's mine and I can't be with her all the time? I never thought I'd be a dad, but if I had thought of it, I'd want Julie to be the mother. This is so screwed up." Just saying that made me sad for this little girl.

"You may feel differently after she's born . . . if she is yours." Alex shrugged. "Look, man, I know the type of guy you are. You'll want to be there for her, for them."

"No. I mean, yes, if the baby's mine, then of course I'll be there for her. But how could you think I'd be there for Nikki? Especially after all of her lies. Making me think that I did something with her that I haven't even done with Julie is enough for me to despise the ground she walks on." My nostrils flared. "Shit, Alex, what if it was Leah having your baby instead of Aubrey? What if this was happening to you? Your wife, a woman you love, is having your baby. You can't compare that to my situation."

Alex's lips formed a fine line. "Fine, I see your point. But please don't ever bring up Leah again, especially in front of Aubrey."

"I'm sorry. I hate her almost more than I dislike Nikki, and you know I love Aubrey. I just can't think clearly right now."

We walked over to the bar. Tyler was talking to Carly, one of the waitresses, so Alex got us both a drink.

Alex popped the cap off a beer bottle and set it in front of me. "Do you want to know what I think?"

"Sure." I took a swig and focused on what he was about to tell me.

"I think that if this baby isn't yours, you have a lot of groveling to do. Actually, you have a lot to do regardless. I've never seen you this torn up. Figure it out, and get your girl back. Maybe this new information will help." Alex lifted a bottle to his mouth.

"Yeah, from your mouth to Julie's ears." I stood. "I need to call my brother."

"Tell Bentley I said hi."

"Will do, man."

I grabbed my beer and walked over to a booth. I stared at my screensaver, a picture of me and Julie. We had been so happy when we snapped that selfie. Her smile was bright, and her eyes sparkled. Why couldn't I have realized then that I wanted forever with her? Why had it taken losing her for me to realize she was it for me? Julie wasn't like any other woman I knew. She was the one, and I'd lost her because I'd denied the woman I loved the one thing she wanted—our future. I stared at the picture while saying a silent prayer she'd forgive me for being so blind and quick to reject her. Alex was right. I needed to get her back.

chapter 12

Julie

WORK. THAT WAS what I needed to concentrate on. I threw myself into creating the marketing proposal for the vineyard and the club. The reality of how intertwined my worlds were had solidified for me that we needed to coexist. Ours wasn't a normal breakup. We ran in the same circles—both personally and professionally.

I was done lying to myself. Yes, I was a strong woman, but seeing him again had ignited a fury of emotions that were difficult to keep at bay and unnoticed. It would be impossible to hide my feelings from Aubrey when he and I were at her home on Sunday. Part of me didn't want to hide my feelings, but I needed to protect myself.

When Brett had held me, it was as if his skin seared mine—but not in a painful way. His words were honest, and it took every ounce of my strength not to tell him I wanted him back. The feel of his chest rubbing against mine when we made love, the feel of his fingers tracing the curve of my neck, the way his gaze roamed my body as he appraised me in approval and made the pit in my stomach tingle, his soft lips molded with mine—those were the desires that exploded in me when I was close to him. It broke my heart to not act on them, but how could I?

I stared into space and wondered if we could get back there one day. Then thoughts of Nikki and her baby rushed in. I vigorously shook my head in an attempt to clear it of any ill thoughts. Mark knocked on my door. His easygoing demeanor was what I longed for. That used to be me, but now I was strung so tightly that if someone pulled my string, I'd spin for days.

"Hi, Mark. What's up?"

He closed the door as he sauntered in, and he sat down. "Luca called Brian and told him your presentation was flawless, but I'm concerned about you."

His gaze made me keenly aware that he saw through my facade. I leaned forward on my desk. "You're concerned that my presentation was flawless? Or are you here because you're wondering what happened with Brett?"

He relaxed his shoulders and leaned back in the chair. "I'm not surprised about your execution of your marketing plan. But I'm surprised that you think I don't see how conflicted you are. It's written all over your face. I know you, Jules, and I've been where you are. Your eyes don't lie. They don't hold the gleam I'm used to seeing when you pull off a major deal."

I turned my head slightly. "It's difficult. You know how it is. Remember when Jessica up and moved to London and left you?" I'd never forget the devastation and hurt she'd caused him.

He nodded, and his brows slanted in a frown. "Of course I do. It hurts me that you feel that way." His eyes were filled with understanding. "Julie, when I see how this breakup has changed you, I feel as though I'm going through it myself. When you were away on business, it took every ounce of control I had not to go beat the shit out of Brett, but I didn't do it out of respect for you."

I smiled tightly and nodded. "Thank you. I wouldn't want you to get into a fight over me."

"So tell me, how was it when you saw him?"

I regarded him quizzically for a moment. "When I first saw him, all my old feelings came rushing back like a tidal wave. As I sit here and recollect that moment, they aren't old—just suppressed." My lips quirked to the side. "He's hurting too."

Mark's face relaxed, and he let out a huff. "I'm sure he is. I'm also pretty confident he's kicking himself for letting you go." He walked to my side of the desk and squatted beside me.

I swiveled my chair to face him, and he took my hands. My head lowered to look at him.

"No man in their right mind would turn you down. You're a special woman, and I never want you to forget that. I know what Brett did was unforgivable, but for once, put yourself first. I know you, and even if you could forgive him and take him back, you still might not because of the baby . . . if it's his."

Tears trickled down my cheeks. "That's the hardest part." Mark handed me a tissue from the box on my desk, and I blotted my eyes. "Thank you. Even if I do forgive him, how do I forget? How do I get past the fact that he was with her in a way he'd never been with me?"

Mark let out a huff. "I can't tell you that. I know I'd never do that to Val, even if we weren't together. I can tell you, as one of your closest friends, that sometimes people make mistakes. Don't misunderstand. I think he's an ass for doing what he did, but sometimes the male race doesn't think with the right head." He smiled and shrugged. "You deserve what I have with Val."

I let out a muffled laugh. "Yes. I know." Mark was right I did deserve a loving relationship and that was what I'd thought I had with Brett.

He winked and stood before taking his seat. "So now that we've covered the important stuff, tell me about the meeting."

For once, my smile didn't feel forced. "Thanks, Mark. You're a pretty terrific guy, and Val is a lucky woman. You're great together."

He blew on his nails before he rubbed them on his shirt. "Yeah, I know."

After I filled him on all the particulars, he went to his office to create the online graphics. Having Mark on our creative team was a huge help. He was extremely talented and an extraordinary person.

By the time I finished my proposal and sent it to Brian for final approval, I was ready for a break. Thankfully my boss told me to take the rest of the day off, which I kindly accepted. After I finished some errands, I headed over to Aubrey's house. I needed my girl time.

Brett

"Hi, bro." I was in need of brotherly advice. I hoped Bentley had some words of wisdom for me.

"Hey, little brother. I've been thinking about you. How are you?"

The concern in his voice reminded me of when we were kids and he'd broken my arm during a flag football game. Apparently he forgot he wasn't supposed to tackle me. It was the weekend of my lacrosse tournament, and I couldn't play, though I did play the guilt card for months. He became my gopher and chauffeur, so it wasn't a total loss.

"That's what I called to talk to you about. I went to the ultrasound, and we found out she's having a girl."

"Figures." Bentley chuckled, and I shook my head. "Can you imagine having to fight off your daughter's suitors?"

"If she's mine."

"Right. I can't believe you didn't cover it up. That's sex ed 101," he said.

"Yeah, well, I did cover it up. But I used a condom Nikki gave me, so who knows if she tampered with it." That thought alone irritated me.

"Wow, this woman sounds desperate."

"She's completely delusional." Maybe changing the topic would help me feel better. "What's new with you?"

"I've met someone. She's really special. Remember I told you about that actress in Jersey?"

"The one you wrote a scathing review about? Wait, that's all of them." I chuckled, but he didn't.

"I write honest reviews, but yes, her. She's special."

My cheeks rose as I smiled. "That's great news. I'm happy for you."

"You should go see Mom. She might have some words of wisdom for you." He switched the topic effortlessly.

"I'm actually heading there now. I'll catch up with you later."

"Bye, bro."

Pulling into my parents' place made me feel at home even though I didn't live there. My mother, the one woman I knew truly loved me and wouldn't steer me wrong or make me feel like shit. I walked in and smelled her freshly baked chocolate chip cookies. She was in the kitchen, wearing her apron and humming as she slid cookies onto a cooling rack.

"Did you know your favorite son was coming?" I laughed.

With her back still to me, she said, "Bentley, honey, is that you?"

She turned and winked, and we laughed. That was why I loved my mother. She had two sons who both thought we were her favorite, and she would tell us each we were, though not when we were together. It was a long-standing joke between the three of us. I guessed we were momma's boys.

"No, it's your other favorite." I chuckled and kissed her cheek. I sat at the breakfast bar as she placed a small plate of cookies in front of me.

"Milk or coffee?" she asked.

"A beer, if you have one." I bit off a chunk of cookie.

"Beer and cookies? That's revolting. But you drink orange juice with pizza, so I guess for you, it isn't that strange." Her smile was bright and cheerful and exactly what I needed. She handed me a Stella Artois. "Here you go."

"Thanks." I took long draw and a few more bites of the warm confection.

"So what's wrong?" She untied her apron and sat next to me.

"I went to the ultrasound today." I hated this. When I'd told my parents they might become grandparents, they weren't completely upset—until I explained the situation. I pulled out the sepia photo Nikki had given me at the doctor's and handed it to my mother. "It's a girl."

She held the thin paper, and it trembled in her grasp. "Brett, sweetheart, a girl? Oh, wait until I tell your father." Her eyes glistened, and she blinked away tears.

"Yes, that's what the technician said." I took another sip of my Stella. "Mom, what am I going to do if she's mine?"

She handed me the picture. "What do you mean what are you going to do?"

I exhaled. "I know that I'll take care of the baby and love her, but what about her mom? What about Nikki?"

"Brett, sweetheart, I can't answer that for you." She placed her hand on mine. "What else happened? Not that this isn't plenty, but I can tell when you're not telling me the entire story." She bit a cookie, waiting for my reply.

"So much has happened I don't even know where to start."

"The beginning." Her calm voice soothed me.

"I saw Julie." I looked down and shook my head. "God, Mom, how do I get her back? I love her so much. I truly can't believe how dumb I was."

"Look, sweetheart, sometimes life decides we need a challenge. This is one of yours and most likely won't be your last. I know you can handle whatever comes your way, or your father and I didn't do our jobs correctly."

I nodded. "I think Nikki tried to trap me. I found out that I did use protection, but she gave it to me. I won't marry her, Mom. I can't. You and dad raised us in a loving home, and I can't pretend I love her. If this is my daughter, I don't want her to realize one day that her parents were unhappy and she was to blame." Now I was the one with tears in my eyes. "None of this is this innocent child's fault. I want her to be happy and feel loved."

My mom hugged me. "Brett, why don't you find out if she's yours? I've never seen you so stressed out. You're my baby, and I don't like when you aren't happy."

I wiped away a stray tear. "I want to, but Nikki said it's too stressful because of a big needle or something. I don't want to harm the baby because I'm impatient."

"Brett, sweetheart . . ." She placed her hands on my cheeks and traced my eyebrows with her thumbs the way she had when I was a kid. "It doesn't have to be invasive anymore. I heard a woman talking about it at the club. Her neighbor is in the same boat, and she said it can be done with a simple blood test. Why don't you talk to Aubrey about it? Maybe she knows."

My first thought went to Nikki, wondering if she knew about this and withheld it from me. I stood and finally felt a twinge of hope. "Really? Thanks, Mom."

I pulled her into a hug. I would always need her in my life, and if the baby was mine, I would always be there for her in the same way.

After I grabbed another cookie and said good-bye to my mom, I hopped in my car and headed to Alex and Aubrey's house. They didn't live too far from my parents' place, but the roads seemed longer and never-ending. I passed a flower shop and decided to bring Aubrey a bright bouquet. It wasn't anything fancy like the orchids Alex showered her with, but it was a thank you for being an amazing friend.

Once I pulled up at their house, I took a deep breath and prayed my mom was right. Even if she was, I'd need to convince Nikki to go along with the test. That would be my next challenge, but I was up for it. I grabbed the bouquet and walked up the porch steps.

Aubrey opened the door before I could knock. Her belly was starting to pop, and she looked adorable. "Hi, Brett! I heard a car pull up and saw you." She pulled me into a hug, ignoring the bouquet. "I'm so glad to see you."

I released her and presented the flowers. "These are for you."

"They're beautiful! What's the occasion?" She lowered her nose and inhaled their scent. "They smell lovely. Come on in." She moved out of the doorway, and I followed her inside.

"No occasion. I just wanted to." I shrugged.

She walked into the kitchen, and when she came back out, the flowers were in a crystal vase, which she placed on the dining room table. "Okay, spill it. I highly doubt you came by because you were just in the neighborhood. Do you want a beer or something?"

"I actually was in the neighborhood. I'll pass on the beer. I just had one at my mom's." I raked my hand through my hair. "But you're right. I did come here for a reason."

"Ha! I thought so." Her lips curled into a beautiful smile. "Are you okay? I know you saw Julie. Is this about her?" Her voice was tentative, as though she was scared to bring up our meeting.

"Kind of, but not entirely. Like I said, I was at my mom's, and we were talking about Nikki's ultrasound today."

"Oh my God! Do you have a picture? Do you know what she's having?" Aubrey's voice was full of excitement and anticipation.

"Yeah." I pulled out the picture and handed it to her. "It's a girl."

Aubrey placed her hand on her chest as she stared at the photo. "Brett, wow. She looks perfect." She handed it back.

I studied the photo for a minute before I placed it back in my pocket. "She's actually why I'm here. When I talked to my mom, she said there's a non-invasive test available to determine paternity. Do you know anything about it? Not that you would need it, but I thought maybe you'd heard of something."

"Hold on. Let me go grab the folder my obstetrician gave me. There are so many pamphlets in there, and I think there may be one about that. But like you said, I didn't need it, so I didn't read it." Aubrey left the room.

I rose and paced the hardwood while gnawing the side of my thumb. My heart raced. I needed to find out if I was going to be a father. If I wasn't, then I would do whatever I needed to in order to get Julie back. But then again, if I was the father, I would still try to get her back. I wanted her. I needed her.

Aubrey walked out with a green-and-white pamphlet, and she gave it to me. “Here it is. I looked at it briefly, and it appears the test is a simple blood draw that won’t affect the baby at all.”

My smile grew, and I wrapped my arms around Aubrey. “Thank you so much. I need to make an appointment and talk to Nikki. You’re the best, Aub.” I tightened my arms before releasing her, and I headed toward the door. “Love you, and tell Alex that he’s a fortunate man.” I smiled and shut the door behind me.

With a bounce in my step, I headed to my Rover. I was about to open the door when a car pulled up behind mine in the circular drive. Julie. My heart jackhammered against my ribs. I let go of the door handle and walked toward her car. She sat behind the wheel even after turning off her car. I didn’t want her to start it up and reverse out of there. I slowly raised my hand to greet her.

I made my way to her door and opened it for her. She unclasped her seat belt, and I couldn’t avert my eyes from the woman I loved. I offered her my hand.

“Thank you.” She placed her fingers in my palm and stepped out of her car.

We were so close the temptation to hold her was stronger than it had been at the club. “Hi.”

“What are you doing here? Is Alex home?” Julie crossed her arms and put space between us.

“No, I came to talk to Aubrey. I didn’t know you’d be here.”

She looked at the pamphlet in my hand.

“Yeah, about this.” I held it out to her. The smell of vanilla washed over me as her beautiful blond waves blew in the wind.

"What is it?" She narrowed her eyes. "You know what? I don't need to know. I only came here to surprise my friend." She stalked away from me.

"Wait." I hurried to her. She needed to know. Even if she didn't care, I had to tell her. "It's for a paternity test that I want Nikki to agree to."

Julie shrugged one shoulder. "Whatever. It isn't any of my business."

I lowered my head and felt completely overwhelmed. When I lifted it, she was staring past me at the house. I needed to move so she could go see Aubrey. But instead of stepping aside, I stuck the brochure in my back pocket, placed my hands on each side of her neck, and stared into the beautiful eyes I'd missed.

I leaned in and placed a soft kiss on her forehead. My body and heart craved her taste. I rested my forehead against hers as I cupped her cheeks. Our eyes met, and I did my best not to shed the tears I felt building. "It will always be you, Julie. No matter what happens. Just you . . . forever. There will never be anyone else for me. You own my heart and fuel my soul. Even if you don't want me to, I'll always love you." After a beat, I moved aside.

She walked away, and I couldn't divert my gaze as she hurried up the steps to knock on the door. She looked back at me, and I saw sadness etched in her features. I needed to make this right. I needed her to let me back in and give us another chance.

But first, I had to talk Nikki into taking the test. I decided then and there I'd do whatever I needed to make that happen.

chapter 13

Julie

ONCE THE DOOR closed behind me, I let out a breath and grinned.

Aubrey embraced me. "Jules, I'm so happy you're back. Are you okay? I was on the phone with Alex when I heard you pull up, but I saw you talking to Brett, so I thought I'd leave you two be for a bit." She stroked my hair. "Come in. I'll pour you a glass of iced tea."

I sat on her supple leather sofa and watched my friend pour my drink and water with lemon for herself. She handed me my glass and joined me.

I smiled as I placed my hand on her belly. "Wow, you look great. It's true what they say about pregnancy. You're glowing and absolutely radiant." I lowered my head to her stomach. "Hey, sweet baby, it's your Auntie Julie. I can't wait to meet you." I kissed my fingers and placed them on Aubrey's tummy.

"You're going to be a wonderful aunt. Speaking of, I was going to wait until this weekend to talk to you about this, but since you're here, Alex and I would love for you to be this baby's godmother."

My eyes widened as I stared at her. I looked at her protruding belly and back at her eyes.

"You don't have to answer right now. You can think about it." Aubrey rubbed tiny circles on her stomach.

I felt pressure in my eyes, and my cheeks tingled. "I don't need to think about it. Of course I would be honored to be the godmother to your sweet angel." My cheeks hurt from the smile that stretched across my face.

Aubrey pulled me into a hug. "Yay, I'm so happy! I can't wait to tell Alex." She released me and took my hand. "Jules, I should let you know who we're going to ask to be the godfather." My smile faltered, and Aubrey's did as well. "Brett. Alex is going to ask him soon."

I nodded and pulled myself together. "He should. They're like brothers. Don't worry about me. I'll be fine. Look, I can't avoid him anyway. I just returned from Italy, and I've already seen him three times. It hasn't been too awful."

"Jules . . ." Her voice was laced with sadness, and that was the last thing I wanted. We should have been celebrating.

"No, Aubrey, don't. I'm fine, really I am. Brett and I can be friends, especially for this little bundle of sweetness." My hand went to Aubrey's tummy. "Hi, baby. You're going to have the best baby shoes ever."

She giggled. "I can't believe I'm having a baby!"

"I'm so happy for you. How has your anxiety been? Are you holding up okay?"

"Yeah, everything's wonderful. I've been writing and sharing my journal with Alex. We jot things down for the baby too. He's so amazing. He even started his own journal for our child."

"You're a lucky woman. He's pretty spectacular. You'll both make great parents." I wondered what type of parents Brett and Nikki would be. Would he take them to Disney, go for walks through Central Park? I sighed. Even though he said they wouldn't be together, who knew what the future would bring.

Her hand went to mine. "Jules, did Brett tell you why he was here?"

"Yes, he said he was talking to you about a paternity test he wants Nikki to take." My body shuddered at the thought of him sleeping with her. Of all the women who constantly threw themselves at him, he had to pick her. My stomach rolled at the thought of them being intimate in a way we'd never been.

"He's pretty hell-bent on getting to the bottom of this. You know, he still loves you." Aubrey took a sip of her water and peered at me over the glass.

"Yes, so he tells me. A part of me will always love him too, but if he's going to be a father, that's it. He'll have a child and be with Nikki—if not in marriage, then in a parental bond. For every birthday, school play, dance, first date, wedding, and every monumental event, Nikki will be a part of it, and rightfully so. But that's what I wanted for us." I stood and contemplated having wine rather than iced tea, but I hadn't tasted the drink I'd had. "When I look at him, my heart feels sad. I can see his pain. It's gut-wrenching. Sometimes I want to tell him none of it matters and that we can try again, but then my head goes back to the baby. I need to do what's best."

"I know, and I truly think you're handling this well. Look what happened to me when I saw Alex kiss Leah." She wiggled her shoulders. I was sure a chill had run up her spine because I knew one had run up mine.

"We were so close, and sometimes I wonder why I didn't ask what he wanted or how he envisioned our future. This is partially my fault, and that's the part I'm trying to work through. But a bunch of guesses and what-ifs doesn't change reality." I looked at my watch.

"Do you have a meeting?"

"No, Brian gave me the rest of the day off. I was wondering where Luca was and if he needed anything. He's been trying to get in as much sightseeing as he can before he leaves." I smiled as I pictured him running all over the city.

"Alex told me he thought Luca was a nice guy and quite fond of you."

I tilted my head. "He's a friend, that's all. You know I've tried dating, and it doesn't work. Luca is suave and extremely easy on the eyes, but he isn't Brett. One day I hope I'll meet a man I don't compare to the man who holds my heart."

"Jules, do you hear yourself?"

"What?" I sipped my drink.

"The man who holds your heart, the one you compare everyone to? He's not dead. Yes, he made a mess of things, but think about being friends with him. Maybe you two can start from scratch."

I kissed her on the top of the head. "My friend, the incurable romantic."

"Your friend wants her friend to find her happily ever after, like I did."

"You're a lucky woman, and Alex is a luckier man. But happily ever after? I don't think I'm the fairy-tale type. My life is more like a horror movie." I took my glass into the kitchen and set it on the counter before I headed back to Aubrey. "Thanks for everything. I should get going." Aubrey stood, and I embraced her. "Thank you so much for asking me to be the godmother. I'll be the best one I can."

She walked me to the door. "Can you still come over on Sunday? We're going to barbecue."

"I wouldn't miss it. I'll bring dessert." I kissed her cheek. "I love you."

"Love you too."

As I drove home, my cheeks hurt from the massive smile plastered across my face. *A godmother*. I wondered when Brett would find out if he was the father or not. I shook my head. Would I ever stop thinking about him?

My phone rang, and Aubrey's name popped up on the screen. "Hi, did I forget something?"

"No, Alex called, and he wants me to go to the club later tonight. Do you want to go with me?"

"Sure, why not? We haven't done that in a while. Do you want to come to my apartment, and we can go together from there?"

"Alex is sending a car for me."

I laughed. "Of course he is."

"Oh, shut up." She snickered. "We'll come pick you up so you don't have to drive."

"Have I ever told you how great your hubby is?"

"Yeah, yeah, I know. Okay, I'll see you later. I need to find something to wear that doesn't make me look like I should have baby written across my belly with an arrow pointing south so there's no question that I'm almost six months pregnant."

"You're beautiful no matter what you wear. I'll see you later."

"Bye."

I pushed the button on my Bluetooth and realized I'd most likely be seeing Brett again. Suddenly, I felt the need to look amazing. Instead of going home, I went to Saks and did some shopping.

Brett

BACK AT THE club, I headed to my office and read about the paternity test. Aubrey was right—all that was required was a blood test. I grabbed my cell. This was a topic that warranted a phone call or a face-to-face conversation, but a text would suffice.

Brett: We need to talk.

Nikki: Hey, babe. What's up?

Babe? Yeah, I needed to get to the bottom of that.

Brett: I'm calling a clinic about a paternity test. Don't worry about stress on the baby. It's a simple blood draw.

Nikki: No. I won't do it.

I closed my eyes. I needed to tread lightly and amp up the Chambers' charm.

Brett: Nik, I want to know if this is our baby. I need to know if we're going to have a daughter. Please, if you care at all, do this for me.

Saying "ours" made my stomach reel. I'd never wanted Nikki to be the mother of my firstborn, but if this baby girl was mine, I'd never let her know that. I'd make sure she knew only how much I loved her.

Nikki: She is yours . . . like I am.

I scrubbed my face with my free hand and decided to call instead. She answered on the first ring.

"Hey, Brett." Her syrupy voice made a chill run down my spine.

"Nikki, please consider this test. You'll most likely be getting blood drawn anyway. I'll try to arrange to have a sample sent to the lab so you only need to have it done once. Then I'll go and have mine done." I decided to include her since she wanted to be with me any chance she got. "Do you want to come with me when I go? Then we can go back together to hear the results."

"Really? You want me to go with you?"

I heard the jubilation in her voice. I needed to use that to my advantage. "Of course, this is about you too." My insides churned at how she would misinterpret my gesture. "Plus, if she is mine, we'll need to make the necessary preparations." I knew what that sounded like. Her head would immediately go to Brides-R-Us, while mine went to my attorney's office to make custody arrangements.

"Okay. If we can do this together and all it takes is a small amount of my blood, I'll do it. But I'm calling my doctor to verify all of this before I do anything." She sighed.

"Fantastic. I wouldn't expect you not to check it out. Thanks, Nik. Let me know what he says, and once you give the go-ahead, I'll call the lab for an appointment." I disconnected the call and tossed my phone on my desk. I reclined in my chair and finally let out a breath of relief.

My door opened with a quick knock. "Hey, man." Alex walked in and sat across from me.

"Hey."

"Heard you went to see my wife today. Brought her flowers and everything." He smirked.

I smiled and chuckled. "Yeah. You're a lucky guy. She's the best."

"Don't I know it." Alex's face got that dreamy look that made me smile. Ever since he'd met her, he'd been a goner. "Heard you ran into Julie too. How was that? Better than the last time?"

"I don't know. All I know is, thanks to my mom and your wife, I now have the information I needed to talk Nikki into having a paternity test."

"Yeah, Aubrey told me about that. I didn't know you'd talked to Nikki already." Alex crossed his legs, resting his ankle on his knee. "She agreed?"

"I just hung up with her before you came in. My next call is to the lab. Nikki is going to run it by her doctor, but I highly doubt it will be a problem."

Alex gave me a pensive stare. "What happens if the test comes back positive and you're the father?"

"Well, I guess I'll be having a daughter soon." I leaned forward. "Look, if she's my baby, I'll make sure that I have as many rights as Nikki, and I'll provide for her. She won't want for anything—especially my love." I pictured a sweet girl in a pink dress, swinging on a swing in a lush green backyard. She giggled every time she glided back and forth while she kicked her feet in excitement—except in my imagination, Julie was the one pushing her, not Nikki. I let out a frustrated breath. "That's what I'll do. Being there for her is my only option."

Alex's head bobbed. "That's what I thought you would do. What about Jules?"

"I'm going to win her back. Don't ask me how, but I need her the way you need Aubrey. Shit, I was so stupid. If I would have heard her out, and if she would have given me some time, this wouldn't have happened. All I needed was time."

"Don't say that to her—she'll never forgive you. I get that you needed time, and you both played some dumbass games that night, but I hope you've learned from my mistake. Never try to hurt the woman you love by grabbing the first woman with a pulse—especially a conniving one with an ulterior motive." Alex stood. "If you need time off, take it."

I nodded. "Thanks, but I need to keep busy."

I grabbed the silver frame on my desk and stared at the picture of Julie and me at the Statue of Liberty. We were laughing and having a great time. I traced her face with the tips of my fingers and whispered, "Please come back to me."

The club was getting busy, and Alex had informed me that the girls were coming by tonight. I needed to tend bar for a bit, but Tyler and Mike had the later shift. I was so proud of this place. We were making a name for ourselves, and with the wine room in full swing, we were bringing in a nice profit. My attorney had been able to keep Samantha's hands out of the till, so to speak. One crazy bitch down . . . one to go.

Before I saw Julie, I knew she'd walked in, but she and Aubrey weren't alone. Luca was walking beside her, and the three of them were laughing. I should have been consumed with jealousy, but I was happy to see her smiling. A wave of possessiveness washed over me when I saw his arm around her, but I let it keep rolling. My goal was to rebuild a friendship, not be an asshole.

After I served a group of guys their drinks, I noticed Alex and the girls sit at the end of the bar. Luca had stepped away. When she saw me, Aubrey smiled as if she had a dirty little secret. Her lips curled, and if I wasn't mistaken, she shot me a wink. I had no idea what that was about.

"Hi, Brett," Aubrey called.

I walked around the bar and gave her a kiss on the cheek. "Hi, Aubrey." My head turned to the right. "Hey, Jules." I wasn't sure if it was habit, instinct, or need, but my lips found Julie's cheek too. When I felt hers on mine, I knew we were headed in the right direction.

"What am I, chopped liver?" Alex chuckled, but I grabbed his face and planted a kiss on each cheek. The ladies laughed while Alex shook his head. "I'm sorry I said anything."

I chuckled as I went back behind the bar. "What's your pleasure?"

Julie shifted in her seat and rolled each shoulder until her posture was pin straight. Her pink tongue licked her glossed lips, which made me want to do the same. She didn't say anything at first, but after Aubrey ordered a Pellegrino, Julie ordered her usual martini.

When I brought them their drinks, Mark and Val had shown up, and Luca was back. I said hi to everyone and shook Luca's hand. He wasn't a bad guy, and after I'd looked over the proposal, I realized the club stood to make a lot of money from a partnership with his family's winery. Luca said he'd wanted to see the club in action, but since he was leaving to return to Italy tomorrow, he needed to go pack. He said goodbye to everyone, gave Julie a kiss on each cheek—yes, I was watching—and he left.

After a bit of time, Mike came in to start his shift, so I was free to hang with everyone. I grabbed myself a cocktail. We all headed upstairs. It was perfect—well, almost perfect.

I slid out of my seat and held my hand out to Julie. "Want to dance?"

She tentatively nodded and placed her hand in mine. It felt so natural, almost instinctive. We excused ourselves and went downstairs to the dance floor. People were swaying to the beat of the music. I moved Julie to the back corner, hoping for some alone time. I held her right hand and placed my other on her back. We kept time with the music. I wanted to hold her close, but I made sure to keep a balloon's space between us.

"This is nice." Her green eyes had a bit of their sparkle back.

I moved my lips toward her face, and her breathing altered. Her fingers flexed on my hand, and I felt the muscles in her back tighten.

Once I was close to her ear, I whispered, "Yes, it is. Thank you for dancing with me."

We stayed on the dance floor for a few more songs. When we tried to walk off, we were blocked by Nikki. She was practically snarling. I half-expected her to yell at me, but she was more interested in Julie.

"So you're not giving up?" She put her hands on her protruding belly, and Julie's eyes followed them. "How much more do you need to realize you're never going to have him?" She grabbed my arm and attempted to tug me toward her. "He's going to be a father. What are you going to be? A homewrecker?"

Julie's face flushed, and my mind was about to blow. Before I could say anything in her defense, Julie said, "I'm not a homewrecker, nor would I ever be, but

Brett is my friend. So if you're having his baby, then get used to me because I'll be around."

Pride coursed through me, but Nikki looked as though she could snap at any moment. I needed to protect my baby and Julie.

"We'll see about that. Now I need to talk to Brett about this paternity test, so if you could excuse us." She yanked on my arm. "Now, Brett!"

Julie walked away.

I was fuming! "What the hell, Nikki?"

She spun around to face me as she leaned on a stool and rubbed her stomach. "Do not talk that way in front of our daughter."

I ran my tongue over my teeth and tried to soften my tone. "What do you need?"

She stared at me. "I don't want you talking to her."

The chick had lost her mind. "If you're referring to Julie, you can forget it. You don't dictate who I'm friends with."

"Do you want this test done?" She twisted her head to the side. Her lips contorted in an almost demonic way.

That's it. I was done playing Mr. Nice Guy with her. "Here's the deal, Nikki: either you get the test done, or I'll take you to court and get an order for you to comply." I had no clue if I could do that, but I assumed she didn't know either. If it wasn't an article in *Cosmo,* she probably didn't know about it.

Her face turned all shades of red. "You can't do that."

There was a quiver in her voice while mine remained steady. "Try me."

"You know what? Go ahead and be with your friends. Soon enough we'll know the truth." She straightened up and stepped forward. “Once our baby is born, she’s off-limits. My husband will not hang around with his ex.” She looked at her friends who had walked up behind her. “Come on, ladies, let’s get out of here.” With that, she walked away, and her entourage followed.

Husband? What? I went upstairs to the VIP area while I tried to forget what she’d just said.

“You okay, man?” Alex’s features were clouded over with anxiety.

The waitress put a fresh whiskey neat in front of me. I nodded and took a sip. “No, I’m not okay.”

Aubrey placed her hand on Alex’s. She was as concerned as he was. “What happened when you were talking to Nikki?”

I glanced at Julie, who was looking at Aubrey. “She wanted me to stay away from Julie.”

“What?” Julie’s head snapped toward me.

I took another sip of the amber liquid. I loved the burn going down my throat, and I needed to feel it right now. “Don’t worry about it. I told her that wasn’t going to happen. Can we not talk about her? Seriously, there has to be something happier we can discuss. I just wanted to be honest about what she said.” I looked at Julie. “I’m sorry she’s such a bitch, but she’s jealous.”

Julie let out a breath. “She has nothing to be jealous of.”

I drained my drink. Julie was right that Nikki shouldn’t be jealous. I wasn’t in a relationship with Julie; we were just friends.

I raised my glass, and the others followed suit. “To my godchild.”

“Our godchild.” Julie smiled at me.

Without taking my eyes off her, I said, "Our godchild."

Everyone clinked glasses, and for a brief moment, it was almost like old times. *Almost.*

chapter 14

Julie

WHEN LUCA AND I pulled up to JFK, he handed me a picture of himself and Jennifer Anniston's wax figure, which made me laugh. He brought such fun and lightness to my life. I would miss him.

"Thank you for everything, bella. You're a wonderful, strong woman. I can see in your eyes that there is still sadness, but not as much as there was in Italia. Yes?"

"I'm not as sad as I was before. They say time heals all wounds, but I'm not there yet. I just don't want to be angry anymore. I don't want to harbor ill feelings. It's exhausting, and worst of all, it isn't me."

A car horn blared, and a man yelled at me to drop off and move on. We both exited the car while still being screamed at by the impatient driver. I popped my trunk, and Luca grabbed his bags.

He set them down and embraced me. "You call me if you need anything, and I don't mean with only business matters." He kissed my cheeks. "Try to remember, *no rosa è senza spine.*"

I snickered. "I have no idea what you said."

His deep brown eyes looked into mine. "'No rose is without a thorn.' Remember that. *Ciao,* Julie."

"Ciao, Luca."

No rose is without a thorn. How true that was.

When I got back to my apartment, I tried to make sense of everything that had transpired since I'd met Brett.

I'd instantly lusted after him.

He quickly became one of my closest friends.

I fell in love with him.

He broke my heart.

I let him.

I poured myself a glass of wine and fixed myself a nice hot bath. Once I'd immersed myself in lavender-scented bubbles, I began to relax. My eyes fluttered closed, and all of my thoughts, as usual, went to him . . . always him . . . only him.

We'd told each other we'd stay friends, and deep down, I'd known being his friend would be inevitable. It was time to search into the deepest part of my soul and figure out how to get past my hurt and come to terms with how his life, how our lives, were.

Mistakes. We all made them; it was how we corrected them that mattered. To live a life of what-ifs would be completely draining and pointless. When I thought about it, that was all we'd done. What if Brett hadn't said anything to Aubrey? What if she hadn't said something to me? What if I had never gone to see him? What if I hadn't tried to make him jealous? What if Brett hadn't slept with Nikki? And the big one—what if Nikki hadn't gotten pregnant?

I scooped up a mound of the lavender-scented suds and watched each tiny iridescent bubble vanish, like my reasons why I shouldn't fully accept how things were now and be by Brett's side. The water was cooling down, so I got out of the tub and wrapped myself in a towel. In my bedroom, I put on a pair of yoga pants and a hoodie, grabbed my phone, and lay down in bed.

My phone chimed with a text from Aubrey, confirming that I was bringing dessert to her house the next day. After I said I was, I scrolled through my pictures. A few months ago, that would have been self-torture. I looked at a picture of Brett eating a chili dog from my favorite street vendor, one of me sitting on a park bench in Central Park and holding a flower Brett had given me, pictures of the four of us at Alex and Aubrey's wedding.

The last one I looked at was a candid of Brett laughing as he chatted with a club patron. His smile reached his sparkling eyes, creating the cutest laugh lines. That was what I missed the most, and although I didn't know if I could bring his smile back to that full mega-watt force, I wouldn't be the one to lower the dimmer switch. That was when I made the decision to text him.

Me: Hi. You there?

I knew he was working, so I didn't know how quickly he'd respond, but his text was almost instantaneous.

Brett: Yes. Are you okay?

Me: Yes, why do you ask?

Brett: Because you're texting me. I thought there was a problem.

My chest tightened. How awful our situation had become when even sending a text was an oddity.

Me: I was thinking about you. Are you busy?

A few minutes passed. I made myself comfortable under my down comforter while I waited for a reply.

Brett: Sorry. I had to get Mike to cover for me. I'm all yours now.

I paused. *All mine now.* I didn't know how much time passed, but he must have noticed my hesitation.

Brett: I mean I'm not busy.

Me: You're still going tomorrow, right?

Brett: To Alex's? Yes. Is that okay? If you're uncomfortable, I won't go.

I looked at the screen and pressed the call button next to his name.

"Hi, Jules." His voice was deep and a tad unsteady.

I needed to lighten this up and try to relax him. "Hi. So about tomorrow . . ."

He stopped me before I could say anything. "Really, if it's going to ruin your fun, then I don't need to go."

"Of course you won't ruin my fun. I'm bringing dessert, so I needed to know how much to bring." I squeezed my eyes closed and chastised myself saying something so utterly ridiculous. "That was a lie. I'm sorry."

He chuckled. "Have you been drinking?"

I laughed. "No, but I'm thinking I could use a Chambers martini right about now." I fiddled with the lace eyelet trim on my sheets. “This shouldn’t be this hard.”

“Just be honest, Julie. Why did you call?”

Here goes. I let out a breath and said a silent prayer that I could articulate what I needed to say. “I was thinking about us tonight when I was taking a bath.”

He made a noise that rumbled through the receiver. “What have I told you about getting wet without me?” A laugh escaped him, which made me smile.

At the memory of when we’d first started getting to know each other, tears trickled down my cheeks.

“I’m sorry, that totally slipped out.”

His apology made my heart clench.

“Jules?” My name sounded as though I were a wish.

“I needed to let you know I’m glad you’re going tomorrow.”

“Well, that makes me extremely happy.” He paused, and I heard muffled chatter. “Hey, I need to get back to work. But thank you for calling. I’ll see you tomorrow.”

“Brett?”

“Yeah.”

“I need you to know that I don’t blame you for all of it. It wasn’t all your fault. It takes two to get together and two to break apart.”

“Yeah, but I started it.”

“Okay, I’ll agree with that.” I tried to laugh, but it sounded like a broken sniffle.

He laughed. “See, we’re agreeing on things already. I’ll see you tomorrow.”

We disconnected our call, but before I turned off the phone, I changed my screensaver back to the picture of me and my friends. *One day at a time.*

The next morning, I woke up a bit more rejuvenated. I looked forward to spending time at Aubrey's. I opted to wear my sexy black string bikini and a pink sundress. I slid on a cute pair of flat sandals and headed out.

It was a beautiful sunny day, which meant traffic to Aubrey's would be a bitch, but it would be totally worth it. I stopped at a bakery to pick up a key lime pie, which happened to be Brett's favorite. As I drove, I cranked up my radio and belted out tunes.

I pulled into their driveway, and Brett must have just arrived as well. He was standing at the front door, looking great in a pair of black board shorts and a pale green T-shirt that hugged his strong arms and V-shaped back.

He turned and walked toward me. "Hi."

"Hey, there." I grabbed the pie out of my car and closed the door.

He glanced at the pink box tied with white string. "What do you have there?"

"Key lime pie that needs to get in the refrigerator before we have key lime gazpacho."

"Hmm . . . that happens to be my favorite dessert." His grin was wide, and the sparkle in his eyes made me smile.

It would be a good day. *Finally.*

Brett

THE SUN BEAT down on me as I sat on Alex's patio. He was at the grill while Aubrey was inside making side dishes with Julie. Alex grabbed us both a beer and sat next to me.

"So when are you getting the paternity test done?" Alex took a swig of the pale ale.

"Tomorrow. All I can hope for is quick results, but it may take a week or two." I sipped my brew.

"How are you feeling about it?"

Alex's question surprised me. "What do you mean? How do I feel about having the test done or that I'll finally have the answer?"

"What I mean is, have you thought about what your next move will be? Don't get me wrong, I know you don't want Nikki to be the mother of your child, but are you prepared if that is the outcome? You've been dealing with this for months." He shook his head. "I know our situations are completely different, so I can't imagine what you're feeling, especially if she damaged the condom."

"I don't know. When I heard the baby's heartbeat and found out it was a girl, I immediately wanted to protect her. So if she's not mine, I don't know if I'll be relieved. I think I'll still worry about her, especially given who her mother is." Alex opened his mouth, but I cut him off. "Before you say anything, the only thing Nikki wants out of this is me—you know that as much as I do. It was revolting how disappointed she was when we found out she was having a girl. That woman is missing brain cells, and part of me hopes that little girl is mine so I can guard her from a life without love—no matter how she was conceived." When I heard chatter, I set down my bottle, stood, and looked toward the door.

Aubrey was standing there with Julie. Alex and I looked at each other, and I wondered how much they'd heard. The heat in the air tripled around me, and I began to sweat.

Alex got up and took the bowl out of his wife's hands. "Let me help you with that, sweetheart."

Julie walked over to the table and placed a platter of fruit on it before she shrugged out of her pink sundress. Her black bikini made my mouth water and my heart skip a beat. She didn't even notice. I watched her lower herself onto a floating chaise in the pool.

"She's such a bitch with that body of hers." Aubrey laughed as she rubbed her belly as she sat at the table next to Alex. "If she wasn't my closest friend, I'd cuss her out."

"I think you're stunning." Alex kissed his wife.

"On that note, I think I'll go cool off with Julie." I didn't know why I bothered saying anything. Neither of them were paying attention to me.

I took off my T-shirt as I walked toward the pool. Julie was floating on the raft with her eyes closed. My lips curled before I did a cannonball off the diving board. Julie screamed and fell into the water. She sputtered as she wiped back her long hair. She splashed me, which made me laugh harder. Of course, I retaliated.

"I can't believe you did that, you big jerk!" She smiled. "I'm soaked!"

"You're in a pool. What did you think would happen?"

She went to splash me again, but I caught her around the waist and brought her up against me. I smoothed back a strand of her hair and tucked it behind her ear. I cupped her neck and felt her quickening pulse. Unable to resist her, I pulled her face closer to mine. Every pore in my body needed her, craved her. When she didn't back away, I brought my lips to hers. Our lips didn't move as we breathed each other's air, felt each other's skin. When a sigh escaped her, my left hand pressed on the small of her back, drawing her closer to me.

She parted her lips, and we were once again Brett and Julie. The couple who were once in love, the man and woman who needed each other. My hands went under her perfect ass. Her legs wrapped around my waist, and the growing erection in my board shorts pressed against her. Nothing else mattered as time stood still around us. Our tongues danced as my hand moved from her neck to tangle in her wet hair.

Our kiss broke, and we stared at each other. Other than the birds chirping, we were surrounded by complete and absolute silence. Alex and Aubrey were on the patio and out of earshot. A warm breeze made the water ripple around us.

"Brett . . ." she whispered, and her eyes softened.

All I could do was hold her. I brought her head to the crook of my neck. She rested her cheek on my shoulder.

"Julie, I've missed you so much. Can we please start over? All I want to do is be with you."

Her chest rose with every breath she took. I felt a hitch every now and again and said a silent prayer she wasn't crying. I didn't want to let go, but I needed to make sure she was okay, so I loosened my grip on her, making her legs unwrap.

She stood and looked me straight in the eye. "I've missed you too, but . . ."

"No! Please, don't say it. Believe in us and my love for you." I placed my hands on her shoulders. "You're my soul. I need you. If you're not ready, we'll take it slow, one day at a time, and I'll prove to you that I'm worthy of your love. I won't rest until you trust me with your heart again. I'll cherish it and never take it for granted." I never broke eye contact with the love of my life.

Her tongue swept over her lips as though she were trying to taste us again. I'd have been happy to remind her, but she didn't need that. All she needed was space.

"One day at a time?" She shyly smiled. "No more heated kisses or dunks in a pool?" Her eyes narrowed, creating the cutest crease above her nose.

"Yeah, one day at a time. But as for the pool thing . . ." I laughed, and she swatted my arm. "Sorry, Jules, no promises there."

We dried off and made our way to the patio to reunite with our friends. The table was set, and the steaks Alex had grilled were waiting for us along with the dishes Julie and Aubrey had prepared.

"Did you two have a good swim?" Aubrey beamed and winked.

I couldn't help but smile. My cheeks had even begun to sting, and it wasn't from the sun.

"Wow, you're looking good, Mr. Chambers," Aubrey said.

"Hey, I'm right here, Mrs. Logan." Alex leaned over and planted a possessive kiss on his wife.

"Yes, honey, but I always tell you that you're the sexiest man alive." She rubbed his arm. "Julie, don't you agree? Doesn't Brett look great?"

Julie turned the same shade as her dress. Her brows shot up, and she glanced at me. "Yeah, I suppose he looks okay." Julie sat down and put salad on her plate.

Alex clapped my back and laughed. "Boy, you have her eating out of the palm of your hand already. Good to see you haven't lost your touch."

"Why don't you worry about your grilling skills? Let's hope this steak is as good as it looks." Aubrey giggled, knowing full well that Alex prided himself in being the "grill guru."

We all sat around, enjoying our meal and each other's company.

I didn't want to bring up tomorrow's blood test, but I needed to. If we were going to be friends and honest with one another, then I had to be able to talk about it. "So Nikki and I are getting tested tomorrow. According to the brochure, the clinic takes walk-ins, so I'm not waiting."

The sound of flatware against plates ceased as all eyes turned toward me. Alex had already known, but the girls hadn't.

"I think that's great." Aubrey patted my wrist.

"Me too." Julie surprised me with her admission.

I turned toward Julie, who was wiping the corners of her mouth with a napkin. "You do?"

She nodded. "I think you need to know. Not only for you, but for Nikki."

"Nikki?" Alex's voice was tense.

Julie raised a shoulder to her ear. "Yes, Nikki. I've been thinking about her lately."

We all stared at her as though she needed an exorcist.

Her eyes roamed across all of us. "Don't look at me that way. I didn't say I loved her. I just think if I got pregnant and the man I thought was the father didn't want to believe that, I'd be hurt." She took a sip of water and looked at Aubrey. "Wouldn't you?"

"Of course I would." She placed her palm on her stomach. "I couldn't even begin to think about that."

"And you'd never have to because you're not like her." Alex grabbed her hand and kissed it.

I rubbed my hand along the back of my neck. "Look, I'm not trying to be the bad guy here, but how could I not wonder? If you walked into a random club in Midtown, there'd be a good chance she'd slept with or attempted to sleep with half of the men in the room. Shit, if she were here, she'd be at one hundred percent."

Aubrey's mouth dropped open as Alex's head whipped in my direction. It wasn't a pleasant thought, but it was the truth.

"I'm sorry I brought it up." Julie gave Aubrey a sympathetic look.

Alex stood and grabbed a drink out of the cooler. "The past is the past. We've moved on, so let's not rehash shit."

I cleared my throat. "I didn't want to start anything here. I just wanted my closest friends to know what's going on."

The rest of afternoon was relaxing. I loved the way Julie's porcelain skin took on a sexy hue of pink and the blond streaks in her hair became a shade darker than white from the sun kissing them. She was laughing and having fun—we all were.

chapter 15

Julie

TODAY WAS THE day Brett was having the DNA test performed. After the way things had gone yesterday, I wasn't even sure how I felt about it anymore. When I'd heard Brett say he wanted to protect the baby because her mother was so vile, I almost hoped he was the father.

I rolled out of bed and got ready for work. I would do my best to try to not think about what was going on with him today, though I knew that would be a challenge. I grabbed a cab and headed to the office.

Mark was in the break room, holding the *Times*. He lowered the paper when I entered the room. "Morning, Jules. Did you have a good day yesterday?"

I poured myself a cup of coffee and sat down. "I did actually. Brett and I talked, and I think we're finally starting to heal." I took a sip of the delicious hazelnut coffee, then I nonchalantly said, "Oh . . . and we kissed."

His brows raised a fraction, and he grinned tightly. "I guess you are healing, but please be careful, okay? There's nothing I'd like more than for you to be happy, and if getting back together with him is what you want, then I support you. But if he hurts you, I will inflict so much pain on him that he'll feel as though he was run over by a truck."

I smiled in approval. "Thank you. But let's hope inflictions of pain aren't necessary."

Mark stood. "Let's hope not."

As usual, work was busy, and before I knew it, it was close to noon. My desk phone rang. "Good morning, Julie Michaels speaking."

"Hey, it's me. You're not answering your cell."

Brett's voice was so deep it sent excitement through my veins. Then I remembered where he'd been, so I kept my voice upbeat. "Hi. I left my phone in my purse. How's it going?"

"We just finished taking the test." He sounded strained but relieved.

"Are you okay?"

"It's funny, but yes. I'm so glad I'll be getting answers soon, but I'm nervous."

"I'd be terrified."

"Do you have time to grab lunch? I'm craving a chili dog and some fries."

The humor in his voice made me smile. I relaxed into my chair. "I'd love to."

"Good, I was hoping you'd say that."

My body jolted up, and my hand went to my chest. Brett stood in the threshold to my office, holding a yellow rose.

"God! You need to stop sneaking up on me."

His hearty laugh filled my office. “Actually, I’m Brett, and this is for you.” He strolled toward me and handed me the flower. “Be careful. There are thorns on it.”

My teeth grabbed my bottom lip as I studied the stem. “Thank you. I suppose every rose has a thorn.” I snickered.

“Are you quoting Poison?” He chuckled.

I smacked his arm. “No.”

He pulled me close to him, and my skin ignited. “You know, if you put our names together, it makes sense.”

My head tilted as I tried to decipher what he meant.

“Put our names together—Brett Michaels.”

“Haha, very funny. No, it was just something Luca said before he left.” I waved, brushing off the words. “So are we going to go eat some greasy food or what?”

“Yeah, let’s go.”

We walked outside, and thankfully a subtle breeze helped diffuse the hot, humid air. Brett placed his hand on the middle of my back to guide me to the closest food stand. A sense of familiarity and security engulfed me.

He looked at the tilted menu hanging off the top of the vendor’s silver cart. “So what’ll it be?”

The cook looked at me. “The usual, Julie?”

Brett’s head turned toward me as I glanced at him. I couldn’t help but snicker. “Hi, Bernie. Yes, please.”

“You’re on a first-name basis with the street vendor guy, and you’ve been away for months? Not to mention you have a usual and he remembers that?”

“Yup. Don’t let this body fool you. I eat what I want and when I want it. Let’s not forget I’m pretty memorable.”

Bernie looked at Brett with an arched brow, and I nudged Brett with my elbow. It dawned on me that Bernie was waiting for his order.

After studying the menu, Brett said, "I'll have what she's having."

Once we had our food, we walked over to a small quad area where business people often took breaks. We found an empty bench and sat down.

I peeled back the foil on my hot dog and inhaled. The aroma of spices filled my nose. "Mmm, it's so good."

"You haven't even taken a bite yet." Brett took a sip of his soda and placed it on the sidewalk in front of the bench.

"I don't need to take a bite to know how good this is. Once you've had a taste, you'll understand. Bernie makes the best sausage, and none will compare after this." I took a bite. When I glanced up, Brett was staring at me. "What?" My mouth was so full of food that it didn't even sound like a word. I snickered. Once I swallowed, I tried again. "Sorry, that wasn't very ladylike. Why are you staring at me? Eat before it gets cold." I took another bite and moaned.

"Seriously, Julie, you're killing me here." He took a big bite and nodded. "This is good."

"Told you." I grabbed my soda and took a sip. "So when will the results be ready?"

He swallowed and wiped his mouth. "At least two business days, barring any problems with the samples." He continued to eat as though it was the best thing he'd ever tasted—which could have been the truth.

"Wow! I didn't think it would be that quick."

Brett placed the last bit of his sandwich in his mouth and crumpled the foil into a ball before tossing it into the can next to us. "I know. Nikki was surprised too."

"Well then, it won't be long before you have your answer." I finished my lunch and discarded my trash.

"I need to tell you something else." He rubbed his hands on the front of his jeans and took a deep breath. "I had the doctor test me for STDs."

I could almost feel my lunch churning in my stomach. "Oh."

"I feel sick that I need to worry about it, but I had to have it done. So I asked the doctor to have the lab run additional tests."

He turned his hand palm-side up, and I studied it before I placed mine in his. Once his fingers wrapped around mine, I felt my insides settle down and my pulse steady. We stood and didn't release our grip. Being hand in hand was familiar, and although we weren't together, it felt right.

"Is this okay?" His voice was soft as our joined hands dangled between us as we walked back to my office. "I'm trying my best not to rush you. I've told you what I want, and I understand your reservations, especially because of my situation."

We stopped in front of my building and faced each other. I grasped his other hand and laced our fingers together. "I'm trying, Brett. To be honest, this is much better than being angry with you. The amount of energy it took to be mad and detach myself from our situation exhausted me. I'd like to move forward and not think about that night, but you could be a father soon. That's why we need to stick to our 'one day at a time' plan."

"I think we're on the right track, but I need you to talk about what's going on with you. There's no need to walk on eggshells because you think I'll get hurt.

Please be my friend—laugh with me, talk to me, let me help you if I can. If you need a shoulder, I have one for you to lean on." I rolled up on the balls of my feet and kissed his cheek. "Thank you for lunch."

"You're welcome and thank you for . . . everything."

I nodded. "You're welcome."

My afternoon was uneventful and productive. I felt energized after my lunch, and I didn't think it had anything to do with Bernie's awesome sausage—it had to do with Brett. However, thoughts of the test results weighed on my mind. God forbid he'd contracted a disease.

"Hey, chica!" Aubrey bounded in my office and sat down.

My hand went to my chest. "Jesus, what is with everyone scaring me lately?"

She laughed. "I didn't mean to startle you. I had a doctor's appointment in the city, and Alex dropped me off here so I could go over a few things with Brian." She took a sip of her bottled water and tilted her head. "Wait, who else was here?"

I matter-of-factly said, "Brett."

"Oh . . . hmm . . . you've been seeing a lot of him lately." She winked, and I shook my head. "Why did he stop by?"

"He was on his way back from the lab and stopped in to take me to lunch." I placed my head in my hands. "Wow, how screwed up did that sound?"

"It is a bit messed up, but it isn't as though you two are back together . . ." Her tone was questioning though still understanding.

"No, we aren't together. It's . . . I don't know." I sat back and looked at her hopeful face. "He's so . . . Brett.

I know that makes zero sense." My thoughts were as scrambled as the storyboards I worked on.

"It makes perfect sense."

"What?"

She smiled warmly. "Alex isn't always perfect, but he's Alex. There's no one else for me." She placed her hand on her belly. "Even after our breakup, when I was in Paris trying to get over the hurt, it was always about him. He once said I could put an ocean between us, but it wouldn't matter. All I needed was time and space, but no amount of time or space would ever make me stop loving him. So I do understand." Her empathetic statement didn't fall on deaf ears.

"You and Alex were meant to be."

Aubrey laughed. "Well, from what I observed yesterday, I'd say so are the both of you. I don't think I'll ever look at my pool the same way again."

"Yeah, that was nice." I sighed, and we both laughed. Then I thought of Nikki's baby. "That can all change in a couple of days when he gets the test results."

"It doesn't have to. Alex told me under no circumstances will he be with Nikki."

"Yes, I know. I suppose we'll wait and see what happens."

"You're a strong woman, Julie, much more than I am. I know you can handle whatever is next."

"Thanks. I'll do my best. Now, enough about me. Tell me how your appointment went."

The radiance she exuded at every mention of her baby was how a loving mother should be. "Everything was wonderful. I can't wait to hold this little one."

"I'm looking forward to meeting my godchild too. Can he or she call me Auntie Jules?"

Aubrey laughed. "Of course. I thought you'd want them to call you their fairy godmother."

"Oh, that's even better. Let's go with that." We broke out into a fit of giggles.

It had been a perfect day . . . perfect.

Brett

I STROLLED INTO THE club with an extra bounce in my step.

Alex's eyes peered at me over the bar. "For some reason, I thought you'd be completely depressed and take the night off."

"Nope, I'm good. I'll have answers soon, and I just saw Julie."

"Did you see Aubrey? I dropped her off at Walker-Stone so she could hang out with Julie for a bit."

"No, we must have missed each other."

"So you and Julie seemed comfortable with each other yesterday," Alex said.

"Yeah. I'm trying to be what she needs right now because she's always what I need. We agreed to take it one day at a time. I don't want to push her away."

"Good call. Okay, I need to get some paperwork done. I'll catch you later."

Thankfully, the club stayed busy all night, and time flew by. I didn't text or call Julie. I wanted to lay low and prove to her that I wouldn't pressure her into anything she wasn't ready for.

The next two days dragged by. I must have looked at my cell phone over a hundred times per hour as I waited for a call about the results. I was off today and thought about going to the gym, but I opted to stare at my phone instead. I was about to put it down when it buzzed in my hand. Nikki.

"Hello."

"Hi, babe, the results are in. I'll meet you there."

The sound of her calling me babe made my skin crawl. "I'm on my way."

I opted for a cab so I wouldn't need to worry about parking, and my cabbie got me to the doctor's office in record time. Nikki was waiting for me in the lobby, and we took the elevator to the sixth floor.

"So are you ready to hear that you're going to be a father?" Her patronizing voice broke the silence.

"Let's wait and see what the doctor says."

My heart jackhammered in my ribs, but Nikki seemed oddly calm. The car came to a stop and chimed. Once the doors slid open, I felt as if all the oxygen had evaporated. We walked through the glass doors, signed in, and after a few minutes, we were escorted to Dr. Franklin's office. He was sitting behind a large wooden desk.

"Good afternoon. Please have a seat." He gestured to the two chairs in front of him.

We sat down, and my knee bounced rapidly as we awaited the news that could change my life forever.

He slid on a pair of black reading glasses and opened a manila folder. He read the papers inside then closed the file and looked at us. "Mr. Chambers, the test concludes that your DNA and that of the fetus are a match. Congratulations, you're going to be a father."

Nikki screeched, and a chill ran through me. I stared blankly at him. My body was completely numb, and I wasn't sure I was breathing.

"I knew it!" Nikki boasted and turned to me. "I told you." She put her hand on my arm, but I barely felt it. "We're going to be a family." She stood and shook Dr. Franklin's hand. "Thank you so much." She looked at me and mockingly cocked her brows.

"Mr. Chambers, as far as the other tests, they came back negative, but you might want to check again in about six months."

I nodded and stood. "Thank you." What the fuck was I going to do now?

We walked out of the office and got back into the elevator.

"I think I should meet your family," she declared.

My head jolted toward Nikki. "What? No."

The door opened. I got out of that tiny box that had felt as though it was getting smaller with each floor we descended.

"Babe, we're going to be a family. Don't you think it's time you realize that?"

Babe. That's it. "Do not call me babe. And we're going to have my daughter, but we aren't going to be a couple."

She pulled my arm and stopped me. "What other tests did you have run? Are you sick?"

"No. I wanted to make sure I didn't contract a disease since you tampered with the condom."

Her laugh was pure evil. "I don't know why you keep saying that. I didn't do anything of the sort." But her face turned three shades of crimson and her eyes never held mine as she spewed her lies.

We were standing on a crowded sidewalk, so I grabbed a cab and told him to take us to the club. I rushed us into the club and didn't look at anyone as we made our way to my office.

I closed the door, tossed my phone on the desk, and pressed the "conference" button on my desk phone to link me to Alex's office in case I needed witnesses. "Look at me, Nikki."

She propped her hands on her hips and cockily looked at me. "Okay, I'm looking."

"Look into my eyes and tell me you didn't do anything to the condom you gave me that night. Tell me you didn't poke holes in it or damage it."

"I didn't do . . ." Her voice faltered, and her eyes shifted.

"Go ahead, keep going." My tone was stern, and my eyes bore into hers.

"What does it matter?" She moved her hands to her stomach. "What's done is done, and this baby is yours." Her sarcastic tone grated on my nerves, but when her mouth twisted in amusement, I completely lost it.

"You bitch! I knew it. Motherfucker! GodDAMMIT!" I spun and cleared off my desk in one swipe including my phone that crashed to the floor. I was sure Alex heard the commotion. When I turned back, her mouth was agape. "Is this a joke to you? Get this through your brainless head—I will never marry you. Do you understand me? Never!" I shook my head in utter frustration and anger.

"Fine." Her hand made circles on her stomach. "Then you won't be with her either."

"The fuck I won't!"

My door swung open, and Alex and Tyler were staring at us.

Alex tilted his head toward Tyler. "Call a cab and escort Nikki out of here."

Ty left with Nikki, and before she could say anything, Alex closed the door. My hands grabbed my hair, and I tugged on the roots until I felt pain.

Alex looked at the papers strewn all over the floor. "I don't need to ask what the results were, do I?"

"No. You don't."

"Brett, I know this isn't what you wanted, but in about a month, you're going to have a daughter."

"Yeah, I know. I need to call my attorney and find out what my rights are." I let out a long breath. "Jesus Christ, Alex, she admitted to fucking with the condom. You heard her! I thought I was fucking her, and she totally fucked me. Did you notice she wasn't even upset? She thinks she's won. Little does she know the battle she started. Fuck!" I bent down to pick up the mess I'd made and noticed the picture of Julie and me. "Do you think the baby heard me?" I hated that I'd yelled and sworn. I prayed my daughter had been sleeping in her happy place and didn't understand the hell I was going through.

Alex gathered some papers from the floor. "Brett, why don't you get out of here? Go home and relax for a bit. Figure out where you go from here."

"Yeah, let me clean this up, and I'll go." I looked at the picture of a happier time. I knew I needed to tell Julie before anyone else—except for my lawyer. He had to be my first call.

"Take a few days. You're going to need them. Smart move getting witnesses," Alex said.

"Yeah, I don't know what good it will do me." I could barely breathe. "Thanks, man."

I called my lawyer on my way to Julie's. She told me that I had rights and could sue for joint custody, but since I worked nights, that might be hard to get approved. Another blow to my day. There had to be a way.

I ran through various scenarios that could work. I could schedule myself to go in later when the baby was asleep and have someone stay with her. Maybe I could hire a live-in nanny. Maybe I should have the guys buy me out and get a day job. All questions and no answers.

However, I would file an "Acknowledgment of Paternity" petition with the court to establish my parental rights. I had rights, and there was no way I would relinquish them. I was this baby girl's father, and although the circumstances weren't ideal, she'd always know I loved her and would protect her until the day I died.

When my cab pulled up to Julie's apartment building, I thought my heart would escape through my ribs. A pizza guy was leaving, so I went in and made my way to Julie's door. Before I knocked, I heard her singing. I couldn't make out the lyrics, but she sounded so happy.

I knocked on the door, and she opened it. Her eyes went wide as I studied her. Her hair was in a high ponytail, and she was wearing a pale blue tank top, which she filled out perfectly, and white shorts. She looked completely flustered and stunned as she removed the earbuds from her ears.

"Brett, I wasn't expecting you." Her lips turned down. "What's wrong?"

"Can I come in?"

"Yes, I'm sorry." She quickly stepped aside. "I was cleaning and must not have heard the buzzer. Did my neighbor buzz you in? I'm sorry if you were waiting long." She was rambling and finally took a breath.

"No, I walked in when someone was walking out. I need to talk to you." I lowered my head and walked across the room to sit on her couch.

"Would you like something to drink?"

"No. Can you please come sit with me?" I wanted her to know about the baby, and I needed her to. . . . well, I just needed her.

She took the iPod band off her arm and laid it on the table with her headphones before she sat down. Her eyes widened as I watched her chest rise and fall. How I wished things were different. If only I could turn back the clock.

"I got the results today. She's mine. I'm going to be a father."

Her breath hitched, and her eyes glistened before a tear streamed down her cheek. She quickly whisked it away.

I stood and paced. "The doctor said our DNA was a match. Jules, I'm going to be a father. What am I going to do? My lawyer said I could fight for custody, but my job may hinder me from winning." My hand scrubbed my face. "I'm going to have a daughter, and her mother is a conniving bitch. She's so awful, and I truly can't believe how stupid I was." I glanced at Julie. She swiped tears away and broke my heart.

chapter 16

Julie

A FATHER. THE BABY *was his.* Brett continued his rant, and I let him get it all out.

"And want to hear the best part?" He looked at me, anger flashing across his face. "As bits and pieces of that disastrous night came back to me, I remembered I *did* wear a condom. How about that shit? I knew I'd never have had unprotected sex, no matter how drunk I was. But I also recall her giving it to me, and she admitted she tampered with it. What do you think about that?" His hands flew in the air, and he threw himself into the chair next to my couch. He huffed out an exasperated breath. "Why? Why did I sleep with her?"

He wore a condom? What did he mean she tampered with it? I'd save those questions for another time. He was hunched forward, and his body was trembling. I crouched in front of him. My hands went to his knees, and he wrapped his arms around me. I brought myself up to sit in his lap, and he burrowed his face into the curve of my neck.

I rubbed his back in an attempt to comfort him. I had no idea what to say, but I didn't shed any more tears. He needed strength. I'd told him I'd be there for him to lean on, and that was what I intended to do.

He raised his head. "Thank you, Julie. Sorry I fell apart." His eyes were rimmed in red.

"Have you told your family?"

"No, the only ones who know are Alex and most likely Tyler. I flipped out on Nikki in my office today."

I quirked my lips to the side. "I'm sure she loved that."

"Well, she's completely delusional and deserved every word I said to her. I just hope my daughter didn't hear me."

"Your daughter." I smiled at his confident voice. He probably didn't even realize how protective he was of his little girl already. "Want to know what I think?"

"Of course." He laced our fingers together.

"I think you're going to be a wonderful dad. You're funny, loving, genuine, and kind. She's a very lucky girl. You have your family and your friends . . . and that includes me."

He nodded. "Thank you. I'm going to need all of you. My brother is in London, but I need to go see my parents."

"It's getting late. Why don't we order dinner and chill out? It's a long drive out to your parents' place. You can even crash here tonight if you'd like." I was being completely selfish. If he left, I'd worry about him all night, so staying with me was a better option.

"Are you sure?"

I smiled and placed a chaste kiss on his lips. "I'm more than sure."

"Thanks, Jules."

"Come on." I scooted off his lap, grabbed his hands, and pulled him upright. "Let's get some menus and order."

He called his friend Pirro and had a platter of different Greek dishes sent over. We laughed as we fought over the last piece of spinach spanakopita then decided to share it. Well, Brett took a bite then fed me the rest.

It was great to see him laughing and not thinking about everything that had transpired today. He had been so amped up when he spoke of Nikki that it concerned me. Together, we cleaned the dishes—I washed, and he dried. Then we decided to watch a comedy.

"Why don't you go pick out a DVD while I change?" His eyes boldly raked over my body, sending a flash of heat through my veins and between my legs. "I'll be right back."

I walked into my room and closed the door. The magnetic force between us was in full power. Not giving in to our feelings would be our next hurdle. After we'd heated up Aubrey's pool, it had become more and more challenging to avoid telling him that I couldn't stop thinking about him.

I put on a pair of sweats and a fresh tank top. Horror struck me as I looked in the mirror. I looked like a disheveled disaster. I brushed my hair and left it loose. I brushed my teeth and was about to put on some lip gloss but opted not to.

When I got back to the living room, Brett was sitting on my couch with a beer in hand. He glanced over and smiled. "Even in comfy clothes, you're gorgeous."

I sat down and tucked my legs underneath me. "So what are we watching?"

He turned on an episode of *Friends,* and I laughed.

"It just started and you're laughing already?"

"When Luca went to the wax museum, he sent me a picture of him and his new friend Rachel." I scrolled through my pictures on my phone and held it out to him. "See?"

He looked over and smiled. "You like him, don't you?"

"I do. He's a good man, and it was nice being around someone who wasn't caught up in the drama of my life."

His eyelids lowered, and he nodded.

"Sorry to put it that way, but when I went to Italy, I wasn't in a good frame of mind. That flight over was horrible. All I did was replay our last night together, the things we said and how we ended. But when I hung out with Luca, it was relaxed, easy."

"I'm glad he was there for you. I truly am. I only wish he was fat and balding . . . or a woman." Brett chuckled. "Wait, he isn't gay by any chance, is he?"

I smacked his arm. "No, he isn't gay. Jeez!"

"Did he hit on you?" He took a swig of his beer.

My mouth dropped open. "No! Of course not!"

"Then he's gay." He chuckled.

I shook my head and focused on the television.

After the fifth or so episode in the *Friends* marathon, we were exhausted. I'd been nestled into Brett's side, and his arm rested around my shoulder. When I let out a yawn and sighed, he shifted.

"Why don't you go to bed?" He stood and held his hand out to me.

I took it, and he pulled me up. My legs felt like lead. I'd been sitting on them for far too long. His arms wrapped around me.

"Thank you for tonight." He gave me a squeeze and released me. "All I need is a pillow, and I'm good to go."

"Are you sleeping on the couch?"

Wrinkles formed on his forehead. "Yeah, that was my plan. Did you have a different one?"

Embarrassment washed over me. *I'm such an idiot.* "No, but you're longer than my couch. It won't be comfortable. You take my bed, and I'll take the couch." *Great save, Julie.*

"I'll be fine, but thank you. You have to work tomorrow, and I don't."

"Okay, there's a pillow and blanket in the hall closet. If you need a toothbrush, there's a new one in the bathroom cabinet above the sink."

"Thanks." He smiled. "Good night, Julie."

"Sweet dreams, Brett."

Brett

MY BODY JOLTED AS I woke up from a nightmare that could become a reality. I sat up and tried to rid my mind of all things Nikki. The clock on the cable box read four in the morning. I was so drained, but when I closed my eyes, all I saw was Nikki taking my daughter away from me.

I tossed the blanket aside and went into the kitchen for a bottle of water. When I closed the refrigerator door, Julie stood in the doorway, rubbing her eyes and looking more adorable than ever. She was a mess—hair all over the place, a small amount of eye makeup smeared under her eyes—but she was still sexy as hell.

"Did I wake you?" I cracked open the bottle and took a swig.

She blinked a few times, probably to adjust to the light, then stared at me.

It dawned on me that all I had on was my navy boxer briefs. "Jules?"

She shook her head. "Um . . . no. Sorry, you caught me off guard. I wasn't sleeping, so I came in here for some water. I wasn't expecting you to be standing here."

The tip of her tongue moved across her lower lip. The knowledge that I still affected her went straight to my dick. If I wasn't careful, I'd have a raging erection in zero point two seconds.

I handed her my bottle. "Want some?"

She took a generous sip and handed it back to me. "I should go back to bed. Why are you up?"

I leaned against the counter. "Bad dream."

"Do you want to talk about it?" She attempted to stifle a yawn.

"No, go to bed. We can talk tomorrow."

"It is tomorrow." She smiled warmly. "Come on, you can lie down with me for a bit and tell me all about it."

We walked into her dimly lit bedroom and lay on our sides, facing each other. Her head was propped on her hands, which were in the prayer position. I told her about my nightmare and how scared I was that it would come true.

"Brett, no judge in their right mind would refuse to grant you your rights as a parent. If you can't get a nanny right away, I'll stay with the baby while you work. See? Problem solved." Her cheeks rose as she grinned.

"You'd do that?" This woman never ceased to amaze me. What a stupid asshole I had been to push her away. If given the chance, I'd never do that again.

"Of course I would. What are friends for, right?" She exhaled, and her long lashes rested on her cheekbones.

"I love you, Julie."

With her eyes still closed, she softly said, "I know. Go to sleep, Brett."

Her breathing evened out as she fell back asleep. I didn't move. I just stared at the beautiful woman lying next to me and realized how lucky I was.

When morning came, I drove Julie to work and headed to my mom's house. I tried calling Bentley, but according to Andi, he was critiquing a play. So telling him would have to wait.

I pulled into my parents' driveway as my dad was walking out. "Hey, son. I didn't know you were coming over. It's early for you, isn't it?"

"Hi, Dad. Yes, I suppose it is. Can you come with me for a minute? I need to talk to you and Mom about something."

He nodded, and we walked inside. My mom was sitting at the table, reading the paper and drinking coffee. She looked as surprised as my dad had when he saw me. I walked over and gave her a kiss.

"Sweetheart, I didn't know you were coming. Would you like a cup of coffee?" She began to stand, but I stopped her.

"Not right now. I came here to tell you and Dad something."

My dad sat next to my mother, and her face softened as she held my father's hand. She knew.

"What is it, Brett? Are you okay?" My dad's voice was deep and laced with concern. He didn't know.

I took a deep breath. "You're going to be grandparents. We got the results yesterday, and the doctor confirmed it."

My father was rendered speechless, but my mom threw her arms around me.

"How are you doing? Are you okay? Do you need anything?" She leaned back to look at me.

"I'm okay. I have to figure some things out, but I wanted to tell you."

"If there's anything we can do, we'll do it. Your family is here for you." My dad came over and hugged me. "Family sticks together, and I know you'll be a great father."

I nodded. "Thanks. You both set the example that I know will help guide me through this."

"How much longer until her due date?"

"A couple of weeks."

"We'll get a special room ready for her."

I smiled and thanked my parents before I headed back into the city to deal with all that came next. In the car, my phone chimed with a voicemail from Nikki.

"I thought you'd like to know that my doctor will be inducing me next week."

That was it. I pushed "call back" on my phone.

"Brett, I knew you'd call." She didn't sound worried. Instead, her voice was buoyant.

"What's going on? Is the baby okay?"

"Yes, she's fine. The doctor thought I should have been bigger when I went to my routine appointment. So, I had to have another ultrasound. My amniotic fluid is low, so the doctor wants to induce me."

"You had an ultrasound and didn't tell me? Is the baby okay?"

"I tried calling you, but you didn't pick up. The heartbeat was strong, and the doctor said she looked good."

I glanced at my phone and saw she had, in fact, left me another message. "Fine. What's next then?"

"Well, we need to go shopping so we can get her room ready. I've been thinking we should live at your place because it's bigger than my apartment."

Have I entered the Twilight Zone? With every fiber of my being, I tried to remain calm. "Nikki, can you hear me okay?"

"Yes." She giggled as though this was all fun and games while I was worried about her being induced. Apparently she didn't realize how serious I'd been over the past few months. But I didn't want to upset her and risk anything happening to the baby.

"I don't know how else to say this to you, so I'm going to speak very slowly, okay? We . . . are . . . not . . . a . . . couple. We . . . are . . . not . . . going . . . to . . . live . . . together." I prayed she caught on.

"Are you still on that kick?" She let out a breath.

I wanted to throw my phone out the fucking window. This was a lost cause. "It's not a kick, Nikki. I'm going to set up my apartment for what she needs, and I suggest you do the same." Then I realized that Nikki may not buy the best things. She'd be more inclined to go to Saks and buy herself an expensive outfit to wear home from the hospital. There was no way in hell my daughter was getting anything but the best. "I'll tell you what—when I buy what I need, I'll have some necessities sent to your place. But don't misunderstand my generosity. I'm doing this for our daughter and only for our daughter."

"Whatever, you'll change your mind."

I shook my head and bit my bottom lip to prevent myself from saying anymore. "What day next week are you going to the hospital?"

"Sunday."

I pulled the car over and came to a screeching halt. "As in *this* Sunday? That's not next week; that's in a few days." *Holy shit*. I broke out in a sweat.

"Whatever. The doctor told me I need to be there by seven on Sunday morning."

"Fine, I'll see you there."

"You're not picking me up?" she asked.

"Are you in pain?"

"No, but—"

"Then I'll meet you there." I disconnected the call and dialed Aubrey. When I told her what was going on and that I needed her help with everything that a baby needed, she told me she'd send me a list.

When I got to my apartment, I opened my email and saw how long the list was. I decided to call in reinforcements—my mom.

By the end of the day, my apartment had been transformed. My office was a nursery decorated in beautiful pictures painted in soft colors. She had a white crib adorned with pink bedding and a pale yellow teddy bear in the corner. There was a rocking recliner next to the crib, a shelf lined with children's books, a changing table and armoire that matched the crib, and some items I couldn't define.

I sat in the recliner and looked around the room—*my daughter's room*. It wouldn't be long until she was there, and my life would be forever changed.

My cell rang. It was Alex.

"Hey, man, I'm glad you called."

"Aubrey filled me in," he said. "What can I do?"

"Can you get the gang together and come over tonight? I know you probably have to go to the club, but it won't take too long."

"We'll be there."

I ordered some pizza and waited for my friends. My buzzer rang, and Alex, Aubrey, Mark, Val, and Julie came in. I called Tyler via FaceTime and explained to all of them what was going on. To say they were stunned was an understatement. Alex, Ty, and I decided to hire a part-time bartender to cover me for a while. The women went to check out the nursery while Alex, Mark, and I had a beer in the living room.

Aubrey came out of the nursery, walked over to me, and hugged me. "It's beautiful, Brett. Your daughter will love it."

My attention was focused on Julie as she walked toward me. "What do you think, Jules?"

"It's fit for a princess. She's an extremely lucky girl." Her arms wrapped around my waist.

I poured every ounce of my love for her into my embrace. I never wanted to let go, but I eventually did.

Mark strolled up and shook my hand. "You're a good guy, Brett. I think the way you're stepping up is great. I'm not sure a lot of guys would do what you're doing."

"Thanks." I pulled him aside. "I know you're worried about Julie, and I want you to know I am too. I promise you I'll never hurt her again."

Mark nodded. "I'm glad to hear it. She's happy again, and I know that's because of you."

I glanced at Julie, who was laughing with the girls. Alex must have said something about his baby because Julie bent toward Aubrey's baby bump and whispered to it.

"I plan on making her happy for the rest of our lives." *If she'll let me.*

Mark smiled, and we joined our friends for a quick dinner. Afterward, they all went home—except for Julie.

chapter 17

Julie

"THE ROOM IS beautiful." I made my way to his kitchen with the empty pizza box and set it on the counter. Brett leaned on the counter, and my eyes lingered on his taut waist and broad chest. "You're going to be a dad. Can you believe it?"

He shook his head with a pensive look in his eyes. "No, to be honest, it hasn't sunk in yet. Do you think I can do it?"

I rested my forearms on his strong shoulders. "Yes, and I think you're going to be wonderful."

His eyes flicked to my lips, and the fire that ignited inside me was fierce. The feelings I'd spent months hiding came to a head. I couldn't continue fighting them, so I gave into myself and to him.

My teeth bit my lip, and I felt his hands cup my cheeks. His mouth met mine. Our kiss was soft, slow, and when our tongues pressed against each other's, all of my pent-up desire poured into him. I drank in the passion of our kiss.

Brett broke our kiss, and I immediately felt the loss. "I want you, Julie."

"I want you too." My breathing faltered when he swooped in for a searing kiss.

He lifted me, and I felt his erection when he carried me to his bed. In his arms, I took off my top and bra. My back arched as his tongue swirled around my pebbled nipple. He alternated between the two, not showing any favoritism. Heat pooled in my core as I fisted his hair. A sexy groan escaped him, and he laid me on the bed. I propped my body up on my elbows and watched him slide off his jeans. He unbuttoned my pants and shimmied them down my legs, along with my thong.

He appraised my curves, and appreciation flashed across his features. "You're more beautiful than I remember."

All I could do was smile as I fixated on his broad chest.

His erection sprang free when he took off his boxers. My hand felt the firm curve of his ass as he opened the drawer in his nightstand and pulled out a sealed box of condoms. My heart jolted with hope that he hadn't been with anyone since our breakup, but even I knew that wasn't the case. He had been with Nikki, which was something I wouldn't—no, couldn't—think about.

He straddled my legs, and his tongue ran up the center of my abs, between my breasts, and up the center of my neck, making me roll my head back. When he reached my chin, his mouth claimed mine with possession as if he were marking his territory. But his mark had never left. I'd always been his.

"God, Julie, you taste so sweet. I can't get enough of you."

His husky voice made me sigh in ecstasy. "Brett, I want to taste you." I tried to sit up, but his hands were on my shoulders, pressing me into the mattress.

"No, tonight is about you. I've dreamt of this moment for months." He peppered me with kisses, moving lower and lower until he reached the top of my thighs. His thumbs traced the insides of my legs until he reached between them. "I've missed this." He kissed my clit, and my hips involuntarily bucked up. I felt his lips curl against my heated flesh. "I think it missed me too." His tongue stroked and licked my sex.

I was lost in his agile movement and could barely see as my insides pulsed. "Brett . . ."

"Let it go, Jules."

His tongue went back to work, and his lips wrapped around me. He suckled and made every ounce of me tense and shudder. When his finger entered me and crooked up, finding my G-spot, I gasped. My legs wrapped around his back as he took in every part of my orgasm. When my legs lowered, he grabbed the condom and put it on. He gazed lovingly at me.

"I haven't been with anyone since you," I said.

His eyes widened, and he let out a breath. "I haven't either . . ." His smile faltered, and he crashed his lips to mine as he slowly slid into me. "I'm so sorry, Jules. If I could take it back . . ."

"I know."

"All I"—he thrust forward—"ever wanted . . ." He kissed my neck. "Was you." He nibbled my earlobe. "Only you . . . always you."

Our eyes met, and his beautiful hazel eyes displayed his love. "I love you, Brett."

His lips twisted into a smooth smile. "I know."

"Good."

We moved in harmony until we reached our pinnacle. His pace picked up, and I grabbed his taut back as we came together. The feel of his weight and the heat radiating off his sweat-slickened skin felt like home. I was in his arms, where I was supposed to be.

Afterward, he went to clean up, and when he came back, he had a wide smile.

"What?" I pulled the soft white sheet up over the swell of my breasts.

"I'm so happy. You've made me so happy." He slid under the sheet and lay down next to me. His hand laced with mine. "Say it again."

"Say what?"

"You love me. Let me hear it again."

My fingers tightened on his hand. "I love you, Brett Chambers."

He blew out a long breath. "Thank God, because part of me died without you."

I nodded. "I haven't been the same either. But it's going to be complicated."

He shook his head. "Only if we let it. We'll work it out, I promise."

"Okay."

"Jules, thank you for coming back to me. I know it wasn't an easy decision."

"No, it wasn't. I didn't have any rights or claim to you when you slept with Nikki. What hurt me the most was that you slept with her bare, a way we've never been together. But when you told me you did wear protection, that eased some of the pain." I shrugged. "I know that sounds ridiculous, but I've never given myself to anyone like that, and I knew you hadn't either. So that cut me deep."

"When Nikki told me she was pregnant, not only was I beyond terrified, I was pissed at myself. I had been with her out of spite, I knocked her up, and I was reckless, but I'd never wanted to hear 'I'm pregnant'—not from anyone. I hope you can forgive me for everything, but I'll understand if you don't because Lord knows I don't forgive myself for letting you go. It's funny—I was scared of commitment after my failed marriage, but that was nothing compared to my fear of not being with you."

I felt my eyes well up with tears. "I forgave you a long time ago. But we need to move on and get ready for your true committed relationship: yours and your daughter's."

"My daughter."

My lips met his. "Everything will be fine. Let's get some sleep. We have a busy couple of days ahead of us."

The following day, Brett went to talk to his attorney, and I went shopping after work. I bought just about every girl-colored newborn outfit I could find. She had everything from onesies to frilly dresses—with matching shoes of course. When I got back to Brett's place, he was finishing up filing all the necessary paperwork to establish shared custody.

"Are you all set?" I asked.

"I hope so. I called a nanny service, and I'm going to start interviewing women next week. I thought it would be better for them to meet the baby. If she doesn't like these women, then they aren't getting the job." He sounded stern and determined.

"That's a good idea."

He glanced at my hands. “Did you buy out the store?”

I laughed. “Yes, do you have a problem with that?”

He sauntered over to me and hugged me. “No, not at all. What did you get?”

I clapped and bounced. When I was done, I showed him everything, including the tiny padded hangers for her dresses.

“Oh, and I got this for you.” I pulled out a navy T-shirt.

He chuckled when he read the front, “World's Greatest Dad.” He kissed my cheek. “I love it.”

“We need to pack a bag for you.”

“A bag?”

“Yes, for when you stay at the hospital. I assumed you wouldn't want to leave.”

“No, I don't.” Fear flashed in his eyes. “I keep having nightmares that Nikki takes the baby and leaves.”

“That's twisted!”

“Yeah, well, she's twisted.”

I had no argument, so I kept my mouth shut.

“Can you stay tonight?”

“I suppose I could be persuaded.” I giggled and headed to the kitchen.

His phone rang, and he let out a huff when he looked at the screen. “What do you need, Nikki?” His eyes went wide, and he started scurrying around the apartment. “Okay, I'll be right there.”

My heart dropped. “What happened? Is she okay?”

“Her doctor sent her to the hospital because she was having contractions.”

"What can I do?" My mouth was completely dry, and my head was spinning.

"Grab your purse and come with me."

I frantically shook my head. "No, that's not a good idea. Nikki will freak out."

"Julie, please, you can stay in the lobby if that makes you feel better, but I need to know you're there." His eyes implored me to comply.

"Okay, let's go."

Brett weaved in and out of traffic while I called Aubrey and asked her to call everyone, including his parents. We made it to the hospital in record time. Brett nearly pulled my arm out of the socket as we rushed through the closest door. We went to the information desk, and his entire body trembled. I gave his hand a gentle squeeze. He looked over and gave me a grin.

"May I help you?" the man at the desk asked.

"Can you tell me where Nikki Webster is?"

He punched the keys on the computer. "Fifth floor." He handed us two visitor passes. "Follow the red line to the elevator, and take that to five. There will be a nurse there to assist you further."

Brett was already jogging away.

I looked back at the man and yelled, "Thank you!"

It felt as though the elevator stopped at every floor. Brett never took his eyes off the red numbers as we slowly climbed. When the doors slid open on the fifth floor, we rushed to the nurse's station and after Brett identified himself, we were given her room number.

Outside her door, I released his hand and stopped. "Go ahead, Brett."

He swallowed hard and kissed me. Once the door closed behind him, my adrenaline dropped, and I started trembling.

"Miss, would you like a chair? You look pale." A nurse was standing next to me, but I hardly noticed her.

"No, thank you. Can you tell me where the waiting room is?"

"Right around the corner to the left."

"Thank you."

When I got to the waiting area, Leah was there. *Great.*

Her nose crinkled. "Eww, what the hell are you doing here?"

I wasn't in the mood to get into it with her. "How's Nikki?"

"Like you care." She went back to reading her magazine.

An older couple sat in the far corner of the room, and heat crawled up my neck. Did Nikki have parents?

"Leah?"

She flipped the page and never looked at me.

"Leah!"

"What? God, I'm reading *Cosmo*."

"Where are Nikki's parents?" I asked.

"Why do you care?"

"Because they should be here." I didn't know if I was doing the right thing or if Brett would appreciate me asking, but I felt it necessary.

"Her father died. She hasn't talked to her mother in years, so I have no idea." She buried her head back in her magazine.

I sent a text to Alex telling him Leah was there and, given their history, it may be best if Aubrey didn't come. He thanked me and told me he'd get to the hospital as soon as he could.

I felt as if hours passed, but it was probably only one before Brett's parents and Alex walked in. I stood and hugged them.

His mom held on to my hands. "How is she?"

"I don't know. I haven't seen Brett since we got here."

She nodded and walked away after introducing me to her husband.

Alex hugged me. When we broke apart, he bent down and looked at me. "It'll be okay. He'll figure it out."

I nodded.

"You think you have everything figured out, don't you?" Leah's voice was like nails on a chalkboard.

"It doesn't concern you, Leah." Alex's voice sounded scolding.

"No, it doesn't. I told her to abort the baby. She could be modeling and making money, but now she's heavier and saddled with a kid."

I gasped, and Alex shook his head. We went to the other side of the room and sat down.

Brett

"NIKKI, YOU'RE ALMOST there. One more push." The doctor's calm voice did nothing for Nikki.

She screamed as she squeezed my hand so tightly I thought every single bone would break.

"The head's out. You can do it—one more push."

A nurse wiped Nikki's forehead with a damp cloth and helped her sit up. Another nurse was standing next to the doctor and holding a blanket while staring at Nikki's vagina, which I wanted no part of. All of a sudden, I heard a baby's cry. Nikki flopped back on the bed.

The doctor held up my daughter, and my heart swelled. "Congratulations, it's a girl."

My jaw dropped open at the tiny human he was holding. He placed the baby on Nikki's chest, and I was instantly filled with jealousy.

She crooked her neck to look at our daughter, and then she looked at me. "We're a family."

I leaned down and kissed my daughter. She was so tiny and perfect.

"Dad, would you like to cut the cord?" The nurse offered me the weirdest pair of scissors I'd ever seen.

I looked at Nikki, and she looked exhausted. I took the scissors and cut the umbilical cord. I couldn't contain my joy. "When can I hold her?"

The nurse asked Nikki, "Will you be breastfeeding?"

"No."

A gush of relief rushed over me. That was one thing I knew for certain I couldn't do, and who knew if Nikki would adhere to special diets.

"I'm going to take the baby and clean her up. I'll be right over here," the nurse said.

My daughter was placed in what looked like a plastic bed with a heat lamp. The way the nurses tugged on her arms freaked me out, even though they didn't seem to be hurting her. Then they stuck something that looked like a tiny turkey baster in her mouth and sucked something out of her. Finally, the nurse listened to my daughter's heart before she placed the baby on the scale then measured her length. She jotted things down.

"What are you writing? How much does she weigh? How long is she? Is she okay? What are you doing now?" I heard the questions coming out of me, but she didn't answer as she scribbled on the piece of paper.

The nurse looked at me and smiled. "I love new daddies. She's two point thirty-three kilograms, 49.53 centimeters, and her Apgar is great."

"I have no idea what that means. What is an Apgar? Is it hereditary?"

Now both nurses were smiling, and one looked as though she was trying too hard not to laugh at my expense.

"Apgar stands for: Activity, Pulse, Grimace, Appearance, and Respiration. So when you had that horrified look on your face as I moved her limbs and suctioned her, that's part of it." She wrapped my daughter up tighter than a burrito in a small blanket and put a pale pink cap with a knot on the top over her brown hair. "Are you ready, Dad? Be sure to support her head."

I looked at my hands. "One second." I rushed over to the wall where a hand sanitizer unit was hanging and made sure I was completely disinfected before I stood in front of the nurse and held out my arms. "I'm ready."

She placed my daughter in my arms. I'd never felt so much love and responsibility.

I kissed her tiny cheeks. "Hi, sweet girl. I'm your daddy." A tear ran down my face, and I turned to look at Nikki. "Look how tiny she is."

Nikki smiled, and the nurse chimed in, "She's five pounds, thirteen ounces and nineteen and a half inches long."

"Wow, you're a teeny thing, aren't you?" I couldn't stop talking to her.

The doctor finished taking care of Nikki and left with the nurses to give us some time together.

"I knew you'd be the best father. See how good we are together? She's beautiful."

"She's the most beautiful thing I've ever seen." I looked at Nikki. "You did great, Nik."

"Thanks. That was hard and painful, and now I'm going to have these dreaded stretch marks. I better be able to lose this weight."

Always about her. That was Nikki, Princess Selfish.

"Who cares about all of that? Look at her. She's amazing." I didn't want to let her go, but I wanted to tell everyone she was here. I knew Nikki would freak out if she knew Julie was in the waiting room, but she would find out soon enough. "Do you want to hold her, Nikki? I want to go tell everyone all about her."

She grinned tightly. "Can you please send Leah in?"

Figured she'd ask that bitch to come here. "I don't want her holding our baby."

Nikki scoffed. "She won't want to. She hates babies."

"Then I definitely don't want her holding the baby."

The nurse came back in. "You have a group of people asking for you."

I smiled, but I didn't know what to do with my daughter. I turned to hand her to Nikki, and she refused. My mouth dropped open before I kissed my daughter's head.

"I'll take her and put her in the bassinet," the nurse said. "She needs to be fed. Would you like me to do that in the nursery?"

"I can do it." Nikki sat up. "Gimme her."

I swallowed hard. "Can you please stay with Nikki until I get back?" My eyes begged for the nurse to understand what I was really asking. "In case she needs help?"

The nurse gave me a curt nod. "Yes, I'll be right here."

I placed her in Nikki's arms and nodded at the nurse. When I made it to the waiting area, my mother jumped up. "Brett!" Everyone else followed suit and stood and stared at me. Alex wasn't here, but Tyler was. I looked at my watch, and it was 2:45 a.m. He must have left to go home.

"She's beautiful." I looked at Julie, who had tears in her eyes.

She hugged me. I told everyone my daughter's measurements. When my mom asked me how her Apgar was, I laughed and said it was perfect, just like my little angel. My parents hugged each other, then my dad shook my hand.

Still tucked up against me, Julie asked, "How's Nikki?"

"She's good, and I think she's tired." I looked around. "Is Leah here?"

Tyler tilted his head to the left, where Leah was sprawled over three chairs, sleeping.

"Nikki wants to see her," I said.

"Well, we want to see our granddaughter. Is that okay?" My mom's voice was dripping with pride.

"Yes, of course. Let me wake up Sleeping Nasty over there, and we can go."

Julie shifted so she was standing in front of me.

"I want you to meet her too," I said.

She smiled. "I will, just not right now. Go be with your daughter. I'll be right here."

I kissed her. "I love you."

"I love you too." Before I walked away, Julie asked, "Brett, what did you name her?"

"We haven't yet. Oddly, we haven't even discussed it. I know what I want, but Nikki probably won't go for it. I'm sure we have time." I had, however, asked the nurse to use my name as the identifier in the nursery.

Everyone except for Julie and Tyler, who decided to stay and keep her company, came to meet my daughter. My mom cried, my dad beamed with excitement, and Leah snarled.

Once they all went home to get some rest, I asked the nurse if I could stay. She smiled and said yes, but she was going to take the baby to the nursery so Nikki could get some rest. When I saw her wheeling out my daughter, I followed and let the nurse know I'd be in the waiting room.

Julie was still there, sleeping with her head on Tyler's shoulder.

I gently nudged her and whispered, "Jules?"

She blinked, lifted her head, and looked at Tyler as if she had no idea she'd been resting on him. "Hi, is everything okay?" She yawned. "I'm sorry I fell asleep."

"It's late." I tapped Ty's knee. "Tyler, wake up. Can you make sure Julie gets home okay?"

He rubbed his eyes and stretched. "Yeah, no problem."

"Before you both go, I want you to meet my daughter."

I took them to the nursery's viewing window and pointed at the perfect baby in the bassinet labeled, "Chambers, Girl." Thankfully, Nikki agreed with me when I'd asked the nurse to use my last name.

"She's so pretty." Julie waved. "Hi, precious baby."

Tyler congratulated me, and after I hugged Julie good-bye, he took her home.

The next day, Julie brought me a change of clothes, and I told her to go get more rest. She looked exhausted. After I pleaded with her to take care of herself, she agreed and said she'd be back later.

Nikki was being completely annoying. "Brett, when can we go home?"

My heart jumped into my throat, and I was ready to choke. It dawned on me I wouldn't be taking my baby home—she would.

"We haven't decided on a name yet. We need to do that before we leave," I said.

She smiled. "I think we should name her Nicole."

"I was thinking Madeline after my mom. We can call her Maddie."

She crinkled her nose. "No way."

The nurse walked in with our baby and gave her to Nikki, along with a bottle. "Do you need help?"

Nikki shook her head. "I think I know how to feed her."

She wasn't the same nurse as the night before, and I was embarrassed by the way Nikki spoke to her.

I smiled at the poor young nurse. "Thank you anyway. We'll let you know if we need anything."

She nodded and said the doctor would be in shortly.

Once the door closed behind her, I glared at Nikki. "Can you take it down a notch? She was doing her job."

"Here, you feed her." Nikki held the baby as if she were allergic to her. "I don't want to."

I gladly took her and sat in the rocker next to the bed. I watched her perfect rose-petal lips mold around the bottle's nipple as she sucked. I was in awe of this tiny bundle in my arms. "That's my girl."

"You aren't going to be with me, are you?" Nikki crossed her arms and pouted like a petulant child.

"No, Nikki. I'm in love with Julie, and we're back together. I told you from the beginning, I never stopped loving her." I brought my attention back to my baby. "My lawyer has drafted papers so we can have joint custody."

"You're a terrible father."

My heart splintered at her words.

"Seriously, refusing to be a family after I gave you a daughter? You made love to me that night, not Julie. She didn't go through hell and have a human come out of her—I did. That should count for something."

I didn't want to get angry while I was feeding the baby, but I felt my pulse accelerate. "Look, I know you gave birth. I've never said I would take the baby away from you, just like I never said we'd be together. Can't you be happy that our daughter is healthy and has two parents who love her?"

She huffed. "Whatever. I never wanted a baby. I only wanted you. So now I have her and not you. Maybe I won't let you see her. I can fight you in court. A mother always wins."

I placed my daughter on my chest and tapped her back to get her to burp, as I had earlier when the nurse woke me to feed her. "That's a horrible thing to say. Do you mean that?"

She shrugged. "I'm tired. Can you leave?"

A little burp escaped my daughter, and I smiled.

"Take her to the nursery." Nikki's words were clipped and nasty.

The next morning, I woke up in the waiting room after the same recurring nightmare. Julie was sitting next to me.

"Good morning, Brett." She kissed my cheek.

"Hey, how long have you been here?"

"Not too long. I didn't want to wake you. I went to the nursery and saw "Chambers, Girl" then I came in here." She smiled. "Still no name?"

"No. Nikki wanted Nicole."

Julie's head jolted back.

"Yeah, that was how I felt, so I said no. She's so non-maternal. I had a feeling she would be, but I figured she'd at least try. She told me she's going to fight me in court and not let me see my daughter."

Her jaw dropped. "She can't do that."

"I'm going to call my lawyer and make sure of it. She'll be discharged today. I don't know what to do." I stood. "Let's go see my daughter. Then I need a cup of coffee."

We walked to the nursery, and I waved at the nurse standing next to my angel. I mouthed that we'd be right back, then I grasped Julie's hand. We headed to the cafeteria to get some much needed caffeine.

On our way back upstairs, I told Julie I needed to try to talk some sense into Nikki. Julie completely understood and said she would go look at the babies. I gave her a chaste kiss before I went to Nikki's room—

where I was greeted by a nurse stripping the empty bed.

"Where's Nikki? Did she move to another room?" My heart raced. A chilling feeling ran up and down my spine.

The nurse pivoted, looking calm while I was the opposite. "She was discharged and left about ten minutes ago with her friend. I told her you said you'd be right back, but that didn't seem to matter. An orderly wheeled her out. I can ask him if she said anything."

My lungs lost function as my chest constricted. Sweat coated my skin as I sprinted to the nursery. *No, no. Please don't tell me she took the baby.* With each step, I said more prayers. My heart jackhammered while my head spun. Then I spotted Julie. Her huge smile faltered when I approached her.

"I think she has your eyes." Julie looked in the window and pointed. "Look, they're open."

When I saw the bassinet with "Chambers, Girl" holding my precious daughter, I let out the biggest sigh. Tears flowed from my eyes.

"Brett? What's wrong?"

I pulled Julie into my arms and held on as tight as I could. "I thought Nikki had taken her. I was so terrified."

Julie placed her hands on my cheeks and wiped my tears with the pads of her thumbs. "Sweetheart, she's right there. Everything's okay."

"She's gone." I shook my head in utter disbelief. How could she leave?

"Who's gone? Do you want to sit down? You're pale."

"No, I want my daughter." The nurse who had been in Nikki's room walked by, and I looked at her tag. "Marie?"

She stopped in front of us.

"Can we borrow Nikki's room for a minute?" I asked.

"Sure, do you want to see the baby?"

"Yes, and the doctor. I need to talk to him."

"Of course, I'll page him and bring your baby right in."

When the nurse arrived, I picked up my daughter and kissed her. "Your daddy will never ever leave you." I placed my cheek on hers and breathed in her scent. I turned to Julie. "Would you like to hold her?"

She frantically nodded. I placed the baby in her arms, and Julie's face lit up like a Christmas tree. "Hi, sweet girl." She rubbed her nose against the baby's. "I'm Julie, and we're going to be great friends."

In my dreams, Julie would have been her mom. She was a natural. Her gentleness and comfort warmed my heart, but right now, I needed to deal with my nightmare. The doctor came in, and I asked about Nikki. He told me he'd given her discharge papers.

Then the doctor looked at the baby. "Is Nikki still here?"

"No, she left."

"Without the baby?" The doctor put his hand on his chin and tilted his head. "I didn't notice any signs of postpartum depression, but that can come on at any point. I'm sorry, Mr. Chambers."

"Don't be. She isn't depressed—she's twisted. Nikki never wanted this baby unless I was part of the package. Apparently since it wasn't going her way, she bailed." I huffed and looked up. "But I never thought she'd stoop this low and leave her daughter." My lips grazed my girl's sweet skin. "Can I take my daughter home? I have papers that state I'm the father. I gave them to admissions when I arrived on Sunday."

He nodded. "I'm aware, but your daughter needs a name before you can take her home."

"Okay, can you give us a few minutes?"

He nodded and walked out.

"How could she leave her?" Julie was rocking back and forth, staring at my baby. "What are you going to do for a name?" She looked lovingly at my daughter then at me.

Before I could answer, a woman from the hospital staff walked in. "Hi, I'm Andrea. Congratulations." She looked at her clipboard and clicked the top of her pen. Her expectant eyes turned to me. "So do we have a name for this pretty girl?"

I didn't even need to think about it. "Madeline."

"And the middle name?" Andrea glanced up with arched brows.

"Um . . ." I looked at Julie. "What goes with Madeline?"

Julie shrugged.

"What was your mom's name?" I asked.

Her lips turned downward. "Kate. My mom's name was Kate."

"There you go. My daughter's name is Madeline Kate Chambers."

Julie gasped, and I took the baby from her arms. "Hi, Maddie." She made a gurgling sound, and I chuckled. "See, she likes it."

Andrea smiled.

"Can I please have a copy of Nikki's admissions paperwork as well?" I wanted everything Nikki had signed to be in my possession.

"Sure. I'll be back with the documents, then you can take Madeline home."

Home. We were going home.

chapter 18

Julie

BEING IN BRETT'S apartment now was different than it had been a week ago. Seeing Brett put Maddie down in her crib gave me such a unique feeling—almost indescribable.

He turned on the monitor and walked out of the nursery. "Any luck contacting her?"

When I shook my head, he rubbed his temples. Poor guy was so tired. Maddie was a great sleeper, but we'd been trying to get her on a schedule. That wasn't happening though. We were convinced she was nocturnal.

"I had Tyler try her cell phone and Leah's, and they both went to voicemail. He went to her apartment, and her neighbor told him she'd left with suitcases."

He studied me for a moment. "When did her neighbor see her? Could it have been when she left for the hospital? She had a bag then."

I frowned and said, "Last night."

"She's been in New York this entire time? How could she not come see her daughter? I don't get it." He shook his head and twisted his lips. "Why in the world would Nikki abandon her? Don't get me wrong, I can't stand the bitch, but how could she do that to Maddie? She doesn't even know her name."

I shrugged. "I don't know. Do you think it's postpartum?"

"She didn't seem depressed until I told her you and I were back together. So my guess is she left because of us." He sat and rested his head on the back of the couch. "I told her from the start that I didn't love her. I didn't lead her on. I couldn't have been clearer. But I never thought she'd abandon her daughter."

The buzzer rang, and Brett looked toward the door. Dark circles rimmed his eyes. He was exhausted. We both were.

"I'll get it." My muscles yelled at me to sit back down, but I ignored their plea, as I had for the past few days.

When I opened the door, his mom came in with a couple bags of groceries and a beautiful young woman.

"Hi, come in." I stepped aside, but not before his mom hugged me.

"Julie, I'd like you to meet my niece, Lyn. She's a Broadway actress." Madeline's pride made Lyn blush.

"Hi, Julie, it's nice to finally meet you." Lyn smiled.

"Hey, two of my favorite family members are here." Brett staggered over to kiss his mom and hug his cousin. "Lyn, it's so great to see you. I haven't seen you since my birthday party."

Sadness washed over me when I realized I had missed that party.

"I'm surprised I haven't seen you at the club, trying to get busy with Tyler." Brett waggled his brows and winked.

"Brett Chambers!" his mother scolded.

We laughed, but Lyn's face turned red.

"What?" He turned to me. "You should have seen them, Jules. They were completely undressing each other with their eyes in my parents' backyard." Brett chortled. "Good thing there weren't any children there."

I gave Lyn a sympathetic look. "He's overtired. Please ignore him."

Brett went to take the bags from his mom, but she scurried into the kitchen and started putting things away. "We're here so you two can get some rest. So scoot, and don't worry about anything. Grandma and Lyn are here."

The thought of a pillow under my head made me more exhausted than I had been.

Brett grabbed my hand and turned to his mom. "The monitor is on the counter, the formula is in the cabinet, and be sure to burp her more than once. The diapers and wipes are in her room."

His mother stared at him with a tight grin.

"If she gets fussy, all you need to do is rock her for a bit or walk around." We were almost in the bedroom when he tossed out, "Oh, and Lyn?"

His cousin tilted her head to look at him.

"No boys over while you're babysitting."

I bit my lip to stifle a giggle. His mom shook her head while Lyn gave Brett the finger.

"None of that either. Don't go teaching my baby any bad habits," he said.

I mouthed "I'm sorry" to Lyn before we went into his room. "You're terrible! Your cousin looked completely mortified. Seriously, they came to help."

Brett fell back on the bed. He rolled his head and patted the mattress next to him. I gladly laid my tired body down.

"She's used to my comments. Bentley and I are like her brothers. It's our job to harass her."

"Still . . ." My eyes began to close.

"Believe me, if I didn't tease her, she'd think something was wrong. And just so you know, I wasn't lying about Tyler. The two of them hardly said a word to each other, but their eyes told a whole story."

"I missed your birthday. I'm sorry."

He moved to his side and looked at me. My skin warmed under his palm as he cupped my cheek. "As long as you're here for all of my future birthdays, it's all good."

"I promise." I smiled and yawned.

"Let's go to sleep while we can." He turned off the monitor. "The one in the kitchen was on, right?"

"Yes, I looked to make sure. Get some rest."

"You too." His lips met mine for a gentle kiss. "I love you."

"Love you too."

That was the last thing I remembered until I thought I heard Maddie cooing. I opened my eyes, looked at the clock, and realized I'd slept for almost four hours. Brett wasn't next to me, so my fingers clicked the monitor on his nightstand on, and I heard him. He was singing "Somewhere Over the Rainbow" to Maddie, and my eyes welled with tears. His deep voice was smooth and soft. I propped my head on my hand as his voice filled my heart with more love for him than I'd already had.

After the last verse, I heard a kiss. "I love you, Maddie. I promise you'll always know where I am because I'll never leave you. Even when you need a new diaper like now." His hearty chuckle made me smile.

After a quick shower, my muscles felt so relaxed and my body a bit more rejuvenated. When I went into the living room, Brett was on the couch, giving Maddie a bottle.

"Hey, you two."

He craned his head back and smiled. "Did you sleep well?"

"I did, thank you. Is your family gone?" I grabbed two waters out of the fridge and handed one to Brett.

He smiled. "Yes, they said good-bye."

"They're pretty great. Taking a break felt so good."

His face faltered, and his frown concerned me.

"Did I say something wrong?"

He shook his head before he leaned Maddie forward to burp her. "I appreciate you being here, but you haven't been to your place in a while. If you want to leave, I'd understand. Plus, you need to get back to work. We both do." He slid the nipple back between Maddie's lips. "I need to start interviewing nannies." His eyes focused on his daughter. "I'll find you the best one."

"I've been thinking about that. I may have a solution, but you need to be completely honest with me. If you think I'm overstepping or you don't want to do this, I'll understand. My feelings won't get hurt, I promise you."

He handed me the empty bottle, and I set it on the coffee table.

"What is it? I'd never hurt your feelings." He stood with Maddie and swayed back and forth while his hand made gentle circles on her back.

I steadied my resolve and said a quick prayer that I would be able to articulate what I wanted to suggest. "Well, I work during the day and you work mostly nights. So I thought I'd ask Brian if I could work from home after three in the afternoon. Then I could watch Maddie while you work, and you wouldn't need a nanny." My hands trembled in my lap as his eyes widened. "I told you I'd help you, and the offer still stands."

"What if you need to be in the office for a meeting? I don't want you jeopardizing your career. I know how important it is to you, and you've worked hard to get where you are. You're fantastic at your job."

I approached him as he swayed with Maddie in his arms. I looked at her precious face before looking at Brett. "You both are the most important things to me. If there's a meeting, it'll be on the schedule and we can ask your mom. This isn't the first time things like this have been done. I want to do this. I honestly do." Our eyes locked.

His crinkled in the outside corners as his cheeks lifted. He nodded. "I'd like nothing more than to have you with her when I'm not. But I have a way to make it even easier."

I tilted my head as he laid Maddie in her bassinet next to the couch.

"Move in with us," he said. "I'm going to look for a house because an apartment in the city isn't where I want my daughter growing up, and you can help us pick it out. It'll be ours."

"Brett . . ."

Brett

I COULDN'T TELL IF she was excited, confused, or happy, so I guessed she was stunned. "I don't want to force you. I know we're just getting back together, and now I have a daughter—it's a lot for me to ask of you."

She frantically shook her head. "No, no, that's not a lot at all."

Her arms thrown around my neck as mine wrapped around her back was all I needed to know she liked the idea.

"I'd love to be here all the time. I just don't know if it will be good for your situation. What if it makes matters worse?" Her body arched back as she studied my face. "Call your attorney tomorrow and, for peace of mind, ask what he thinks. You need to contact him anyway, right?"

"Yes, but my attorney is a she. I'll call her first thing in the morning. We can go from there?"

"Most definitely. One day at a time." She smiled brightly and kissed me, continuing to take my breath away.

The following morning, Julie went to work, and I called my attorney. She advised me to get statements from the doctors in regards to Nikki's state of mind when she departed the hospital. We needed a doctor to say that Nikki wasn't depressed, just selfish.

"I want to petition for sole custody," I said.

She advised me to wait five more months. If Nikki made zero attempts to make contact within six months of Maddie's birth, it would be considered abandonment. My attorney didn't think a judge would take too kindly to a woman who left her newborn and never inquired about her wellbeing.

I reluctantly agreed. I wanted this over with, but I saw her point. "Six months. That's it—no more. I want this taken care of, and I don't care what it costs."

They would be the longest five months of my life. Knowing Nikki was out there somewhere made me anxious. But I wouldn't attempt to contact her again, nor did I want anyone else to. I called Alex and Tyler and let them know to do the same.

My next call was to a realtor. Alex had told me about a home in his area that had gone on the market which was vacant, so I made an appointment to go see it. Julie was working, so I grabbed a diaper bag loaded with necessities, buckled Maddie into her car seat, and we were off.

Once I pulled into Alex's neighborhood, I gave Aubrey a call to see if she wanted to come see the house with us. She jumped at the chance. I told her I'd pick her up, and when I pulled into her driveway, she was sitting on their porch. When she saw me, she got up and waddled to my car.

I opened her door for her. "You look like you're going to give birth any minute." I smiled.

Her eyes narrowed. "Thanks."

A chuckle escaped me, and I clamped my mouth shut since Aubrey wasn't amused. Once we were in my car, I looked over at her. She looked great.

"You didn't tell Jules, did you? I want to surprise her."

"No, of course not. You've made her very happy already, and this will blow her mind." She finally smiled.

"Let's hope it's the right house for us." I pulled down the tree-lined street and looked at the beautiful homes with large yards. "Wow, one of these would be great for Maddie."

"How is your little angel?"

"Perfect. I never thought I could love anyone as much as I do her. Then there's Julie, so I'm doubly blessed."

When we pulled up to the house, Aubrey and I stared at it. When we looked at each other, we had the same realization in our eyes. *This is the one.*

The realtor took us around the house, and I pointed things out to Maddie even though she had no idea what I was saying. Her little blue eyes took in everything. I even showed her where her swing set would go.

I offered asking price with a quick closing date. The realtor looked as though she'd hit the lottery when I told her I had an apartment in the city to sell. She said she had clients who may be interested.

When we were back in the car, I turned to Aubrey. "Do you think Julie will like it?"

Aubrey beamed. "She's going to love it."

I looked skyward and thanked my grandparents. Without them, I wouldn't have been able to do this. Aubrey put her hand on her stomach and groaned.

"Hey, are you okay?"

She smiled tightly. "I've been having Braxton-Hicks contractions."

I glanced at her as I pulled out of the driveway. "Um . . . who's contractions?"

She laughed. "Don't worry about it. I promise I'm not going to deliver this baby in your car. I'm fine."

I didn't find any humor in her comment, but she wasn't concerned, so I didn't say anything.

"So when do you plan on making an honest woman out of Julie?" she asked.

"Soon. Do you think she'll say yes?" My eyes shifted to her side of the car. "Aubrey?"

"My guess would be yes, but you need to ask her, not me."

"I'll do that." I pulled into her driveway, but something was off. She was frowning and sitting still, so I asked, "What are you thinking?"

"I'm curious about why your views on marriage seemed to have changed. Please don't misunderstand me, but it wasn't too long ago that you despised the thought of marriage." Aubrey shook her head. "You lost each other because of your views on a formal commitment, and now you're buying a house and want to propose." Her shoulders dropped, and her eyes lowered. "I hate to ask this, but do you want a wife or a mother for Maddie?"

"You think I want to get married so I can provide a mother to my daughter?" I ran my tongue over my teeth. "I love Julie. Yes, I told myself I'd never get married again, but she's different. My love for Julie surpasses anything I thought possible. I told you all those months ago that I was scared, and I still am but for different reasons. I need her because I love her, not because my daughter needs a mother."

Aubrey smiled and nodded. "Great. That's what I thought you would say. Sorry, but Jules has always been there for me and had my back. It would have been remiss of me not to ask what your intentions are. For the record, she loves your little girl. You're a lucky man." She kissed my cheek then got out, opened the back door, and gave Maddie a kiss. "Bye, Brett. Thanks for letting me come today."

Knowing that I'd passed her test, I felt relief wash over me. "Take care of yourself. Go rest and stop having those whatever-they-are contractions."

She laughed and closed the door. Aubrey was right—I was a lucky man, and there was no way I would ever be without Julie again.

About a week later, the realtor called to tell me the house was mine and she'd had an offer on my apartment. Time flew between my offer being accepted and receiving the key. Keeping the surprise to myself was killing me.

When move-in day came, I took my girls to their new home. My mom had helped me furnish it, and all I needed to do was bring over Maddie's bedroom furniture we had just bought for her.

Julie was looking out her window. "Are we going to Aubrey's? You made a wrong turn."

I placed my hand on hers. "No, we aren't. I want to show you something."

When I turned into the driveway, she looked at the glorious colonial-style home. The house was a mixture of cedar siding and stone with a large porch that wrapped around the sides.

"Wow, this is stunning! Who lives here? Is this your brother's place?" She opened the door and stepped out. "The perennials are exquisite. Those colors are so vibrant."

I retrieved Maddie from the backseat, car seat and all since she was asleep. We walked up the porch steps to the double front doors.

"Bentley doesn't live here, but we should go see him soon." I unlocked the front door. "Welcome home, Julie."

She gasped. "What?" Her face flushed, and her eyes widened. "This is your house?"

I took her hand while carrying Maddie in the other one. "No, it's ours. The three of us—our family."

"Oh my God, Brett!" Her head turned to the left and right as she took in her surroundings. She walked toward the fireplace and looked at a picture of the three of us on the mantel. "It's really ours?"

"Yes. Look, Jules, I know we said we'd take this one day at a time and not rush anything, but I feel as though I've loved you forever. If I hadn't been so foolish all those months ago, we would have stayed together and been happy. But I screwed that up." I looked at Maddie. "If I hadn't, I wouldn't have my daughter, so maybe that's why."

Tears filled her eyes as she stared at Maddie. "I love her so much, Brett. I wasn't sure . . ." Tears streamed down her cheeks.

I set down the car seat, took Maddie out, and held her close to my chest. "You weren't sure of what?"

"If . . ." Her breath hitched. "I feel terrible for even saying it."

"Honesty, Jules."

She placed her hand on Maddie's back. "If I could love her." She wept as she took Maddie and hugged her. "But I do, I truly do, as if she were mine. Please know that." She peppered soft kisses on Maddie's head. "Sweetie, please know I do love you."

I wrapped my girls up in my arms. "She knows, and I understand. Come on, let me show you the rest of the house."

Once we were done with the grand tour, we headed back to my apartment to put Maddie down for her nap. Julie and I made ourselves comfortable on the plush sofa, and she rested her head on my lap. My fingers played with her soft hair.

"Jules, what you said back at the house about loving Maddie?"

She looked at me with loving eyes. "Yeah."

"I've been thinking about something for a while, and I spoke to my attorney about it." I felt my pulse quicken as nerves crept in. "I want you to be ours and for her to be yours."

"I'd like that too." Her lips quivered, and my heart clenched.

"Will you marry me?"

Julie sat straight up and looked at me with wide eyes. "What?"

I got down on one knee. "Julie Michaels, will you be my wife?"

"Yes!" She stood and pulled me up with her.

Our kiss was quick at first, then my lips claimed hers with unbridled passion. She would be mine, and I couldn't wait to make it official.

"I love you, Brett Chambers."

"I love you, Julie Michaels."

We went into our room. I opened my dresser drawer and took out a small velvet box. When I turned, she was looking at a picture of us when we first met, and my heart broke a bit over all the time we'd lost.

"I'm so sorry for everything, Julie. When I think back to when I freaked out because of my past when all you wanted was for us to have a future, it kills me."

"It's okay." Her eyes glistened as she tightly grinned.

"No, it isn't. Samantha was all take. She was in it for what she could get, and I should have realized that you are the complete opposite. You're all give. You've never acted as though anyone owed you anything or that you were entitled to anything." I linked our hands. "You're so special, and I promise you a lifetime of happiness. You own me—heart, body, and soul—and I'll do my best to prove I deserve you." She sniffled, and I kissed away her tears. "I had a romantic evening planned, but why should anything we do be conventional?"

My shaking fingers opened the velvet box, revealing a two-carat round diamond in a stunning platinum setting. She covered her mouth, and I smiled. I took her left hand and slid the ring on her finger.

"It's beautiful." Her eyes met mine. "Thank you."

"You and Maddie are the most important women in my life. We should be thanking you for loving us. Jules, I don't want to wait. I'd like to call my lawyer and start adoption proceedings so Maddie will have you for a mother. What do you think?"

Her head bobbed up and down. "Tomorrow wouldn't be soon enough."

"So much for one day at a time." I placed a chaste kiss on her lips.

"We are taking a day at a time, but they're our days and our time, which we've wasted enough of. Don't you agree?" Her genuine smile warmed my heart.

"Yes. I couldn't agree more."

I laid her down and made love to her until Maddie woke up. It was then and there I knew my life was perfect.

The following day, I contacted my lawyer and told her my plans. Unfortunately, she said I needed to prove that I had tried to contact Nikki for permission, which was difficult since I had no idea where she was. I decided to call my friend Ben Stone, who was a cop, to see if he could find out where she was.

A few nights later, Julie and I were packing the rest of our things to move into our new home. Maddie was with my parents, so we were trying to get everything done while we were alone. My phone rang, and I saw it was my pal on the force.

"Hey, Ben. Did you find anything?"

"Yeah, she used her debit card at a coffee shop in SoHo two days ago. I ran a check on the card, and I have an address for you. Do you want me to go check it out? It isn't in the best neighborhood."

Chills ran up and down my arms. "No, but thank you. If you could send me the address, that'd be great."

"You got it. I hope it helps. Take care, Chambers."

"Thanks for everything, Ben."

I rubbed my temples as I waited for the text. Once I had it, I forwarded it to my attorney.

"He found her, didn't he?" Julie's voice was laced with concern.

"Yes, he did, but I'm going to leave it up to my lawyer. I'm not going near her."

"Okay." She went back to packing, her tension showing on her face.

I'd have done anything to make that go away, but sadly, I couldn't.

Once we had everything packed and the movers came to take Maddie's crib, we headed to our new home.

chapter 19

Julie

EACH DAY WAS filled with the stress of wondering when or if Nikki would resurface. It had been a few weeks since Ben found Nikki, and we still hadn't heard anything. I'd never seen Brett so tense, and I couldn't do a thing to alleviate any of his anxiety.

My phone dinged with a text from Alex.

Alex: We're at the hospital. Aubrey's being admitted.

Oh my God! I needed to get there! Then I looked into the living room at the baby gliding back and forth in her swing.

Me: I'm with Maddie. Brett isn't here. I'll get a sitter and meet you there.

Alex: It's okay. Who knows how long it will be?

Me: Okay, but you better call me later. Kiss Aubrey and tell her I love her.

Alex: Will do.

I was so excited for Aubrey. Every single one of her dreams was coming true. Mine had as well, but I still had to deal with the vile woman who'd abandoned her baby. Maddie was so perfect. Her hair was coming in, and it had the cutest waves. Thank God she looked like her father and, more importantly, seemed to have his disposition. Maddie didn't complain about anything. She was a wonderful baby—after she'd gotten out of her nocturnal phase.

Brett called and said he needed to go to the club to cover for Alex. He told me to call his mom if I wanted to go see Aubrey, but I told him what Alex had said. Not to mention, every time I thought of leaving the house, I got an eerie feeling that something would go wrong. It was completely ridiculous, but I'd have felt better if Ben had told Brett that Nikki was out of the country rather than a borough over.

A few hours later, Maddie was in bed, and I was reading when Alex called to tell me that they had a little boy. He sounded so elated and proud.

"Mom and baby are doing great," he said.

I kicked myself for not being there, and even though I knew Aubrey understood, I should have gone to see her. "I'm so glad. What's his name?"

"Jackson Alexander. He's eight pounds, twenty-one inches long. He has ten toes and ten fingers and a head full of dark hair." He chuckled. "Everything is perfect, Jules."

"I'm so happy for you guys. Tell my godson I love him, and tell his mom I can't wait to see her. Congratulations, Alex."

"Thanks. Will you let Brett know? I need to get back in."

"Yes, I'll be happy to," I said.

"Great, love you."

"I love you too." I clicked off and sent Brett a text. Instead of replying, he walked into our room. "Shit!" My hand covered my chest. "You scared me. I didn't expect you so soon."

He looked at me as though I was crazy. "Jules, it's after two in the morning."

"Oh, I must have gotten too caught up in this book to notice the time. Alex called."

Brett stripped out of his clothes and got into bed with me. "Did she have the baby?"

"Yes, a little boy. Jackson Alexander, and according to Alex, he's perfect."

He took my Kindle and set it on the side table. "I think you're perfect." A giggle escaped me as he pulled me close. "How was our angel tonight?"

"She's great and asleep."

A low rumble escaped him. "We should probably sleep."

"Probably." I bit my lip and sighed.

"I think I'll make love to my fiancée first."

"Mmmm . . . okay."

"I'm glad we didn't go forward with our 'take it slow' plan."

I sighed. "I do prefer this plan much better."

His smile was radiant as he brushed my hair away from my eyes. "Me too."

Brett stripped me of my clothes and grabbed a condom. "I can't wait until we don't need to use these anymore."

"You don't need to use it now if you don't want to."

His eyes lit up then darkened with desire. "Are you sure?"

"I've been on the pill for years, and the doctor said you were clean. So yes, I'm sure." I laced my fingers through his hair and stared up at him.

His hand traveled down my flat stomach until it was between my legs. "You're always ready for me. I love that I can do that to you." He slid one finger in then two. "So wet . . ."

"Only for you."

The dizzying current that flowed through me with every stroke of his finger was pure bliss. His body shifted, and he slowly slid inside me. My head rolled back. I wrapped my legs around him and pulled him closer . . . deeper . . . until my body was filled with him.

"Fuck, Jules, you feel so good. I never knew it could feel like this."

As our hips moved in unison, our mouths met, and our tongues did a dance of their own. Desire ran through me with each thrust of our bodies. We picked up our pace. The yearning in his eyes sent me over the top as he flipped us over. I slid up and down his length as his hands gripped my ass, steadying my movements. He controlled the pace until I was ready to explode.

"Brett . . ." I could hardly speak. My body trembled and leaned forward so we were chest to chest.

He rolled us over, and I held onto his muscular back as he quickened his speed. He swallowed my moan while he groaned in ecstasy.

"That was incredible." His warm breath caressed my ear, and all I could do was nod. He chuckled as his dick bobbed inside me. "Have I rendered you speechless?"

"A little, yes."

When our eyes locked, it was different. The love we'd had before seemed to have been amplified by a million. When he slid out of me, I instantly missed him.

"Let's get cleaned up before our daughter wakes up," he said.

"Our daughter . . . I love the sound of that."

"Me too. It's perfect."

When Aubrey came home from the hospital, I took half a day off work to visit her and the baby. My godson Jackson was absolutely perfect.

"Aubrey, you look amazing. If I didn't know, I wouldn't be able to tell you just gave birth."

Alex walked into the room. "My wife is a MILF, but only for me." He kissed her on the head. "Right, baby?"

She rolled her eyes. "Sure, honey. Don't you have somewhere to be?"

He shook his head while I snickered. "Don't encourage her, Julie. The only reason I'm leaving is so you two can have girl time. I'm headed to your house to chat it up with your man."

"Speaking of which." I held out my left hand.

Aubrey squealed and startled poor Jackson. "Oooh, sorry little man." She readjusted him, and he started eating again. "When did this happen?"

"Right before you went into labor."

She gasped. "Why didn't you call to tell me when I was in the hospital?"

"Because this is a special time for you. I knew I'd tell you when you were home and settled."

"Wow, that ring is nothing short of spectacular." She moved Jackson up to her chest and rubbed his back. "So what's the latest on Nikki?"

The sound of her name made me feel as though an elephant was sitting on my chest. "Brett wants me to adopt Maddie after we're married. So he found her address and sent it to his lawyer, and she'll be served with adoption papers." I leaned back into the leather chair. "I'm so scared. What if she doesn't sign off on the adoption papers?"

"Try to stay positive. She hasn't been in Maddie's life since she delivered her."

"I know, but I'm nervous. That little girl is Brett's life. She means absolutely everything to him. If anything should ever happen, I don't know if he could handle it." *Shit. I know I couldn't handle it.*

Aubrey stood and placed a sleeping Jackson in the blue gingham bassinet. "He'd never let anything bad happen. Brett's pretty tenacious. Look at the two of you." She smiled as she looked at me. "He's a fighter, and so are you."

"Yeah, I know. It's just hard. All the uncertainty. I'm so scared. The last time things felt this perfect, it all fell apart." I let out a breath.

"Guess what I made, and I didn't even know you were coming over." She crossed into the kitchen. When she came back, she was holding a plate.

I couldn't contain my smile. "Muffins?"

"It was as if I knew you would be coming over and in need of comfort food." She extended the plate to me.

"They look great." I glanced at her, my lips quirked up. "Out of a box, right?"

"Is there any other way?" We both laughed. "I guess I can blame Jackson now for not having time to bake anything that isn't in a box."

"Hey, don't go blaming my godson for your shortcomings in the kitchen!" I popped some of the muffin in my mouth while trying not to laugh.

"Fine, I'll blame Alex."

We laughed.

"Thanks for being a great friend. I feel better already."

"You should," she said. "So when are we all going to get together?"

"How about for Thanksgiving? I'll talk to Brett. We'll host his family and you guys, unless you have plans with your family."

"My parents are still in Paris, and Alex's dad is in Tokyo. He left for a business trip right after the baby was born, so we'll be there. Can I bring anything?"

"Yeah, muffins."

Brett

WHEN JULIE TOLD me we were having Thanksgiving at our home, I was thrilled. Then I asked her if she had ever cooked a turkey, and her face paled.

"Don't worry, I'll call my mom," I said.

"Thank God, because I haven't the first clue what to do."

I took Maddie from her. "Hi, beautiful girl." I gave her a squeeze and spun her around. "I missed you today. I'm not working tonight, so we can plan our first holiday as the future Mr. and Mrs. Chambers."

"Yay! I'm so excited!" Her face scrunched up. "Wow, I think someone needs a new diaper." She took Maddie from me. "I'll be right back."

I called my family and made sure we were all set for Thursday. My mom was planning on hosting at her home, so all we needed to do was change the location. I was happy Bentley and Andi were able to come as well. I thought having a family Thanksgiving at our place was a great idea. It would be the perfect opportunity to announce our engagement and that we planned on Julie adopting Maddie.

Thanksgiving morning, I was greeted by a wonderful aroma, and clanging, coming from the kitchen. I went downstairs and stopped at the sight of Julie holding a wooden spoon while reading a cookbook to Maddie, who was obviously her assistant.

"So what's the difference between a sweet potato and a yam?" She looked at Maddie. "Do you think that's important?"

Her little feet kicked as her chair bounced, and she let out a squeak of happiness.

"Me either." Julie let out a frustrated sigh and rubbed the back of her hand across her forehead.

I burst out laughing.

Julie's lips twisted, and she glared at me before returning her attention to Maddie. "Daddy thinks he knows everything."

"Daddy doesn't know everything. I thought they were the same thing, but I'm probably wrong." I took a deep breath. "It smells great in here." The room was filled with familiar holiday scents, and I couldn't wait to start making our own traditions.

"Your mom came by earlier and prepared the turkey, so all I needed to do was put it in the oven. I took off my ring so she wouldn't see we were engaged." She held up her hand and wiggled her fingers. "It's back on now."

The doorbell rang.

"Let's do this." I picked up Maddie and grabbed Julie's hand.

"Brett, are you sure I look okay?"

"Yes, babe, you're perfect. Now come on. Let's go say hi to our guests."

I opened the door and was greeted by my brother and Andi.

"There's my goddaughter." Bentley took Maddie from my arms and kissed her head. "You look so pretty. Wait until Grandma sees you."

"Does someone want her Grandma?" My parents walked in. My mother kissed Maddie on the head then walked over to me and kissed my cheek. She pulled Julie into a hug.

Julie embraced my mom. "Hi, Madeline."

"You know, you could call her mom." I held up Julie's left hand.

Everyone bombarded us with hugs. The women were all in tears, and my dad and brother congratulated me with a few bro hugs.

"Welcome to the family. It's good to meet you." Bentley kissed Julie, and Andi followed suit.

"Knock, knock."

The door opened and Alex, Aubrey, and Jackson came in. Alex handed me two bottles of wine from Calabrese Vineyards, and when I showed Julie the labels, she smiled. I knew she missed Luca, but I also knew they still chatted when she was at work. I was banking on him being gay. It made me feel better about their relationship.

Aubrey handed Julie a plate of muffins, and they burst out laughing. Alex and I shrugged. Those two spoke their own language, and we didn't dare try to decipher it.

"Come on in and sit down," I said.

The men congregated in front of the TV while the women headed off to the kitchen. I looked around my home, our home, and joy filled my heart. My entire family was together, and that included Julie. She completed the picture.

In a little while, we all sat around the table to enjoy the wonderful meal. The doorbell rang. I couldn't imagine who it could be since everyone we knew was there, except Tyler.

My goofy smile vanished when I saw Nikki on my porch.

"Hi, Brett." She flashed me a smile.

I was waiting for venom to leak from the corners of her mouth. "Nikki. What are you doing here?"

"I came for my daughter."

I was sure my heart stopped. What the hell was she talking about? "Excuse me?"

She walked in and stood in the family room. I closed the door and tried to gather my wits. Nikki was in my house, and she wanted Maddie. Over my dead body, and not even then would she take Maddie away from us. When I turned, she looked oddly calm. I was anything but.

"You need to leave. You're not welcome here. We're having a family dinner." I crossed my arms and tried to remain steadfast.

"It's been long enough. I decided I want her back. I am her mother after all." She adjusted her shoulders and stood straight while she looked me right in the eyes.

Something was off, but because she was Nikki, I couldn't pinpoint it. All I knew was my dinner was about to revisit me.

"She doesn't even know you, Nik. You can't come here and think you can walk out with her. It's not going to happen. You need to go."

Before I could say more, Julie walked in, laughing, with Maddie in her arms. "Brett, you should have seen what this one did with her sweet potatoes." Julie's laugh ended abruptly, and the color in her cheeks drained when she saw Nikki.

Nikki gasped. "There she is." She strode toward Julie, who tilted her body to shield my little girl. "Give me my daughter. I want to hold her."

Julie's eyes widened, and a look of terror flashed across them. "Brett?"

I hurried to her side and took Maddie out of her arms. "Go get my parents."

When Julie walked away, Maddie twisted her body and reached out to Julie.

A brief look of discomfort crossed Julie's face as she came back and kissed the top of Maddie's head. "I'll be right back, sweet girl."

I turned to Nikki, who had her hands on her hips, then she held them out. "I'm her mommy, not her. Now let me hold her."

I saw the vein in her neck throb. There was no way I would comply with her request. Julie walked back in with not only my parents but all our guests. We were a united front, and I needed that.

"So is this is how you're going to play it?" Nikki looked at the small crowd behind Julie as my mother came forward. Nikki tossed her hands on her hips and tilted her head.

My mother was not amused or affected by Nikki's stance. "I don't think this is the time or place for this discussion. Why don't you leave your number, and Brett will call you in the morning."

Maddie began to cry, and the room fell silent.

"Can't you see you're upsetting her?" my mother said. "I won't stand by while you attempt to destroy this family—my family."

"I'm her family. I'm her mother, and you of all people should understand that. What if someone wouldn't let you hold your child?" She was toe to toe with my mom, who wasn't backing down.

"Listen, young lady, I didn't abandon my child. We all stood by you and Brett when Maddie was born and told you we'd be there for her for the rest of our lives. So don't you speak to me or anyone in this room that way." My mother's face reddened, and my dad put his hand on her shoulder.

I handed Maddie to Julie. "Please take her to her room." I kissed them both and looked at our friends. "If you all can give us a minute?"

Jackson was asleep in Alex's arms as my guests walked toward the kitchen.

"How did you know where we lived?" I hit the red button on my cell to record our conversation and placed it back in my pocket.

"I followed you home from the club the other night. I got a notice from your lawyer stating that you want Julie to adopt our daughter, and the answer is no." Nikki perused our home. "Nice digs you got here. Did you say 'where we lived' as in you live with *her?* She's here with my daughter?"

"We're engaged. Julie is a wonderful mother, and Maddie means the world to her."

"I can't believe you named her that after I told you I didn't like that name." She stretched out her arm and looked at her nails. "I'll change it when we go to court."

"Okay, Nikki, what is this really about?" Any patience I had dissipated, and I just wanted her out of here.

Her face softened. She looked at my mother, who walked back in the room. "I'll tell you, but I don't want her here." She turned up her nose at my mom, who looked as if she would lose it at any moment.

"Mom, can you please make sure Julie is okay?"

She nodded but addressed Nikki. "If you look around, you'll see there isn't a better place for that little girl. She's loved and well taken care of." My mom kissed my cheek and left.

"Do you want to sit down?" I swung my arm out toward the couch.

Nikki moved to the sofa and placed her purse on her lap.

I sat in the chair next to her. "Okay, you have me, so what do you want to say?"

Her lips curved into a smile. "See, that's what I want."

My brows furrowed. "You lost me."

"You. I want you. I can tell you're a wonderful father, just like I knew you'd be, and I want to be a part of your life with our daughter. We could be so great, Brett. I've given you enough time, and I think you owe it to me to at least try to be a family." She reached for me, making me recoil like a snake.

"Nothing has changed except for the fact that you walked away from your little girl when she was barely two days old. Julie and Maddie are my family. I'm sorry, but you aren't taking my daughter."

Nikki stood and headed toward where Julie had taken Maddie.

I jumped up and blocked her from going any farther. Exactly like that day at the hospital, my nerves spiked, and my adrenaline rushed through my veins. My nightmares had become a reality, and I was panicked. "No, you're not going to do this. You can't do this."

She pushed herself around me and busted into the nursery. Julie was holding Maddie and swaying back and forth. Tears streamed down her cheeks, and my heart crumbled. Her eyes pleaded with me for a sign, a signal, something indicating what I wanted her to do. I didn't have any answers. I felt as if time were suspended and everything and everyone moved in slow motion.

Nikki turned to me. "Let me at least hold her, just for a minute. Then I'll leave, and you can talk to my lawyer in the morning."

This wasn't happening. I shook my head as I felt pressure build in my eyes. I closed them, willing them to stay dry. I took a deep breath and took Maddie from Julie. "Daddy's right here, honey."

I tentatively handed Maddie to Nikki, but not before I hugged her and kissed her cheek. My hands shook as I placed her in Nikki's hands. I stood close in case Nikki dropped her.

Nikki cradled her and looked completely awkward. Maddie didn't like being held like that unless she was going to have a bottle, but Nikki didn't know that. How could she? Maddie started fussing, and my instinct was to reach for her. Nikki's nose scrunched up, and she scowled at Maddie. As soon as Nikki saw my eyes on her, she forced a smile.

"I think she knows who I am." Nikki looked mockingly at Julie. "You can leave now."

I grabbed Julie's hand. "No, she's staying right here."

chapter 20

Julie

MY HEART ACHED more than it ever had. I was frightened beyond all measure. I didn't know what to do. The last thing I wanted was for Nikki to hold me being here against Brett.

"It's okay, Brett. I'll go join our guests, and you can talk to Nikki." I glanced at the woman who was the bane of my existence. A shit-eating grin stretched across her Botoxed face.

"No, it isn't okay. Please stay." He leaned in and whispered, "I need you."

That was all I had to hear. I nodded and took my place at his side. Maddie began to fuss, and I went against everything I knew and left her in Nikki's arms. The tension on Brett's face and the tightness in his muscles told me he felt the same way.

"Come here, sweetie." Brett took Maddie, who reached for him. He took in a deep breath as though he needed to breathe in her sweet baby scent.

My heart broke as Brett held on to his daughter as though she would vanish.

"Let's go, Nikki. Julie, please bring Maddie to the kitchen."

I didn't want to leave them, but when I walked into the kitchen, I was thankful I wasn't alone. Brett's mother was pacing the tiled floor.

"Will you hold her?" My voice trembled as I offered her Maddie.

"Honey, he loves you and this little girl. That tramp won't get away with this. We have great attorneys. Just be there for him." She swayed with Maddie in her arms.

I felt my throat tense as I tried not to burst into sobs. I nodded at Madeline and went to be by Brett's side, but not before I glanced into the dining room and saw our family and friends sitting at the table. I caught Aubrey's sympathetic and worried eyes, and I almost lost it again. My shaky legs carried me into the living room where I took my place next to my fiancé.

"Brett, this can either be difficult or simple." Nikki shot me a dirty look, and when I wiped a stray tear away, she noticed my ring. "Nice rock."

I quickly pulled my hand behind my back. It was instinctive but ridiculous since she'd already seen it.

"We're engaged, Nikki. Can't you see that we're giving Maddie a good home? She's happy. Isn't that what's important?" Brett said.

Nikki scoffed. "But she isn't with both of her parents." She narrowed her eyes at me. "Her real parents. So it's going to go like this." She stepped forward, and her eyes darted between us but focused on Brett. "Either it's you, me, and our daughter, or it's her and I. I don't want Julie to be a part of my daughter's life. It's your decision, Brett. No judge in their right mind would keep me from her. So if you think you're going to fight me and win, guess again."

My heart dropped, and I was sure my lungs stopped working. I felt my entire body shutting down. I let go of Brett's hand, and he grasped it again.

"You want a fight? Go ahead and bring it. You don't think a judge will rule in my favor?" He stood so close to her she flinched and pulled her head back, but her eyes never strayed from his. "You're the one who left and has been doing God knows what for the past few months. You missed everything: the first time she rolled over, laughed, ate cereal . . . every fucking thing! Christ, Nikki, you didn't even know her name! So you want to take me to court? Be my guest! Now get the hell out of my house!" Brett's voice echoed through our home, and his face scrunched up in disgust.

"Five million."

"Excuse me?" Brett's eyes went wide, and I may have blacked out for a moment.

"Give me five million dollars, and she's yours. I'll sign the adoption papers, and you two can be on your way to your happily ever after, but I'm not coming out of this empty-handed." She stepped forward. "Do you know what I went through to get you, Brett? I'm not leaving with only stretchmarks and extra weight. You want your daughter? You have two choices: leave Julie and be with me, or pay me five million dollars." Her face was so serene it was creepy.

His face hardened. "What makes you think I have that kind of money?"

"Look at this place." She threw her hands out. "This has to be at least one million, and you own part of the club. If your little girl and your fiancée mean so much to you, then you'll figure it out. Or you move her out and me in. But I can guarantee you there is no way in hell Julie will get to reap all the rewards of being a Chambers while I get left out in the cold. Don't forget whose body you created that baby with. It was me you wanted. It was my name you called out, my body you gave multiple orgasms, my mouth you kissed. Not hers. Don't you remember how good it was when I wrapped my lips around you? How you moaned my name? You wanted me, and it felt so good." Her eyes flicked to me. "I'm sure you can understand what I'm saying, Julie. His hands, his fingers, and that tongue . . ." She licked her lips. "The best I've ever had."

Brett's face turned beet red as he let out a hearty chuckle that held no amusement at all. "You're completely delusional. None of that happened. Your lies won't break us, and I won't stand here and let you fill Julie's head with fabrications. Do you understand me?"

Nikki barely flinched, and her sneer didn't falter.

Brett's body was rigid, and the muscles in his corded arms flexed as his hands balled into fists. "The only thing that happened was we fucked. Your memory is as skewed as your mind. Do you want to know what I remember? I remember feeling sick after I left your apartment. I didn't even kiss you. I used your body. It was unadulterated fucking since the love of my life had just walked away. The only good thing that came out of my lapse in judgment was Maddie." His back expanded, and his face reddened. "I despise you."

I slumped over at his words. He had wanted her that night, and they'd created a beautiful child. There was no denying that fact. Maddie was her daughter, not mine. Nikki's descriptions made me feel as though

I had been there, and horrible images flooded my brain with no way to erase them. I couldn't look at Brett. I wasn't sure what to do. I was consumed by jealousy, and I was sure my heart was bleeding as my chest constricted like a vise. I hoped I could survive it.

"Nikki, you need to leave." I wasn't sure when Alex had walked in, but he started to usher her out.

She stopped and looked at me. "If you honestly love them, you'll do the right thing and let them go. Fighting me would be pointless. My lawyer said I could tie this up in court for years. She'll be in middle school before this is resolved. Is that what you want, Julie? Do you want to be responsible for my daughter losing years of a being happy with her parents? Would you be able to sleep at night knowing that because of you, she comes from a broken home?"

"Get out of my house!" Brett yelled.

All I could do was close my eyes and pray I was having a nightmare.

"Let's go." Alex opened the door, escorted her through it, and quickly closed it.

Once I heard the click of the deadbolt, I crumbled. Brett pulled me to his chest, and all I could think was that I should leave. Then Aubrey was by my side, and I left Brett's arms to weep in hers.

"Shhh, it'll be okay. We'll do whatever we can."

Aubrey's words would generally have soothed me, but I had a feeling nothing could make me feel better. Nikki had made valid points, not to mention painted quite a picture for me.

"You can't let her get to you." Aubrey leaned back and placed her hands on my shoulders. "There's no way anything she said was true. Brett loves you and only you. She would say anything to get to you. Don't let her."

Brett enveloped me in a strong hug. "I'm so sorry she spewed all those lies, but you have to know that's what they were. I didn't make love to her. You're the only one I've ever made love to. Please believe me. I can't lose you—not again."

"You can't pay her off—that's illegal. The easiest solution is for me to leave. You can't lose your daughter. I'd rather you lost me."

"I'm not going to lose you either, Julie. We'll fight her." His strong arms tightened around me.

I knew he loved me, and deep down, I knew Nikki was lying, but her words still hurt.

Brett took my hand. "Let's go have dessert with our family and try to salvage our holiday. I'm not going to let her ruin this day for us."

He was right, and I would do whatever I needed to put a smile on my face, and that's exactly what I did. "You're right. Let's go I could use some pie right now."

His face lit up and his eyes darkened. "Me too." The playful undertone to his voice and the glint in his eye made the heat rise in my cheeks.

We spent the next hour enjoying the comfort of family and friends, which was exactly what Brett needed—we all did.

By the time everyone left, I was completely drained. Maddie was asleep, and I was exhausted and worried beyond measure. I peeled off my clothes, tossed on a T-shirt, and climbed into bed. Brett got in wearing nothing but boxer shorts and a worried expression. I needed to do something to help him. It would break me, but my broken heart was worth Brett keeping his daughter.

I turned so I was on my side with my hands under my face. "I hate to say this, but Nikki's argument had merit."

The muscle in Brett's jaw ticked. He rolled over to look at me. "I'm not me without you." His body tensed, but his voice softened. "You're my heart."

My body stayed still as images, words, and feelings whirled around in my brain. I knew I couldn't let her vile words destroy what we'd rebuilt. I'd forgiven him a long time ago, but forgetting was so much more difficult. I was sure that had been her plan when she arrived—to paint a scene that would be engraved in my memory. Mission accomplished.

"We're engaged, and you've been a part of Maddie's life, and she hasn't." Brett trailed his knuckles down my cheek and rested his palm on my neck before he pulled me close to him.

"I can't believe this is happening." A sigh escaped me. "I don't think you're giving her enough credit. Look at what she did to get pregnant." I rested my head on his chest, and his fingers played with my hair.

"Let's talk to the lawyer tomorrow and see what she says. I loved you and only you. This is all my fault, and you've taken the brunt of it. I'm not going to lose you or Maddie—do you hear me? I'll go to the end of the earth and back to make this right." He kissed the top of my head.

"I love you, Brett."

"I love you more than you'll ever know, and I'll never stop."

I couldn't sleep. Nikki's voice, along with Brett's, rang through my head. I knew he thought he could win in court, but what if he couldn't? What if he lost his little girl because of me? No, that wouldn't happen. I looked at the clock. It was two in the morning. I knew Maddie was asleep, but if I was going to go through with this, I needed to do it now. I slid out of bed carefully, not wanting to wake Brett. His face so handsome and peaceful, his lashes resting against his cheeks, that it solidified my resolve—I was doing the right thing no matter how painful it was.

After I dressed, I made my way into Maddie's room. My eyes filled with tears waiting to spill over. Her little lips were suckling her hand. I watched her chest go up and down with each gentle breath she took.

I whispered, "Hey, little girl."

She moved a bit, and even though I knew she'd fuss a little, I picked her up and sat with her on the rocker in her room. Thankfully, she didn't fully wake.

"I love you, Maddie." My voice hitched, and tears streamed down my cheeks. I studied every inch of her: the way her long dark eyelashes rested against her tiny cheekbones, her chubby fingers, the legs that would carry her through life, lips shaped like petals in the prettiest pink hue, and perfectly round ears. I prayed she would hear everything I said to her.

Brett

IS JULIE TALKING? My arm slid over to her side of the bed. I could have sworn I heard her voice. I thought that after our hellacious night, she might be having a bad dream, but she wasn't there. Then I heard her again.

"I know you don't know what's happening right now, and thankfully you won't remember."

I looked to where her voice was coming from. The green light on the baby monitor was lit as I listened to her. Hearing Julie with Maddie warmed me from the inside out.

"Your daddy loves you very much. I know you feel that." Her voice hitched.

I sat up in bed and continued to listen while holding the monitor.

"I love you both so much. There's nothing that could make me happier than being your mommy, but I'm not your mommy, not really." A sob escaped her, and my chest ached.

"Your daddy is going to need you to be strong for him. I want you to live a life full of laughter and love as hard as he does. Someday a little boy will catch your attention, and you'll fall in love like I did with your daddy. My hope is you'll always be happy, smart, and loving. Don't listen to anyone who says you can't do something because you're a girl. They only say that because they don't have the confidence in themselves to do it, but I know you do. Be sweet and kind to others, and do your best not to fall into the mean girls' clique. There will be times when life may seem difficult, but you have your daddy's resolve. You'll be a fighter. Always know I will never stop loving you. A day will never pass without you being in my thoughts, but I need to go away for a while."

Julie's cry rang through the speaker. *What did she say? She's leaving? No fucking way!* I jumped out of bed and tossed the monitor on it before I ran to Maddie's room. My heart was in my throat. I stood in the doorway with my eyes trained on my two girls.

Julie was rocking and holding a sleeping Maddie. "You have a wonderful family who will love you and teach you things. You may think you don't need their advice, but listen to them because they want the best for you. I know you won't remember me or anything I'm saying to you right now, but I really wanted to be your mommy." Her voice hitched as she caressed Maddie's head with her cheek. "I'll always love your daddy, and you are so lucky he's yours. He'll protect you, comfort you, and be your compass when you're lost. I'm sure he'll be overprotective, but that's his job, and one day you'll understand that. I love you, sweet angel." She kissed Maddie's cheek and laid her down in the crib.

Julie's hand covered her mouth as her body shook with sobs. As she turned to leave, her eyes caught mine, which were leaking hot tears. She stared at me and didn't move.

"No." I frantically shook my head. "No, Julie."

Julie put her index finger in front of her mouth. She quietly pulled the door closed, and we walked into the living room.

I pivoted and looked at her. "You're not leaving." My voice cracked, and I wiped my tears away. "You can't, Julie. I won't let you. You said Maddie was going to need me. Well, I need you." My hands raked through my hair, and I looked up and prayed for guidance.

She stood stock still and stared at me. Her eyes were bloodshot, and I was sure mine looked the same. I scrubbed my face with my hands.

"You're not leaving us. I won't let you." I closed the gap between us. "There's no way in hell I'll let that happen. How could I bear it if you left? How could you?" I cupped her cheek. "Do you hear me? No way! We will figure this out. I'm not going to fail my girls—you're my family."

I took her hand and led her to the bedroom. We sat on the bed and faced each other.

"I know everything you said is what you think needs to happen, but you couldn't be more wrong," I said.

She sighed as she attempted to calm her breathing, and I felt it in every pore of my body.

"Together, Jules. Okay?"

Her head bobbed as she threw herself into my arms. "I'm so scared. I can't be what separates you two—I won't survive it. How can I live with the fact that I'm the reason why everyone is in pain? You can say that I'm wrong, but I'm not."

I rubbed her back. "I'm scared too, but you're wrong. Even if you weren't part of the equation, I still wouldn't be with her. She's trying to break us apart. She's jealous she'll never have what we do—real love. I'm not sure she even knows what that is." I kissed Julie's forehead and let my lips linger. "She's not going to take Maddie from us. That little girl is as much yours as she is mine. You were willing to give up your happiness for hers. That's what a real mother does—she sacrifices for her child. Nikki doesn't know the first thing about being selfless, and there is no way in hell she's getting her hands on our daughter."

I held up her left hand and kissed her ring. "You're my future . . . our future, mine and that sweet little girl's. You told Maddie I'm very protective, and you're right. I'll guard us from whatever comes our way, and I'll guarantee that when the bell rings, my hand will be hoisted in the air as the victor because I refuse to lose our family. But you need to be by my side, Julie."

Her chest jerked as she tried to catch her breath. "I promise, and I'm sorry. I've never been so torn in all my life. There's nothing I want more than to be here for you and to love you." She looked in my eyes, and a flicker of strength flashed in her eyes. "Let's do this . . . together."

"That's my girl."

Our lips met, and I poured my love into her with every touch of my tongue and every breath I gave her. When our kiss broke, she looked at me. No more words needed to be said.

The sun had barely peeked through the slats on the window coverings when I heard sweet cooing. Maddie was such a happy little girl, and she had no idea what had transpired with Nikki—thank God.

chapter 21

Julie

I PEEKED IN THE door. "Hey, sweet girl."

She was lying in her crib and reached for me.

"You're wide awake this morning, aren't you?" I picked her up and kissed her soft cheeks. "Let's get you changed and have some breakfast."

The last thing Maddie wanted was to lie down and get cleaned up, so I tickled her tummy to distract her as I secured her diaper. After I changed her, Maddie smiled at me, and right then, I knew Brett was right. I had actually known before that moment, but this solidified it for me. We were a family, and I'd do what I could to protect those I loved. Her adorable giggle made me grin from ear to ear. She looked at me with so much trust that my heart swelled. I'd never thought I could love her more than I had the day before, but with each passing moment, my heart expanded, and she owned more of it.

I secured Maddie in her high chair, which was slightly reclined and had colorful toys that hung overhead. She swatted them as I wound up the small music box that was attached before I went to prepare her breakfast.

"My favorite way to start my day." Brett strolled in looking sexy as hell in his red-and-blue plaid pajama pants. My mouth watered at the sight of him. His arms wrapped around my waist, pulling my back to his bare, muscular chest. He rested his chin on my shoulder. "So what's on today's menu?"

"Baby bananas and Farina. Would you like some?"

He looked over my shoulder at the beige food. "I think I'll let her enjoy it."

I giggled. "I'll make you bacon and eggs."

"No, just coffee. I'm not hungry, and I need to figure out our next move before I go to the club."

Maddie squealed when I placed her breakfast in front of her. "Here you go, sweetie."

Her eyes widened as she immediately grabbed the food.

Brett chuckled. "Let me help you." He picked up the baby spoon and fed her. Her feet kicked her seat, encouraging him to speed it up. "You're a hungry one this morning, aren't you?"

Watching them together was the best part of my day. He was such an amazing father, and the love in their eyes was beyond pure. It was so natural, as if they were meant to be together. I placed a cup of coffee and one of Aubrey's muffins in front of him.

"Looks like Mommy wants me to eat too."

Mommy. I stopped in my tracks and stared at him.

"You are her mommy, and she knows it." He looked back at Maddie. "Right? Isn't your mommy so pretty in the morning when her hair's all messed up?"

"Really?" I tightened my ponytail holder and smoothed my hair back before I handed him a bottle for her.

"You're gorgeous no matter what time of day it is or if your hair is tousled all over the place." His eyes bored into mine. "Although I like when I'm the reason your hair is messed up. What did you and Aubrey call it?"

I snickered. "JFL."

"Yeah, that's right." He covered Maddie's ears with his hands. "The just fucked look." After he shot me a wink, he released his daughter and looked at her. "You will never have messed up hair because of that reason."

I couldn't help but laugh. God help the boy who ever knocked on her door.

Once Maddie was satisfied—and wore more food than she'd consumed—we cleaned her up and set her on her U-shaped pillow in the family room to play.

"So what's the plan?" I asked.

Brett took a sip of his coffee. The worry that flowed from him broke my heart. His hand found my knee, and he traced it with his thumb.

"First, I don't want you to worry," he said. "Once I get to my attorney's office and let her listen to the recording of Nikki's ultimatums, that should be enough for a judge to deny her any rights. She isn't fit to be a mother, and I honestly don't think she wants to be. What bothers me about yesterday is that until we served her, she never once came looking for us. I didn't think she was even in the same state. No one had seen or heard from her, then finding out she'd been here all along? Well, that irks me to no end." He raked his hand through his hair. "Don't get me wrong. I didn't want to see her, but how could she not be curious about her child?"

We looked at Maddie, who was playing with stuffed blocks that rattled and played musical tones. She loved them.

"I don't know. I could never do that." I shrugged.

His eyes found mine. "No, you couldn't. No decent person would, not to mention someone who wanted her daughter back. What does she have to gain now?"

"Money." My right shoulder rose as he looked between Maddie and me. "I know she said she wanted you, but I think she sees that sweet baby as a monthly paycheck or a large payout." That thought thoroughly disgusted me. "She wants me out of the picture and for you to be with her even though she knows full well you don't love her."

"Love? I don't even like her. The only good thing she has ever done is given birth to Maddie, and I'll be damned if she thinks that entitles her to anything." His face reddened. "Men have been called deadbeats or sperm donors for ignoring their children's needs, so why should giving birth make her a mother in anything but the physical sense? She hasn't reached out until now, and for what? Cash? She doesn't even know the name of Maddie's pediatrician."

"Look, Nikki isn't a stable woman. We both know she's conniving, and now that she knows we're engaged, she's going to pull out all the stops. It would kill me to walk away, but if it would save you pain and heartache . . ."

He pulled me onto his lap. "I'm not going to have this discussion again. I appreciate your willingness to sacrifice your happiness, but you won't be doing that.

I need you. *We* need you. I'm going to give my lawyer a call."

"Okay, I hope she can help."

Maddie cried.

"She probably needs to be changed." I pushed myself off Brett's lap and went to Maddie. "Let's go, sweetie."

Brett

I WATCHED MY TWO girls walk out of the room as I made my calls. Once I'd told my attorney, Victoria, what was going on, she wanted to see me as soon as possible. I called Mike and had him cover me at the club.

I found Julie in Maddie's room. "Jules, I need to head into the city to see my attorney. I'm going to call my mom to see if she can watch Maddie for us. I want you to come with me."

She nodded. "Okay, I just need to hop in the shower. Maddie is cleaned up and dressed and will be ready for a nap as soon as we get to your mom's."

My eyes ravaged her body as I watched her strip out of her clothes and scurry into the bathroom. I looked at Maddie. "Your daddy is a lucky man." I kissed her forehead and put her in her swing.

Once Julie was finished, we traded places. That was how our life was now, taking turns so one of us could be with Maddie, and I wouldn't have changed a thing.

In the car on our way to my parents' house, I looked at Julie, and she seemed peaceful. Once we pulled into the driveway, she glanced at me and smiled. We got Maddie out and headed toward the door.

My mother beamed as she held out her arms. "There's my precious baby."

"Aww, Mom, you know I love when you call me that." I chuckled, and Julie snickered.

My mom took Maddie and peppered her cheeks with kisses. "You know I meant you, right? Your daddy thinks he's so funny."

"Thank you for watching her today." I leaned over and kissed my mom.

She looked at me with joy in her eyes. "This little one is always welcome here, especially when you need to go take care of business." Her eyes found Julie's. My mom loved Julie was as if she were one of her own. "How are you doing, sweetie? Are you holding up okay?"

"Yes, thank you. It was a rough night, but I'm doing fine." She linked her hand with mine.

"Thanks again, Mom, and we'll be back soon. Everything you need is in her diaper bag. She just ate, so she should be ready for a nap."

Julie and I went to the car after we showered Maddie with affection. It was so hard to leave her, even when she was in great hands.

Once we made it to the Law Offices of Allibaster and Drake, we were escorted to a conference room. Victoria was already waiting for us.

She stood and held her hand out to Julie. "I'm Victoria Drake. You must be Julie?"

Julie smiled. "I am. It's nice to meet you."

"Please sit down and tell me what's going on."

I cleared my throat. "Nikki followed me home from work and showed up at our door yesterday. She claimed she wants Maddie."

Julie shifted in her chair, and I rested my arm on the back of it.

Victoria was writing on a yellow legal pad. "You said you had a recording?"

"Yes." I placed my phone between us on the table and hit play. Hearing Nikki's voice made my stomach roll, and I saw Julie's knee bouncing up and down.

When the recording stopped, Victoria said, "Well, she doesn't hold back, does she? So first she wanted Julie gone, and for you to be with her, and then she wanted five million dollars?"

"That's right. Our family and friends were present as well. She never once said she loved Maddie or claimed to have missed her. She seemed more concerned with hurting Julie than getting to know Maddie." I swallowed hard. "She's not fit to be in Maddie's world. I don't have five million dollars, and I don't want to buy her off, but I'll do what I need to get her out of my life."

Victoria pinned me with her eyes. "Absolutely not. Let's get her in here with her attorney, Mr. Henry. I bet he doesn't have a clue what she did. I've met him. He's a good lawyer, and he would never have advised her to come to your home demanding money or making threats."

"So what's our next step?" Julie asked with determination etched in her features. "You don't know me, Victoria, but I'll do anything for this little girl not to be taken from Brett—"

I interrupted her. "From us."

She smiled. "Yes, from us."

"And I'll do everything in my power to ensure that doesn't happen. Please excuse me for a moment." She left the room.

Julie and I stared at each other. "This will be okay," I said. I wasn't sure if I was attempting to reassure her or myself.

Victoria walked back in with a smile. "Well, it seems as though Nikki already filled him in but with much different details. Mr. Henry had no idea about her financial demands. I'm going to schedule a meeting between us to see if we can resolve this without having to go to court."

"So where does that leave us?" Julie placed her forearms on the table and leaned forward as if she was ready to take charge of the meeting. Her business savvy was surfacing, as was my pride in her.

"We wait. He'll call. I'll give him—" Her phone rang, and she looked at the screen. With one index finger up, she answered the call. "Drake."

My eyes were glued to her, waiting for any indication of what the other attorney was saying, but Victoria showed no emotion whatsoever.

"I think that would be in your client's best interest." She glanced at us. "That will be fine. My clients are in my office, and I'll inform them. See you next week—and, Mr. Henry? Be sure to advise your client that we don't intend to lose and keeping this out of Family Court would be wise. I wouldn't want a judge to charge her for extortion." She listened while I began to sweat. "I'm not sure a judge would agree. If we go in front of Judge Hutchinson, he'll eat this up. You know how he feels about paternal rights. Not to mention getting his name in the law review for pioneering a cause." Victoria leaned back in her chair and swirled the top of her pen between her lips. "I'll look forward to your call."

After she hung up, all I could do was stare at her with my mouth open. "Extortion?"

"It's a stretch, but she asked you for an extremely large sum of money in exchange for you to remain with your daughter and Julie. I'll have my associate study some case laws, but it could work." She gathered her notes.

"Could Nikki go to prison? I wouldn't want that." The thought of being responsible for Maddie's biological mother going to jail made me nauseated. "I couldn't do that to Maddie."

"Understood. Trust me, once Mr. Henry describes the evidence against her, I highly doubt she'll proceed. Please email me a copy of the recording."

We all stood and shook hands.

"Thank you, Victoria. I'll look forward to hearing from you," I said.

On the way back to my mom's, the tension in the car was thick. We both wondered what may or may not happen.

"I don't want Nikki charged with a crime either," Julie said, her voice so soothing. "But I also don't want that to be used against her."

"What do you mean 'against her'? How could we do that?"

"I don't want her to think we'll press charges unless she signs the adoption papers. I want her to either sign on her own or because the court tells her to. We can't stoop to her level."

"Don't worry about it. Something tells me we won't have to." I pulled up to my parents' place. "It'll work out. We need to believe that."

Julie nodded. The crisp air blew her golden tresses over her shoulders.

"Come on, beautiful, let's go see our girl."

Over dinner, we explained everything to my parents.

Afterward, we took our daughter home, and after we placed her in her crib, we went into our room. Julie strolled out of the bathroom after changing into a pair of short pajamas. The way her body moved awakened me, and made me think of anything but going to sleep. Her slender arms rose above her head, exposing her taut stomach.

I could feel my cock stir, but Julie let out a yawn as she crawled into bed next to me. I pulled her close and snuggled up to my girl, inhaling her sweet scent as I closed my eyes.

"Sweet dreams, Jules."

"Sweet dreams, Brett."

chapter 22

Julie

"I LOVE THE WAY your lips feel against mine. I love the softness of your breasts in my palms, the taste of your skin as I run my tongue from your pussy to your hardened nipples and back down. I love to watch the way your skin prickles and your hips buck as I blow on your clit."

His words were my undoing, and I let out a guttural moan.

"The way I can feel how warm and wet you are when I slide my finger in you. Do you like that, Julie?"

"Yes! More, please . . . I need more!"

He added another finger and moved them in a circular motion before pulling them out and bringing them to his lips. "So sweet and all mine."

"Brett, please!" I swallowed hard and tried to catch my breath.

"Tell me, what do you want?"

"*You!*" My body tensed up as my orgasm took hold of me.

He grabbed my breasts as he filled me with his length.

"Oh my God, Brett!"

"Jules?"

I felt as though I was being shaken.

"Hey, Julie?"

My eyes slowly opened.

Brett hovered over me with a shit-eating grin on his face. "Are you awake?"

I looked down. My hands were on my T-shirt-covered breasts. Heat rose in my face as I quickly moved my hands to my sides. *I'm awake now.*

"You called my name." His eyes perused my body. I felt my legs go limp and fall to the sides. "Did you orgasm in your sleep?" He kissed me and put his hand between my legs. "You're so wet. What is it with you and dreams?" A look of satisfaction flashed across his features, and he tossed me his ever-sexy wink.

Embarrassment consumed me and, apparently, took away my vocal ability.

"You don't need to dream about me. I'm right here."

"I . . . um . . . I don't know what happened." I could still feel my girly parts throbbing in need of him.

"How about we make that dream a reality?"

All I could do was nod. In a heartbeat, we were naked, and he was inside me.

"I love making love to you," I said.

"You're so ready for me. Want to tell me about that dream?" I shook my head, and he moved his hips back and forth. "That was the sexiest thing I'd ever seen."

I scrunched my eyes closed. "Don't talk about it. It's embarrassing."

"Open your eyes. I want you to see the difference between dreams and the real thing." His abs flexed with each roll of his hips. His biceps became more pronounced as he quickened his movements.

"Brett, so good. It feels so good."

He slid his hand between us and pressed his finger on my hardened nub.

My legs wrapped around his. "Now, Brett. Please . . ."

I felt his legs stiffen as he released inside me. I grabbed his perfectly formed ass and held him close, relishing the warmth of his skin as I pulsed around him. The weight of his chest on mine was the best feeling in the world. It made me feel safe and more loved than I ever had before. Brett was my world, and he'd just rocked it.

Maddie's small cry came over the monitor.

I sighed. "We need to get up."

He kissed me. "I'll get her. You go shower."

Being in this home with Brett and Maddie was where I was meant to be. They were my world. Leaving the house was becoming more and more difficult, but I needed to head into the office and finalize things with Luca's family. As I left, Maddie reached for me and cried. Brett would pacify her, but when I got in my car, no one was there to cheer me up.

The stress of waiting for Nikki and her attorney made it nearly impossible for me to concentrate. I talked to Luca, and we finalized the partnership deal between the club and his winery. He was pleased to hear Brett and I were getting married, and I promised to send him an invite though I wasn't sure when the wedding would be.

A delicious aroma wafted into my office. When I looked up, Brett was standing in my doorway with Maddie and one of Bernie's specials.

"Delivery of the usual for Julie." Brett chuckled.

I took Maddie from his arms. "Hi, my sweet thing!" I gave her a gentle squeeze. "Thank you for surprising me."

"Well, I have a reason for our visit—aside from giving you a food orgasm." He waggled his eyebrows.

I covered Maddie's ears and shut my office door. "Seriously?" I shook my head. "Don't say orgasm in front of her."

He chuckled. "Okay, make sure you don't either."

I twisted my lips and sat at my desk with Maddie on my lap as Brett unwrapped our food. "So what's the other reason?"

"Victoria called. We're going before a judge in two days."

The food I'd put in my mouth felt as if it were coated in tar. I could hardly swallow. "Okay. So does that mean Nikki is fighting us?"

"I'm not sure. All I know is Victoria said to be there. I'm going to have Alex and Tyler come too since they heard her say she did this on purpose by tampering with my condom."

A chill ran up my spine. "Makes me sick."

"I know." He nodded toward Maddie. "But she's pretty fantastic."

My knee bounced her up and down, making her giggle. "Yes, she's the best."

After we finished lunch, I had no desire to stay at the office. Since I was splitting my time between there and home, I decided to leave with my family.

Brett

A COUPLE DAYS LATER, we dropped Maddie off at Aubrey's and headed to the courthouse. My parents, Alex, and Tyler were meeting us there. I prayed Nikki would do the right thing.

The waiting area walls were gray and felt as cold as the blood running through my veins. I adjusted my tie and turned to Julie. "Do I look okay?"

Her hands smoothed the lapels of my suit which, in an odd way, comforted me. "You look great." She took my hands and brought them to her chest. "I know you're nervous, and to be honest, I'm terrified, but we've done all we can. The judge will have to see that, right?"

I held her as tightly as I could without crushing her. "I've been praying all morning for that very thing. We can't lose her."

"They're ready for us," Victoria said, standing in the now-open doors that led to our future—to Maddie's future.

"Here we go." I kissed Julie's hand, never releasing my hold on it.

The clicking of heels caught my attention. I turned and saw Nikki, accompanied by her attorney and Leah.

"Come on." Julie tugged on my arm. "We don't want to start anything negative."

"You're right."

We walked into the courtroom. I sat at a long wooden table with Victoria on my left and Julie directly behind me. I heard people filing in behind us and turned to see my parents, Bentley, Andi, Tyler, and Alex.

Alex placed his hand on my shoulder. "How are you holding up?"

"I'm okay. Thank you for being here." I smiled at the small gathering behind me. When I glanced at Nikki's side of the room, only Leah was behind her. If I didn't loathe her so much, I'd have almost felt sorry for her. *Almost*.

The court officer walked in, and my pulse raced. "All rise. The court is now in session. The Honorable Judge Joseph Hutchinson presiding."

We all stood as Judge Hutchinson entered the room. He sat, his broad body cloaked in black, between our table and Nikki's. "This proceeding is to determine parental custody of minor child Madeline Kate Chambers." He shifted papers around on his desk. "Petitioner is Mr. Brett Chambers." His eyes lifted to me, and I nodded. "The respondent is listed as Ms. Nicole Webster." When he looked at Nikki, she was whispering to Leah.

Nikki's attorney nudged her, and she rolled her shoulders back. "Yes, that's right."

The judge did not appear amused. "I didn't ask you a question, Ms. Webster, and when you address the court, you will do so by saying, 'Judge' or 'Your Honor,' understood?"

She nodded, and he glared at her. "I mean, yes, Your Honor."

"Please be seated."

The sound of chairs shifting filled the room.

"Ms. Drake, you may proceed," the judge said.

Victoria stood. "Thank you, Your Honor. I'd like to call Brett Chambers to the stand."

Julie squeezed my hand before I made my way to the chair.

The court officer addressed me. "Please raise your right hand."

I did.

"Do you solemnly swear to tell the truth, the whole truth, and nothing but the truth so help you God?"

"I do." I sat down, and Victoria approached me.

"Mr. Chambers, is it true that Ms. Webster is the birth mother of your daughter, Madeline Kate Chambers?"

"Yes, we call her Maddie."

Victoria smiled and nodded toward the judge. I glanced at him, and he nodded as well.

"Two days after Maddie's birth, did Ms. Webster leave the hospital without Maddie?"

"Yes." My tie felt like a boa constrictor getting tighter with each question.

"Did Ms. Webster make any attempt to see Maddie over the past few months?" Victoria asked, pacing the courtroom.

"No. Well, she came to my home on Thanksgiving."

"Why did she come to your home?"

I cleared my throat. "She wanted my daughter."

Victoria was now standing closer to Nikki's table. I looked at Julie, and she smiled reassuringly at me.

"What did you tell her?" Victoria asked.

"I told her no." When my eyes landed on Nikki, her lips twisted.

"Did Ms. Webster make any demands?"

"Yes. She said she wanted my fiancée, Julie, out of my life so the three of us—myself, Maddie, and

Nikki—could be a family." I frowned as Julie's eyes glistened with unshed tears.

"Anything else?" Victoria asked.

"Yes. Nikki said if I wanted to keep Julie and Maddie, then I'd have to pay her five million dollars."

"You're a liar! I never said that!" Nikki's voice boomed through the room.

All of a sudden, the room filled with light chatter, and the judge hit his gavel numerous times.

"Order, this court will come to order." The room settled, and he looked at Nikki's attorney. "Mr. Henry, please control your client. One more outburst, and I'll hold her in contempt."

Mr. Henry stood. "Yes, Your Honor."

"Proceed, Ms. Drake."

"Thank you, Your Honor." Victoria returned her attention to me. "Do you have any proof she demanded money in exchange for you to have custodial rights?"

"Yes, I have a recording and witnesses."

Victoria handed the judge's clerk a flash drive labeled, "Exhibit 1."

"Mr. Henry, is your client aware of this recording?" The judge's voice was stern, and he didn't look at all pleased.

Mr. Henry's face paled. "Yes, we are, Your Honor, but we haven't had time to have it tested for authenticity."

Victoria stepped toward the bench. "Witnesses are present to testify if need be. Their names are on the list I provided to Mr. Henry and the court."

"You may proceed, Ms. Drake."

The judge's presence was extremely intimidating, and I was thankful I had nothing to hide.

"Mr. Chambers, do you live alone with Maddie?"

My eyes met Julie's. "No, I live with my fiancée, Julie Michaels."

She gave me a tight smile, which brought one to my face as well.

"How is her relationship with Maddie?" Victoria stood to my side, her back to the empty jury box so that I had a clear sightline to Julie.

"Julie treats Maddie as if she were her own. She bathes her, feeds her, makes her laugh, and soothes her when she cries." My jaw tightened, and my heart beat pounded against my ribs. "Maddie is lucky to have her . . . and so am I." I smiled at Julie.

"Thank you." Victoria looked at Mr. Henry. "Your witness." She sat down while Nikki's attorney stood.

He buttoned his suit coat as he walked toward me. "Mr. Chambers, when you found out Nikki was pregnant, were you pleased?"

I heard my blood swoosh into my ears. "No, not exactly."

"So is it safe to say you were upset?" He raised his eyebrows and looked from me to the judge.

"Yes, but—"

He cut me off. "Answer the question."

Swoosh . . . swoosh . . . swoosh.

"It isn't that simple." I thought of Maddie. It broke me to think she would find out about this one day. "Yes, I was upset."

"I see." Mr. Henry stood in front of Nikki. "Isn't it also true that you demanded a paternity test because you thought Ms. Webster was lying?"

"Yes." The sound of my pulse intensified. S*woosh . . . swoosh . . . swoosh.*

"In fact, weren't you drunk the night my client conceived Maddie?"

"Objection. Relevance?" Victoria stood and addressed the judge.

"Your Honor, I'm trying to establish the frame of mind Mr. Chambers was in when he impregnated my client."

"Overruled." The judge looked at me. "Please answer the question."

"Yes, I was drunk. I also wore protection. Why don't you ask your client about that?" S*woosh . . . swoosh . . . swoosh.*

"Your Honor, please." Mr. Henry crossed his arms and stood in front of the judge.

"Mr. Chambers, yes or no is sufficient."

"Sorry, Your Honor."

"One last question, Mr. Chambers." Mr. Henry stalked in front of me. "Did you want Nikki's baby to be your child?"

I didn't know what to say, so I stayed silent. The pressure behind my eyes and the pulsing in my ears were more powerful, and I couldn't shake them. I thought back to when Nikki had said she was pregnant, and I remembered how upset I had been. I remembered the anger and confusion that had coursed through me. But when I'd seen that ultrasound and received the paternity test results, everything had changed.

"Mr. Chambers? You're still under oath. Please answer the question."

"No, not at first—"

"Thank you, Mr. Chambers, that's all." Mr. Henry smugly sat next to Nikki and patted her hand.

Victoria stood. "Your Honor, I have a few follow-up questions."

"Proceed."

She glanced at Mr. Henry before walking toward me. "Mr. Chambers, how did you feel the day you heard your baby's heartbeat for the first time?"

I took a minute to gather my thoughts. "I felt protective and vowed to myself that I would do whatever I could for her . . . if she was mine."

"Because at that time, the paternity hadn't been established, correct?" Victoria asked.

"That's correct."

She paced. "Once you found out the baby was yours, how did you feel?"

"Confused. But like at the ultrasound appointment, I knew I'd always love and protect her. I have family and friends who have supported me." I looked at the judge. "When I brought Maddie home, I had no idea what to do or what a baby needed, but with their help and time, I've figured it out. There's no one in this world I love more than my daughter." I returned my focus to Victoria.

She smiled. "Thank you. That will be all."

The judge addressed me. "You may step down."

I went back to my seat as Victoria said, "I'd like to call Nicole Webster to the stand."

The bailiff swore Nikki in, then Victoria began. "Nicole, do you want to be a mother to Maddie?"

"I never wanted to raise her alone. The only person I wanted to do this with was Brett." She looked at me and shook her head.

Victoria linked her hands behind her back. "I see. And after you were discharged from the hospital and left without your baby, did you intend on returning?"

"No."

Bile rose in my throat. How could she have done that?

"So it wasn't until Mr. Chambers filed adoption papers and you saw a big payday that you attempted to see your daughter?" Victoria's voice was stern and laced with a hint of sarcasm.

Mr. Henry stood and glared at Victoria. "I object Your Honor. There's no validated evidence that Ms. Webster asked for anything in exchange for her daughter."

"I'll withdraw that question until I call my witnesses. That's all I have, Your Honor."

Nikki's lawyer stood as Victoria sat. "Ms. Webster, what was your intention when you went to see your daughter on Thanksgiving?"

"I wanted to . . . I needed to . . . I wanted to see her." Her voice was shaky at best.

"Thank you. That will be all."

Nikki was excused and sat beside her lawyer.

To say I was shocked would have been an understatement, then it dawned on me that anything Nikki said to counter her previous responses would be a lie. Naturally Mr. Henry didn't want his client to commit perjury.

The judge asked, "Ms. Drake, do you have any more witnesses?"

"Yes, Your Honor."

Nikki's attorney asked the judge if he could speak to Victoria a moment, and after he complied, Mr.

Henry was at our table whispering to Victoria. She nodded, and he walked back to his side of the room.

Mr. Henry said, "Excuse me, Your Honor? Ms. Drake and I would like to have some time with our clients to discuss a resolution."

"The court will take a sixty-minute recess. At that time, if the parties have not reached an amicable agreement, we will proceed. For those of you in the courtroom who are on the witness list, please don't go far." He hit his gavel on the block. "Court is in recess."

As we emptied out of the courtroom, Victoria pulled me aside. "Mr. Henry would like to discuss this between the four of us and try to come to a conclusion. I think he sees the writing on the wall. But if you're uncomfortable at any time, we don't need to agree to any terms. We can let the judge decide."

I nodded. "Give me a minute to speak to Julie and my family." Once I was with my family and friends, I could finally breathe.

My mom placed her hand on my arm. "What's going on, sweetheart?"

Once I'd explained what Victoria had said, they all stared at me.

"I'm nervous too, but if we can resolve this now, I'm all for it." I pulled Julie into an embrace. "Stay close."

She craned her neck to look up at me. "I'm not going anywhere."

The small conference room adjacent to the courtroom was cold and sterile. Aside from pictures of past presidents and the American flag, the room held only a table and chairs. My attorney and I sat across from Nikki and her lawyer.

"Mr. Henry, you wanted this meeting. The floor is yours," Victoria said.

"Yes, well, in regards to the recording, my client is willing to concede she did mention money. I'd like for our clients to talk so we can try to resolve this matter."

"Very well. Why don't we hear from my client since he's the one who has started these proceedings?"

"That's fine. Go ahead." Mr. Henry sat back.

I rubbed the back of my neck with my palm. "I'm trying to be as pleasant as I can be, but I need to know why Nikki wants to have Maddie."

Nikki's eyes narrowed.

"You won't be getting a large sum of money. I will sue for joint custody, and I will be marrying Julie. I don't want to sound like an asshole, but you left her. How could you do that? You knew from the beginning that I was in love with Julie, or you wouldn't have had to pull the stunts you did. So tell me—why? Why after all this time do you want to be a mother to Maddie?"

She tilted her head from one side to the other. "I figured you'd either be with me or pay me. I didn't really think you had me on tape. I thought you were bluffing."

"I'd never bluff with the welfare of my child," I said. "This isn't a game to me. You started this, and I want to end it right now. Alex and Tyler heard you say you tampered with my condom. You're on tape trying to extort money from me. But you know what baffles me? Not once have you asked about Maddie. No 'How is Maddie doing today?' or 'Does she sleep through the night? What toy is her favorite? ' You don't even know how much she weighs or what diapers work best for her. How can you not care enough not to find out these answers?"

I shook my head in disgust. "Maddie woke up happy this morning and had cereal with her formula—which is soy, by the way because she has a hard time digesting any other kind. She sleeps about five hours a night and likes to have the mobile on overnight. Her red block with a little zebra stitched on the sides is her favorite toy. At her last well visit, she weighed sixteen pounds, five ounces, and we use cloth diapers because the paper ones give her a rash. Maddie has the cutest little giggle, and she loves when I sing to her even though I don't have a good voice. Julie and I love her, and we want to raise her. Can you honestly say that you want to be her mother? That you love her and want to care for her? If you can prove that, I won't keep her from you, but you won't have her all the time. I won't give up my family, which includes Julie. I don't even think you ever really loved me, Nik. I think you were in love with the idea of me."

Nikki bit her lip and let out a breath. "You're right. I don't want this."

"Nicole—" her attorney said.

She stopped him. "Brett's right. I wanted him and what he could offer me. Maybe we're not in love with each other, but I hoped that would change."

I felt as if I was having an out-of-body experience.

"I don't know anything about her, nor do I want to be a single mom. All I ever wanted was to be Mrs. Chambers, and I thought that would happen." She looked at me with disdain. "The one time you aren't Mr. Nice Guy is when I needed you to be."

"I never said I would marry you. In fact, you knew marriage was the last thing on my mind. That's what started this entire thing."

She shrugged. "I thought I could change your mind. I thought once I had your kid, you would want me. But in the hospital, you cared more about that baby than me, so I left. Maybe that was wrong to you, but it was right for me. My modeling career is finally getting back on track, and I may move to Los Angeles."

"I did care and do care more about Maddie." I couldn't believe she was still hung up on that. My heart jackhammered at the thought of letting her take my daughter across the country. "I'm really trying here, Nikki, but I don't know how much simpler I can make it. And as far as Los Angeles goes, that's not going to happen if we share custody."

Her eyes narrowed to slits before she leaned over and said something to her lawyer. I looked at Victoria, who held up her index finger. So I waited.

Mr. Henry said, "Ms. Webster will sign the petition for sole custody as long as you don't bring charges against her for offering you money."

An audible sigh escaped me before I agreed to her terms. "But there's still the matter of our petition for adoption. I plan on marrying Julie, and I'd like Julie to adopt Maddie once we're married."

"Ms. Webster?" Victoria looked to Nikki for a reply.

"No. I hate her." Her voiced dripped of disdain etched with jealousy.

Her attorney asked, "Does that mean you deny the request, Nikki? Please be advised the judge can overrule your decision."

"Looks like the court will decide on the adoption," Nikki said.

Her attorney looked annoyed. If I had to guess, he probably wanted to resolve everything now. Mr. Henry pulled out a set of legal documents from his briefcase and placed them in front of Nikki. My heart raced as I watched the ink roll from the pen onto the paper that would change my life more than it had already.

Nikki set the pen down and looked at me with empty eyes. "She's all yours."

"I'll inform the clerk," Victoria said.

We left the room, and Julie ran up to me.

"What happened?" Her eyes sparkled, yet they were rimmed in red.

Before I knew it, I was surrounded by my family and friends. "Nikki signed the custody papers."

Everyone started talking and congratulating me at once.

"But she hasn't signed the adoption papers," I said.

Julie's smile disappeared and was replaced by a frown. "She despises me. Brett, I don't have to adopt her. I can be just her stepmother. You've been through enough. Let's go." She grasped my hand.

"No, we're going to see this out until the end."

Victoria walked up. "We need to go back in."

When court was back in session, the judge seemed pleased we'd come to an agreement on custody. "I see we still have the adoption issue at hand though."

"Yes, Your Honor. My client does not want Ms. Michaels to adopt Madeline," Mr. Henry said.

The judge nodded. "We are moving on to decide the matter of adoption. Ms. Drake, call your first witness."

Victoria stood. "I'd like to call Julie Michaels to the stand."

I watched my beautiful fiancée walk with confidence to the stand even though I knew her nerves were frayed. The bailiff swore her in.

Victoria approached Julie. "Ms. Michaels, I have a few questions for you."

She quietly cleared her throat. "Okay."

"What can you tell me about day-to-day life with the minor, Madeline?"

Julie's face lit up. "She's wonderful." Julie beamed as she looked at the judge then at me. "Maddie is a happy and content baby. When she wakes up, she's usually cooing rather than crying. She enjoys her baby food better than her bottle, except at night—her bottle helps her sleep. Her favorite toy is a red block with a zebra on it. She loves to drop it on the floor so we'll keep picking it up." Julie snickered. "She loves when her daddy sings to her, especially when he sings 'Somewhere Over the Rainbow.'"

I heard Alex and Tyler chuckle. My mom shushed them, which made me smile, and I made a mental note to kick their asses.

Julie continued. "Recently, Maddie has been sleeping for more than four hours during the night. She's a very happy baby. The only times she ever fusses are when she needs to be changed or is hungry. And when she first tried to roll over, her arm would get stuck, but she figured it out. That little girl brings me more joy than I ever thought possible." She looked at the judge. "I understand I'm not Maddie's biological mother, but I couldn't love her more if she were my own. If I thought my leaving would benefit her, I would—I've even offered to—but as much as she needs me, I need her." Julie swiped a tear from her cheek.

Pride filled me as I watched her and, more importantly, listened to everything she had said.

"Thank you." Victoria looked at Nikki's lawyer. "Your witness."

He stood. "I don't have anything for Ms. Michaels."

The judge said, "You may step down."

After she stood but before she stepped down, Julie looked at Nikki. "We aren't doing this to hurt you. I know I'm not your favorite person, and I don't need to be, but Maddie is one of my favorite people, and I will love her until the day I die. We're doing this to benefit her, not to harm you."

When she left the witness area, Julie smiled at me.

I couldn't help standing to hug her. "I love you, Julie."

"I love you too."

The judge hit is gavel. "Court is still in session. Please refrain from personal conversation and contact until court is adjourned or in recess."

I sat down. "I'm sorry your honor."

I heard whispers from Nikki's table.

Then her attorney stood. "Your Honor, my client has decided not to fight the adoption, but she has one request."

"Which is?" the judge asked.

"If her daughter ever asks about her birth mother, Ms. Webster would like Mr. Chambers to tell her that she did what was best for her."

My head snapped toward Nikki. Her face was flushed. *Did she grow a conscience?*

"We agree, Your Honor," I said. I couldn't help myself.

The judge gave me a pointed look before saying, "In the matter of Chambers vs. Webster, the request for adoption is accepted. Court is adjourned, and this case is closed."

Sounds of joy filled the room as my family and friends hugged. I shook Victoria's hand then grabbed Julie and planted a kiss on her lips.

Nikki walked up to us and spoke to Julie. "Not that you deserve to hear this, but since I'm telling the truth, you may as well know I lied about what happened the night Brett and I were together. You were the one on his mind, not me. He should have been saying my name, but he didn't."

She turned, walked out with her attorney and never looked back. We stood there, stunned. A wave of relief mixed with shock washed over me. Julie's expression mirrored mine, and for once, I was thankful to Nikki.

"Let's go get our girl and celebrate." I tossed my arm around Julie's shoulders, and we left the courthouse in much better spirits.

chapter 23

Julie

EVERYTHING APPEARED BRIGHTER than when we'd left that morning. I felt as if the foggy cloud that had blanketed our home this morning had lifted and been replaced with sunrays.

"I don't want to wait, Jules." Brett set Maddie in her bouncy seat and handed her a toy.

I smiled as she kicked and waved, making the seat move. Her giggle was contagious.

"You don't want to wait for what?" I headed toward the kitchen to get Maddie a bottle.

"To get married. I don't want to put it off."

"I'd marry you now if we had a license."

"Jules, don't you want a big wedding? I'd feel terrible if you didn't have what you always desired."

"All I need is you . . . okay, and our friends and family. But we don't have to have anything elaborate. We can have it here in our home."

"Really? That would be okay with you?" He lifted the bottle to Maddie's lips as she eagerly sucked on the nipple.

"Yes, it would be perfect."

Thinking about marrying Brett was a dream come true. I didn't care when, where, or even what my dress looked like—okay, maybe I did care about that. I wanted Brett to be able to be knocked over with a feather when he saw me in my wedding dress. But most of all, I wanted us to declare our love for each other in front of our family and friends.

"How does two weeks from Sunday sound?" he asked. "The club'll be closed. We'll call our family and friends today, and I'll call Pirro and have Fao's cater it. Shit, you can have your pal Bernie set up his stand if that's what you want." Brett chuckled as he burped Maddie.

"Fao's would be perfect." I bit my lip. "So we're going to do this in two weeks?"

He set Maddie in her bouncy seat, grabbed me, and spun me around. "We most certainly are." Brett set me down and swatted my ass. "Now call your girls and go shopping."

"Eeeep!"

I grabbed my cell and called Aubrey and Val. Val was free, and thankfully, Alex was home to stay with Jackson.

I grabbed my purse, gave Brett and Maddie a kiss, and bounced toward the door. "Okay, I'm leaving now."

"Hey, Skippy?" Brett laughed.

I laughed too and stopped bouncing.

"Would you mind if Lyn stood up for you too? She's like a sister to me, and you'll need another girl. I'll have Bentley, Alex, and Tyler by my side."

"Sure! I'd love that. Do you think she'd do it?"

"Of course she will. I'll text you her number."

"Cool, I'll call her on the way."

I left the house, dialed Lyn's number, and headed to pick up Aubrey. Lyn didn't answer, so when I pulled up to Aubrey's, I sent Lyn a text asking her if she could meet me at Bergdorf's because I needed her. Hopefully, she would make it. When Aubrey got in and closed the door, we shrieked so loudly I was surprised the windows didn't shatter.

"I'm so sorry to throw this at you at the last minute, but we don't have much time." I pulled down her street and headed toward the city.

"Don't you dare apologize. I'm so excited! So who else are we meeting?"

"Val and hopefully Brett's cousin, Lyn. She's wonderful. You'll love her."

Aubrey smiled. "I met her at Brett's birthday party at his parents' house."

I'd forgotten about that. "That's right. I forgot."

"Wait, is Tyler standing up for Brett?" Aubrey had a shit-eating grin.

"He's going to ask him, why?" Then I remembered Brett teasing Lyn about Tyler. "So they were into each other?"

"You should have seen them, Jules." She giggled. "There was so much sexual tension between them it was palpable."

"I heard! I'm surprised they didn't hook-up. I don't know if Lyn is the wham-bam-thank-you-ma'am type, but I don't think Tyler is the settling-down type either.

Could you even imagine him committing to one woman?" A laugh escaped me.

"Pfft, no. But I didn't think our men would either considering my husband held the title of most eligible bachelor and Brett, well . . ."

"Yeah, Brett was anti-marriage. I remember." I shook my head to clear my thoughts. "But that doesn't matter because they're ours now. Maybe Mark or Ty will be next."

When we got into the city, I scanned the curbs. "I hate the city. Parking sucks. It never bothered me until we moved and we got a driveway."

Aubrey's arm darted out. "There's a spot."

I parked, fed the meter some coins, and headed into *Bergdorf's*. My phone dinged with a text from Lyn. She was there and in the shoe department. I loved her already. When I spotted her, the first thing I noticed was she looked gorgeous. Her blond hair was pulled up neatly on the sides while the back had an abundance of waves that cascaded over her shoulders.

"Hi, Lyn." I gave her a hug. "You remember Aubrey, right?"

Her brows lowered then rose. "Yes, from Brett's party. You were pregnant then."

Aubrey glowed. "Yes. How are you?"

"I'm good. You look amazing. Congratulations!" Lyn hugged Aubrey.

I was happy Brett had thought to ask her to be in our wedding. "Lyn, the reason I asked you to come here is twofold. One, I'm marrying your cousin, and we'd like you to be in our wedding. Will you be my bridesmaid? Brett would be so happy if you agree—and so will I."

She nodded and smiled. "Thank you! Yes!"

"I'm so happy! Brett will be too. The second reason we're here is because we're going gown shopping, not only for me but for my ladies."

Aubrey gasped. "What? I didn't know that."

"Yes, and the gowns are on me, so let's do this!"

We walked to the escalator as Val walked in. We waved her over, and I filled her in. She was thrilled, of course. I loved my girls.

In the bridal section, a woman came out from the back to help us select something. When I told her when the wedding was, she flinched. "That's not a lot of time. You'll need to buy off the rack."

"What about this one?" Aubrey held up a straight-cut, strapless, hand-painted lace over silk organza. It was stunning.

The woman smiled. "Well, that one was never picked up by the bride because they called off the wedding." She paled. "That's not bad luck or anything."

I laughed. It was perfect. "I'd like to try that on, please." After everything we'd been through, bad luck wasn't in my vocabulary.

I followed the woman into the dressing room. Once I slid the dress on and saw my reflection, my eyes filled with tears.

"It's nice that you're tall. You don't need many alterations." The saleswoman put her hands on my waist and pinched a little of the fabric. "This could be taken in a bit, but our alterations department can handle that. Would you like to show your friends?"

I nodded. When I stepped out of the fitting room, the girls all gasped.

Aubrey started crying. "Jules, oh my God, it's so pretty. You're gorgeous."

Val put her hand on her heart. "It's perfect."

"My cousin is going to freak out when he sees you. It'll serve him right after all the grief he gives me." Lyn grinned.

The saleswoman told me she would go get a veil for me to try on. I wasn't sure if I wanted one, but I decided to try it anyway.

"So, Lyn, since I missed the infamous birthday party, tell me what happened with you and Tyler." I smiled at Lyn, and Aubrey and Val turned toward her.

Her eyes flicked between them, then she looked at me. "Nothing happened." Her cheeks turned a shade of pink, and I cocked a brow. "Really."

Aubrey laughed. "That's not how I remember it. The way he looked at you was hot! He wants you bad!"

The clerk came back and placed a veil on my head. I looked in the mirror and caught Lyn's eye in the reflection. "Did I mention I'm pairing you two up at the wedding?" I shook my head, removed the veil, and handed it to the clerk.

Val and Aubrey nudged Lyn, and she laughed. "You all are worse than my cousins! Okay, he is kinda hot."

"Kinda hot?" we all said in unison.

Val piped in, "The man is sexy as sin and should be walking a runway."

"So what do you think?" I stretched out my arms and twirled.

Lyn smiled. "It's perfect, Julie. Brett is going to flip."

I looked at my reflection. I had to agree with her. "Okay, ladies. Go pick something out for yourselves. I'm thinking all the same color, but I'll leave which color and the style up to you."

By the time, I got home, Brett was feeding Maddie dinner. Her face lit up when she saw me, and my heart swelled.

"Did you find something?" Brett made the *choo-choo* sound of a train as he slipped the spoonful of food in Maddie's mouth, making me smile.

"Yes, my girls and I are all set."

"Great. My family is thrilled, as are Alex and Tyler. I already called the minister, so we're good to go." He wiped Maddie's hands and stood to kiss me.

I took Brett's hand. "I'm going to ask Mark to walk me down the aisle."

"I think that's a great idea."

Brett

OUR WEDDING DAY was finally here. Our home was transformed thanks to my mother and a decorator she'd hired. The women were getting ready at Aubrey's while the guys were here. Even Luca was present—in the form of a life-size cardboard cutout of him and Jenifer Aniston's wax figure. His card had said, *I wish we could be there in person. We hope you both have a lifetime of happiness and love. All our best. Love, Luca and Rachel.*

"So how are you holding up?" Bentley asked as I attempted to make a perfect knot in my tie for the fifth time.

"I wish she was here. She calms me down, and this fucking tie looks like shit." I glanced in the mirror and pulled it apart again.

"Brett Chambers, you do not need to use such language." My mom stood in front of me and tied a perfect Windsor knot in about five seconds flat.

Bentley chuckled, then I heard the rest of the guys join in.

"Sure, you all laugh. Wait until it's your day," I said.

Alex put up his hands. "Hey, don't lump me in with them. I've been there, and I know what you're going through. These other clowns"—he gestured between Mark and Tyler—"they'll get theirs someday, and Bentley is already engaged, so he can't say much."

Mark didn't say a word, but Tyler shook his head with a sarcastic laugh. "No way, man. This clown is fine without a ringmaster."

I chuckled. "Sure, that's what I thought not too long ago. You just wait." I grinned. "I did tell you that you'd be escorting Lyn down the aisle today, right?"

We all turned and faced Tyler.

My mom shook her head. "Boys, leave him alone, and don't bring your cousin into this, Brett." She excused herself and left the room. I'm sure she didn't want to hear what else we had to say.

Mark looked at Tyler. "Lyn is pretty hot. If I didn't have Val, I'd offer to be her escort."

Tyler's eyes shot daggers at Mark, but when he realized we'd all caught his glare, he shrugged it off. "Hey, your call, man. I'll take Val for the day."

All humor left Mark's face.

"Okay, guys, let's put our clubs and loincloths away and go wait for the ladies," Alex said, always the voice of reason, while I checked my tie.

We made our way to the living room, which was now lined with white chairs and a makeshift altar. The minister had arrived, and I made sure he had everything he needed. Then I heard a car door shut, and my heart stopped. My mother made me turn around as she ushered the women through the living room to the kitchen, but not before Aubrey handed a sleeping Jackson to Alex, who brought him to Maddie's room.

"This is a big day, son. Your mother and I are proud of you." My father shook my hand.

"Thanks, Dad. I'm pretty proud of myself too. Julie and I will be very fortunate to have the kind of love that you and Mom have."

Before I knew it, my mom was calling my dad.

He looked at me. "And so it begins."

Soft music played and my parents took their seats in the front row. My eyes went to the back of the room. Bentley escorted Andi, who was carrying a sleeping Maddie. Julie had bought her a buttercup-yellow dress, and she looked like a ray of sunshine. They sat next to my mom as I nervously waited to see my bride. I took a deep breath as Alex and Tyler made their way down the aisle and took their places next to Bentley.

Val turned the corner and walked toward us, followed by Lyn. I glanced at Tyler. He was staring at Lyn, and I laughed internally. When Aubrey headed our way, I nudged Alex. If his smile was any wider, it would have been touching his ears.

Then the music changed, and so did the beat of my heart. When Julie came into view, tears pricked my eyes. She took slow steps toward me with her arm hooked in Mark's. The closer she got, the more difficult it was to breathe. Her hair was pulled up, exposing her beautiful neck and shoulders. She never wore a lot of makeup, and today was no exception. She looked like my Julie—beautiful.

As she took her place next to me, Mark gave her a kiss on the cheek and whispered something that made her eyes water as she looked at me. Then he shook my hand. "You're a fortunate man to be marrying my best friend. Take care of her and make her happy."

I nodded, and he took a seat. "You're beautiful, Julie."

She beamed. "You're not so bad yourself."

The minister cleared his throat and smiled. "Let's begin. We've come together to witness the commitment of Brett Chambers and Julie Michaels. Today, they will recite vows they have written to bind their hearts in marriage. This commitment they make in front of family, friends, and God should not be entered into lightly. Life is full of bumps in the road, and at times, love is tested. Brett and Julie have filled this room with you, their family and friends, not only to share their special day, but to know that you'll be there for them during good times and bad and to help smooth over any bumps that may come their way." He turned toward me and nodded.

Julie and I faced each other, and I took her hand. "Jules, I can't believe this day is finally here. When I think back to the first time I saw you, the first time I heard your voice, and our first kiss, I suppose I knew then that you were the one for me. It took me a while to get here, and I can't thank you enough for standing by my side." I looked at Maddie, who squeaked to remind us she was in the room. "By *our* side."

My eyes filled as I looked at Julie's face, so full of love. "I promise to hold you when you're happy, sad, have a bad day, or just want to be in my arms. You are my soul and my reason for breathing. I promise to never make you cry unless it's in a fit of laughter and to make all of your dreams come true." I winked, and she bit her lip as her cheeks turned a light shade of red. "There isn't anyone in this world I'd rather have by my side to grow old with and to raise a family with. You're my best friend, my Skippy . . ." I smirked, and she giggled. “Thank you for giving me your heart. I promise I’ll never break it. I’ll hold it, cherish it, and honor it for the rest of my life and beyond. Thank you for picking me to share your life with.”

Julie’s eyes leaked tears as she looked into mine. “Well, that’s not fair that you went first.”

Everyone laughed, and the ladies wiped their eyes.

“You, Brett Chambers, are an incredible man, father, and friend. I too remember the first day we met. I knew then there was something special about you, beyond your striking good looks, and even though I couldn’t pinpoint it, I most certainly can now. When you love, you do so with your entire heart and soul. I promise to love you forever, to hold you when you’re happy, sad, or simply want to be in my arms. I promise to keep you calm when that first boy comes to pick up our daughter.”

His brows lowered, and he shook his head, which made me snicker.

“I’ll do my best to be the best wife, mother, and lover. I know it took us a while to get here and our journey wasn’t an easy one, but we’re stronger because of it, and for that I’m grateful. Thank you for asking me to be your wife. I’ll cherish that title forever and do my best to never let you down. I’ll love you for all eternity.”

I softly said, “Thank you, Jules.”

“We’ll now exchange the rings.” The minister took the rings from Alex. “The wedding band is a circle which has no end, like the love you two have for each other.” He handed mine to Julie and hers to me.

I took her left hand and slid the ring down her slim finger. “With this ring, I thee wed.”

Julie slid my ring down my finger. “With this ring, I thee wed.”

The minister closed his book and said the words I'd been waiting to hear. "By the power vested in me by the state of New York, I now pronounce you man and wife. You may now kiss your bride."

Her emerald eyes sparkled like diamonds.

I placed my palms on her cheeks and stared at her. "I'm going to kiss you now, Mrs. Chambers."

She smiled. "I think I'd like that, Mr. Chambers."

Our lips met, and I savored the moment. I knew I'd always cherish our first kiss as man and wife. When we broke apart, our family and friends cheered. Julie bounced on the balls of her feet. Aubrey handed her the bouquet of white roses—without thorns—which she raised over her head like an Olympic champion.

Before we left the altar, the minister signed our marriage license. I spun my wife around, took Maddie from Andi, and held my family in my arms. I vowed to never let go.

epilogue

Brett

IT TOOK ABOUT TWO months for me to plan Julie's surprise, but tonight was the night. Maddie was having a sleepover at her grandparents,' so we didn't have to worry about our daughter. I pulled into a small private airfield and parked next to a fairly large building.

"Are we going somewhere?" She looked at me, and fear flashed across her emerald eyes.

If she only knew the places I planned on taking her tonight—and we wouldn't even leave the ground. I linked our hands together and walked her into the building.

She gasped and covered her mouth with her free hand. "Oh my God, Brett."

The airplane hangar had been transformed into a romantic rendezvous exactly as I'd wanted it to be. A small square table covered with white and silver linens and decorated with candles glowed in the center of the hangar. A canopy of light blue silk and twinkle lights over the table gave the appearance of a clear sky. Soft music played, adding the perfect touch. The look on her face made me realize this was all I needed.

"Welcome to your dream." My arms snaked around her middle, and I drew her close to me. "I love you, Julie, and I promised to make all of your dreams come true."

Her brows lowered as she looked at me, then the light bulb went off. "Oh! My airplane hangar dream." She leaned back and beamed. "I can't believe you did all of this."

We walked toward the table. Her fingers glided along the silver fabric while she looked up and smiled.

I pulled out a chair. "For you, my lady."

She sat down and giggled. Then she looked to her left and laughed. "What do we have there?" Her eyes narrowed, and she shook her head at the makeshift bed covered in fluffy pillows.

After I finished smiling like a fool, I tossed her a wink. We were served our dinners by Anthony, a waiter I'd hired from the Italian restaurant I'd bought our dinner from. He poured a bit of red wine into my glass, and after I gave him a nod, he filled Julie's glass and mine.

I held mine up by the stem, and she did the same. "To many more nights of making dreams come true."

Before she clinked hers against mine, she cleared her throat. "I have something to say. This goes above and beyond anything that I could have dreamt of, and I'm not just talking about what you did to transform this space or the beautiful atmosphere you've created. You, Brett, you're so much more than I ever thought I wanted or needed in my life. I guess you never miss what you don't have, but now that I have you, I'm so glad I'm not missing out any longer. If I didn't have you, I know, in the very depths of my soul, that I wouldn't be complete. You have surpassed any fantasy, thought, or vision I could have ever conjured up, asleep or awake. Thank you for this perfect day. I love you."

We tapped glasses as I forced myself to breathe. This woman took my breath away, and I couldn't have agreed with her statement any more if I'd made it. "*Buon appetito.*"

"Grazie."

Our dinner was perfect, and after our plates had been cleared, I excused Anthony.

When we were alone, I took my girl's hand and brought her to her feet. "Dance with me."

We swayed to the soft instrumental music. My hands went to the small of her back, and she brought hers to my neck. The feeling of her fingers caressing the back of my head combined with the occasional tug on my hair was about to send me over the edge. I cupped her cheeks. Her green eyes caught the twinkling lights perfectly, making them look like emerald stars.

Our lips met. At first our kiss was tender and sweet, but when I felt her tongue glide against my lips, I opened my mouth and gave her access. I was ready to devour my wife. What could be more perfect?

She broke the kiss and lowered herself onto the pillows and blankets. Her body shimmied up the bed, and she pulled a pillow under her head. "You look deep in thought. Care to share?"

I lay down next to her, rolled onto my side, and propped my head up on my hand. "I was thinking how perfect we are for each other and how I never thought I'd meet someone who understood me the way you do.

I love how confident and poised you are and, most of all, how understanding you are."

"That I am. Now stop talking and kiss me. I believe the best part of my dream is still to come."

She was like a gem in an oyster—you know it's out there, but it's hard to find. Julie was my pearl, and now that I had her, I would never let go.

When you can find it in your heart to forgive, love will help you forget.– Brett & Julie Chambers

acknowledgements

This part of the book is always difficult for me. There are so many people who stand behind me and support me while I stay holed up in my office. I hope I don't forget anyone and if I do, please know it wasn't intentional.

First and foremost, I'd like to acknowledge my family. Thank you for putting up with me and my craziness while writing. You three are my world, and I wouldn't be able to do what I love to do without your love and support. I love you more than anything.

My beta readers, Amanda Wilson, Ann Marie Madden, Julie Deaton, Lauren Collins, Lisa Paul, Virginia Carey and Yamara Martinez, thank you for taking the time out of your busy schedules to read for me. Your feedback, comments, suggestions, and more importantly, your honesty, were incredibly helpful. Thank you from the bottom of my heart.

Thank you to my wonderful friend and awesome author, Ann Marie Madden, for "lending" me Ben Stone from Stone Walls to help Brett. Love you sorella!

Lisa Paul, thank you for being my sounding board, but more importantly, for being a great friend! I always know I can count on you, and that means the world to me.

My friends who always have my back, thank you for supporting me. Without all of you, I know I wouldn't be where I am today—losing my mind, so thanks for that! (Just kidding.) You all do so much, and I don't even think you realize it. Just by telling me you enjoy my writing and my characters makes me happy.

To my "Rockin' Reader Group." You ladies are the driving force behind this book. Thank you for believing in me and for pushing for Brett and Julie's story. I hope you enjoyed it.

Thank you, thank you to Yamara Martinez. You've helped me keep my sanity during this journey, although it's your fault for all my "Brett stress." ☺ I value your friendship and support more than I can say. I think you're wonderful and I'm honored to call you my friend.

To Jesey Newman at Sassy Savvy Fabulous, PR. Thank you so much for all your assistance and support. I think you rock!

To all the bloggers, thank you for everything that you do. I truly appreciate all your support. I wish I could list all of you, but that would add several more pages! Thank you for all the time you spend supporting authors and reading our stories. You take time out of your personal lives, and I am thankful.

Special thanks to my editor, Cassie Cox and proofreader, Devon Burke.

Sommer Stein from Perfect Pear Creations, a thank you isn't enough. You create the most amazing covers. I adore you and I look forward to working with you in the future. I am over the moon for this cover, you're the best.

Most importantly, I'd like to thank the readers. We all love to read and talk about the books and characters we love, and I am so thankful to all of you. Thank you for taking the time to send supportive messages. Your enthusiasm keeps me going, and there isn't a thank you big enough for that.

coming soon

Incumbent: The Prescott Series (Book 1)

stay in touch

Website:
www.joanneschwehmbooks.com

Facebook:
http://www.facebook.com/joanneschwehm

Twitter:
https://twitter.com/JSchwehmBooks

Amazon:
http://www.amazon.com/Joanne-Schwehm/e/B00GBC1X2K/

Goodreads Group Page:
https://www.goodreads.com/group/show/156533-joanne-schwehm-s-romantic-reading-friends

Facebook Reader's Group:
https://www.facebook.com/groups/joanneschwehmsreaders/

other books by Joanne Schwehm

Unexpected Chance (Chance #1)
My Chance (Chance #2)

Ryker

The Critic

about the author

Joanne Schwehm is a romance author who was born and raised in Western, NY. She despises being cold, but she warms up either writing or reading sexy romantic books.

Her favorite things are spending time with her family, having fun with her friends, reading, and of course writing.

Joanne is a true romantic at heart and believes everyone deserves romance, modern day fairytales and breathless moments.

24890849R00198

Made in the USA
Middletown, DE
09 October 2015